TEACAKES & MURDER

Book 2

Mike Nevin

HOWCARING.COM

Copyright © 2023 by Mike Nevin

All rights reserved.

No part of this publication may be reproduced, distributed, or transmitted in any form or by any means, including photocopying, recording, or other electronic or mechanical methods, without the prior written permission of the publisher, except as permitted by U.K. copyright law. For permission requests, contact howcaring.com

The story, all names, characters, and incidents portrayed in this production are fictitious. No identification with actual persons (living or deceased), places, buildings, and products is intended or should be inferred.

Cover design by Keroles Raaft

Fourth edition 2024

Published by howcaring.com

Contents

Dedication	V
1. Chapter 1	1
2. Chapter 2	21
3. Chapter 3	37
4. Chapter 4	56
5. Chapter 5	70
6. Chapter 6	88
7. Chapter 7	104
8. Chapter 8	120
9. Chapter 9	131
10. Chapter 10	148
11. Chapter 11	159
12. Chapter 12	179
13. Chapter 13	193

14.	Chapter 14	205
15.	Chapter 15	228
16.	Chapter 16	238
17.	Chapter 17	263
18.	Chapter 18	282
19.	Chapter 19	296
Also By Mike Nevin		309

Dedication

Dedication & Acknowledgements

To my amazing wife Mary, without whom this book would never have been written. Her patience, encouragement and sense of fun keep me going. She is my rock, my love, and my life.

I am so grateful to everyone who helped me with this book. Most of my best ideas came from my wife, Mary. My imagination has merely transformed her stories and ideas into print.

A fantastic writing group in Wellington, Somerset, headed by Peter Blaker, encouraged me along the way. They so loved Hilda; it inspired me to keep writing about her.

My daughter Sandy read early drafts, and my daughter-in-law Rachel lent a helpful hand. Their input has been invaluable.

An American writer friend, Ashley, has been a sounding board and source of encouragement along the way. She patiently read my drafts and pointed out my glaring errors to do with America. Any that snuck into the final book are entirely down to me.

The Cleve Hotel Wellington, Somerset, holds a special place in my memory. It was a delightful location where I spent many hours writing in peace and quiet - in the early years.

Without all my family and friends, I couldn't have finished this book.

Chapter One

May 1998

High Street, Plympton-on-Sea, UK

The Church Bells of St Mark's resounded throughout the bustling seaside town of Plympton-on-Sea. 'Since when is 9 am on a Sunday morning a reasonable time for clanging bells?' Was the usual thought on many minds being dragged from their peaceful rest. Except their thoughts included more uncharitable language. Which I have edited for Sunday use. Perhaps the townsfolk had a point. As this weekly racket served only the faithful few.

On this glorious Sunday morning, the High Street overflowed with market stalls. Missing were the cars and vans impatiently queuing at the traffic lights. The ones that usually struggled through Plympton on their way to more popular seaside resorts. The fuming drivers asking that perennial question, 'will they ever build a bypass?'

Instead of diesel and petrol fumes, a smell of food filled the air. Today was the much-loved annual Plympton Food Fayre. A time of fun and frolics. An opportunity to enjoy local produce and handicrafts. Crowds would soon gather around the stalls that offered free tasters. Everyone loves something free.

All the shops and cafes were open, to join in with the Fayre. They had decorated their shops with bunting and flags. Everything in keeping with the general décor along the High Street. The one business that remained closed was the 'Hidden Garden Tearoom'. It stood out as a place of quiet and emptiness, among the throng of activity.

Hilda Shilton and Pearl Parker were happily sitting in the back garden of their tearoom, blissfully unaware of all the activity. They were early risers, and being a sunny day, they were enjoying breakfast in this garden. Merlin, Pearl's tabby cat was still getting use to his new surroundings. He glanced up suspiciously at Hilda, as if to say, 'what are you doing in my domain?'

As they ate Hilda asked Pearl, 'whatever is that noise dear?' She stared at the high wall surrounding their garden. It directly adjoined the High Street.

'The Church bells?' asked Pearl, following Hilda's gaze. 'They're always a right racket at this time of the morning.'

'No, I mean all the shouts and laughter, very unusual for a Sunday.' The gardens of the tearoom was set back far enough to be quiet most of the time, even during the week. Often people commented on the fact they couldn't believe the garden was in the middle of a town. The traffic sound never permeated the garden. That morning, all the excited laughter and shouts from the street just outside seemed very close.

'I'll go and see,' said Pearl. She bent down and fussed with Merlin as she headed outside. After a while she returned, looking flustered. 'It's the Food Fayre, weren't we going to be open for that?'

'That's today?' said Hilda. She sprang to her feet. 'But Councillor Russell said next week.'

'I knew I should've checked. I said it was odd them putting up signs so early,' said Pearl.

The two of them quickly cleared away their breakfast and got the tearoom ready for customers. Hilda let Pearl start the till up. She still thought of it as strange and other worldly technology. Not something that she wanted to touch in case it bit her. They were very late in opening, but just in time for mid-morning coffee.

***

At seventy-eight, Hilda and Pearl were past retirement age. But that never stopped either of them, especially Hilda. They had moved to 'The Hidden Garden Tearoom,' just a month earlier, shortly after they returned from an adventure in the USA. It was to be both their home and joint catering venture. Paid for by Hilda's reward for returning the duchess of Somershire's diamonds, the tearoom was Hilda's idea. Jewel thief, Jake Vort, AKA The Ghost, had chosen Hilda as an unwitting carrier through customs to the USA. A decision he was no doubt regretting as he sat in prison. Hilda liked to point out to Pearl they had both saved the 'Eyes of Hora' diamonds. Considering the shock, she had given Pearl, at the first mention of opening a tearoom together, that was just as well. It had taken a while to convince her that the idea was sound and desirable. What surprised Hilda's son, William, and his wife Louise was that Hilda would choose to do something that involved such focus and commitment. Hilda was a hard worker, but not known for her structure and application. Nor her staying power. That was where Pearl's strengths came in. She was a brilliant planner and organiser. Perhaps that was why Hilda asked her to join in the venture. Or maybe she just enjoyed their trip around America so much that she didn't want her friend to go home.

***

The St Mark's Church bells that had rung earlier had been summoning the faithful to the 9:15am morning communion. It was a quick thirty-minute service for those who wanted to be in and out before the 10:00am family service. Avoiding all those noisy and messy kids. On this Sunday morning, things differed from usual. As the early congregation left church and headed home along the High Street, they had an added advantage. They could visit the Food Fayre. Unfortunately for the Vicar, Rev John Hanley. The families heading to the 10:00am service also headed up the High St. The earthlier pleasures of food and drink diverted some. As the 10:00am service started, the vicar looked out on a rather sparse congregation.

The Hidden Garden Tearoom benefited from these errant parishioners and was overflowing with customers by 10:15am. Hilda had stocked up on Ice Cream and the ones she had not already sampled herself were selling well.

Councillor Mildred Russell, Hilda's mis-informant about the Food Fayre, was standing across the road. She was watching the crowded tea shop and did not look happy. Having deliberately told Hilda that the Food Fayre was not till the following week. She had not expected them to open and gain business so fast. She hoped they would sleep in and miss it all. Mildred's husband, Lord Leonard Russell, or Len, as she called him, stood next to her. He was smiling as he looked at the cheerful faces of people on the street. People were passing by, laughing, and chatting. Turning to him, Mildred scowled and said, 'why are you looking so happy?'

'It's a sunny day and...' started Len as he looked around.

'You have no idea, do you? I can't believe you sometimes.' Mildred swept off down the street. She had to push her way through the crowds. Len watched her go and then quickly followed behind her. He tripped over a young lad, who was running along chasing after a balloon that had escaped his hold.

In the Hidden Garden Tearoom, things were getting frantic. Normally, Hilda and Pearl employed a couple of servers in the shop. Having forgotten the Fayre, they had also forgotten to ask Kelly and Lauren to come in that day. Leaving Hilda and Pearl rushed off their feet. Hilda was trying to wait on the tables. While Pearl made the food and drinks and took the payments. Hilda was never good at serving tables at the best of times. Adding pressure to the mix made things very hard for her. She was losing track of which tables she had taken orders from. One or two people were getting very impatient and calling out for her attention. Meanwhile, every time Pearl tried to fill an order, the queue at the till built up.

The two girls that Hilda and Pearl employed to help, Kelly and Lauren, were good mates. They had been out that morning visiting the Fayre. As they passed The Hidden Garden Tearoom, they saw a rather fraught Hilda almost drop a tray of tea and cakes. Lauren went over and asked, 'You need us?'

'Life saver... yes, please,' said Hilda, while juggling the tray and a few plates.

'You're on,' said Lauren. Then, turning to Kelly, she said, 'Over ere Kel, we're needed.'

They set to work like a pair of magicians. Order pads seemed to appear in their hands. Food was on tables seemingly before it was ordered. Hilda stared in wonder and relief. Then she realised that she still needed to do some work herself and carried on, taking orders, clearing tables, washing up and helping Pearl make food. The work went by quickly and the stress ease. The angry customers were appeased, and things went smoothly.

At the end of the day, Hilda and Pearl could barely move. Every muscle ached. They were wondering about the wisdom of running a tea shop at their age. Kelly and Lauren had tidied the tables and finished the washing up before they went home. Hilda and Pearl only needed to cash up, switch off the lights, and lock up. As Hilda passed the till, Pearl was just completing cashing up the till.

A pile of leaflets next to the till needed sorting. Groups dropped them off during the week. Some asking if they could be displayed. Others were just local information for them to read. Hilda gingerly picked up the pile of leaflets. They were close to the electronic till, and she didn't want it to zap her. Pearl looked at her open-mouthed and said, 'the till doesn't bite you know.'

'It beeps and whirrs. I don't know what it's planning,' said Hilda, stepping back quickly with her handful of leaflets.

'It's a till. They don't plan things. They hold cash and total the money taken,' said Pearl. She was shaking her head as she continued cashing up. The till was making even stranger sounds as she made it total the takings and print a summary.

Hilda took the leaflets a distance away and said, 'you haven't watched enough sci-fi movies about these things taking over the world.'

'A till, taking over the world!?' said Pearl. She looked at Hilda with both eyebrows raised to her hairline.

'Well... maybe not tills. But robots and things,' said Hilda. She flicked through the leaflets and hummed a nondescript tune.

Pearl shook her head and returned to her task. As Hilda went through the leaflets, she sorted them out. A few were out of date and went straight into the bin. Including one about the Food Fayre. It had the correct date on it. Showing it to Pearl, they both agreed that they had not seen it before. The only information they had on the Fayre was word of mouth to Hilda, from Councillor Mildred Russell. Pearl told Hilda that she must have remembered the date wrong, and Hilda agreed her memory was poor. Neither would have believed that the lovely councillor would deliberately mislead them. What reason could she have? What reason could there be?

Hilda carried on sorting the leaflets. Among them, one caught Hilda's attention. The local Theatre group owned a multi-function premises that had been built in the 1930's. To pay for its upkeep, the committee also showed a selection of movies regularly. Not the latest blockbusters, but a decent range of films. The leaflet was informing the town that the director of an amateur dramatic group, which met at the theatre, was retiring. It also said that the building needed a lot of restoration work, and unless the funds could be raised, they may have to sell it. There was no guarantee that a new owner would keep its use as a cinema and playhouse. The leaflet contained much pleading for money and support. It also asked if anyone knew of a replacement director. There is a well-known expression about cogs turning in a person's brain when an idea is forming. Hilda's brain looked nothing like that. In fact, she just stared open-mouthed at the wall. She then went and sat at a table. Pearl said, 'are you alright? It's not still the till, is it?'

Hilda was silent. That, in itself, was a worry. Pearl stared at Hilda. She waved a hand in front of her eyes. There was no response. 'Hilda, Hilda?' said Pearl.

'Yes dear,' said Hilda.

'I was wondering what was happening. You were in a world of your own.'

'I am absolutely fine,' said Hilda. 'Nothing to worry about.' She headed up to bed, saying goodnight. She had a lot more thinking to do.

There was no need to worry. Unless you happened to be a member of the amateur dramatic group at Plympton-on-Sea. Because Hilda was thinking about that group. She was thinking of getting involved in that group. Not just getting involved; but directing that group. Some people might consider things like experience in directing a necessary requirement for such an idea, not Hilda. Some may think that success in previous ventures would be a minimum requirement, not Hilda. For her, passion and energy were the only requirement for anything. For Hilda, appearing, even by mistake on Broadway, was qualification enough. But then experience had taught Hilda that sheer will, determination, and a smattering of good luck were all you needed to do anything.

You may well have read about her previous experiences on Broadway. It was this she was remembering. All memories of the fact it was an accident, and the mishaps she had experienced, slipped away from her memory. She only remembered the applause. Having accidentally appeared on stage gave Hilda a sense that she could do anything. Not just acting, but directing were her calling. Look out Plympton Amateur Dramatics club here comes Hilda.

Meedham, UK

About twelve miles away from Plympton-on-sea is Meedham. Well, it's twelve miles as the crow flies, not by road. It is much further by road. Why the flight of crows has anything to do with distance, I don't know. Hilda's son William and his wife Louise, who lived there, didn't keep crows. They were not ornithologists. Neither of them was a big fan of crows. As far as I'm aware, they have never tried to fly on a crow. No doubt that would fail, as crows are rather small, and they are much larger. I'm not saying anything about their weight. Louise is a good weight for her height and William just needs to be a lot taller for his. Perhaps a more useful measure of the distance to between Meedham and Plympton is the time to drive on the roads. It took William and Louise about half an hour, traffic permitting, to drive to Plympton. Not that traffic was very obedient most of the time. Hilda took a bus when she visited them, that took her nearer an hour. That was partly because of all the stops and partly the change at Little Hustings. There was often a twenty-minute wait at the crossroads in Little Hustings. Hilda would use the time to buy an ice-cream. She loved ice-creams, whatever the weather.

As both William and Louise worked, they tended to be free to take this journey at weekends. On the roads, not flying on crows. It would have been murder trying to fly on a crow. William worked as an accountant at TSU PLC and Louise was a teacher of 12-year-olds at a local comprehensive school.

The next Sunday after the Food Fayre, they arrived in Plympton. They had wanted to come over for the Food Fayre. After all, that was the day Hilda told them to come. It disappointed Louise to hear she had missed the event. Not wanting to waste their trip, Hilda suggested they visit the parish church. She had been meaning to go since arriving in Plympton but been too busy setting up the tearoom. It wasn't that Hilda was a regular churchgoer. She had gained an interest in God on her American trip. You might call it a curiosity that she wanted to satisfy. A local church seemed the ideal place to quench that curiosity. She had occasionally visited William and Louise's church and planned to visit her friends Gloria and Joys' church. She liked the sound of their church. They made it seem a lot of fun. Exactly the place that suited her character.

When Hilda suggested a trip to St Marks' William looked at his mother long and hard. This was not what he expected. William tried to keep Hilda away from their vicar, the Reverend Pugh, or as she called him Rev Pooh. She thought they named him after the famous bear. He did not appreciate the confusion. Perhaps the fact that his schoolmates had used a similar moniker, but in a crueller way, didn't help. William was one of those people who went to church out of habit. He'd been happy to get out of going that Sunday and instead have a trip to a food fayre. Being told there would be no food and now he was going to church made him very grumpy.

Hilda would not be put off the idea of going to church. Nor would she accept Pearl's excuse of staying behind to make lunch. They set off on the short walk to the Church of St Mark's. Normally, William and Louise liked to dress smartly for church. Perhaps they felt it made them more acceptable to God. It certainly made them blend in with most of the other churchgoers. As they had come for a Food Fayre, they were in casual clothes. Not so casual as Hilda. She was wearing her usual bright purple track suit bottoms, white trainers, blue cardigan, and blue bonnet. Her blue hat always looked incongruous with her bright red curly hair, now dyed, poking out under it. As she walked along, she had a spring in her step, not just because of the trainers. She was looking around at the world in child-like wonder. Her bright green eyes shone out through her tortoise-shell glasses.

St Mark's Church bells were resounding with their usual fervour, announcing the last call for worshippers to get their skates on and rush along to church. No doubt the other locals had their pillows over their ears. As the group arrived, Hilda stopped by the duck pond in front of the church and said, 'oh, I wish I'd brought bread to feed the ducks.'

'We need to get in, can't be late,' said William. He was always anxious about time keeping. If he had to go to church, then he must be on time.

'I'm just going to sit and watch the ducks for a minute first,' said Hilda. She sat on a bench. Louise and Pearl joined her. They all sat and relaxed, enjoying the pastoral scene.

William looked at his watch, then at the few stragglers heading under the arched gate and up through the churchyard to the church door. 'We have to hurry,' he said.

'Don't be such a panic bottom dear,' said Hilda. She glanced at him from the bench. 'You were always such a worrier.'

Louise nodded in agreement. Pearl closed her eyes for a moment. William hopped from one foot to another. Glanced from his family up to the Church. Then said, 'please?'

After a couple of minutes, Hilda got up and skipped up the path. The path was made of paving slabs, and she remembered playing hopscotch on paving like that as a child. But she reached the church door before she found a suitable piece of chalk to draw an outline. No doubt to William's relief. As she arrived at the church door, an usher greeted her with hymn books and news sheets. They pointed her to a pew. Still bouncing along, Hilda ignored the pew showed and headed to the front of the church. She sat in the very front row, directly beneath the pulpit. She didn't realise that St Marks Vicar, the Rev John Hanley, used a small lectern on the opposite side. The rest of the family arrived at the door as Hilda sat down. Having gained their books and papers, they looked for Hilda. William's mouth opened wide when he saw her in the front row. The only time he had sat in the front row in church was at his wedding. Then he had felt extremely uncomfortable. His knees had knocked the whole time through the service. He went up to Hilda and whispered about moving. But while he was doing this, Louise and Pearl sat next to her. She let them pass and sit on the other side of her. Then Vicar and his team of altar servers arrived, processing up the centre, with crosses and candles. William sat down next to Hilda rather abruptly. He was in the aisle seat and looked uncomfortable. But Hilda nudged him and asked to swap. He was quick to agree.

Hilda never looked to cause trouble. She is the most caring, considerate, and loving person you will ever meet. Unfortunately, she is also an enthusiast, full of life and she lacks patience. Hilda struggled to sit still as the Vicar and congregation spoke and echoed lots of old-fashioned words. She loved the singing though. It just ended too soon and didn't include dancing. Holding a hymn book stopped her clapping along to the one livelier song. St. Mark's parishioners were not the most enthusiastic in worship. It was a sombre affair. In their eyes, worship was serious and should be celebrated with decorum and in a manner befitting their view of God. Which was an old man in the sky. A distant, solemn figure sat on a throne, judging them with a long face. In fact, if God was the way he seemed in St. Marks, then it's a wonder anyone wanted to go to heaven. It would be a miserable place. Their church was a place of solemn contemplation and nodded approval. They looked extremely sad. Perhaps, if they were at a football match and their team scored, they would nod and say, 'well done indeed.' Then again, they might just stand unmoved. Or not go at all.

Hilda had a completely different view of God and that was why she wanted to check out churches. On their trip across the USA, Pearl and she heard the good news about Jesus. Hilda thought it sounded like a reason to party. Cynics might say that Hilda would find any excuse to party. But she would say that 'good news is good news and surely worth celebrating?' She believed in dancing and singing. She showed her joy by clapping and shouting. Sitting in St. Mark's, watching all the po faced people, looking so miserable, she wondered if they had heard the same message as her. Maybe they hadn't. Perhaps some were there for entirely different reasons.

Rev Hanley got up to speak. Hilda looked at the pulpit and then at the Rev standing by a small lectern. She pointed towards the pulpit. He didn't notice her hand wave. She tried again. He still didn't notice, but William did and told her to stop. Realising that she needed more drastic action, Hilda got up. William's eyes went wide. Perhaps he regretted swapping seats. He couldn't block her from standing up. She walked across to the Reverend. William gasped. She stood next to Rev Hanley and announced, 'you're in the wrong place.'

There are some who may agree on a deeper theological level with that comment. Hilda meant, of course, the wrong side of the church, not the wrong job. The reverend looked at Hilda in amazement. In his five years of ministry, no one had never accosted him during a meeting. It is a little-known fact that heckling a preacher in church is illegal. That law goes back to the 1700's when such things were commonplace and violent.

Of course, the police are unlikely to enforce such an archaic law and besides, the good reverend was unaware of it. He would not be phoning the local force to arrest Hilda. Although had he known of that law, he may well have been tempted.

Hilda stood at her full five feet three inches. She could be quite imposing, all the same. She looked sternly at the Reverend and said, 'you can't preach from there.'

'I don't preach,' said the Vicar. 'I give a talk.' There may be those who would agree with the opening statement. If preaching is to earnestly advocate a belief. Rev Hanley only earnestly advocated his belief in English cricket. There were some very profound statements being made that morning. Unusual for St. Mark's. Normally, the good reverend only spoke some thoughts he'd been having. It served as a time for the congregation to catch up on their lost sleep. Much as the people in the church looked unhappy, they were at least awake.

'A talk?' said Hilda. 'We all talk, you know dear. I thought you were a man of God. I've found this morning rather depressing. Not at all what I expected.' She seemed to make some interesting theological observations. But then, she was in church. If you can't make theological observations in church, where can you make them?

William cried out, and a few gasps came from the congregation. A couple of ushers started heading up the aisle. Perhaps a little belatedly.

'Could you please sit down?' said Rev Hanley. He was waving his arms around. It was the most animated and excited he'd been all morning.

'I certainly won't be dancing in praise, at this Church,' said Hilda, 'no matter what the words of your hymn said.'

***

Later, as the Shilton family and Pearl all sat around the small dining table at Hilda and Pearl's flat. Empty plates in front of them. William's face glowed like a beetroot. Hilda was humming 'Oh Happy Day.' Which only seemed to make William look more cross. Pearl was smiling and trying to hide the fact. Louise said, 'I agree with the principle of what you said, but it really isn't a good idea getting up like that.'

'Absolutely!' shouted William. Louise glanced at him and he muttered an apology.

'You have to agree, it was dire,' said Pearl. She got up and started clearing away the plates. Perhaps to hide her ever broadening smile.

'Yes but, if everyone who disliked a church service got up and...' began Louise. She stared into the distance, then smiled and shook her head. Then she got up to help Pearl. The two of them whispered and giggled in the kitchen.

'I'm just glad it wasn't our church,' said William. He sounded a little calmer. He shook his head and screwed up his face. It looked as if he was trying to get rid of a foul taste.

'Your church is not as boring as this was,' said Hilda. She looked at Louise for support. 'At least the Rev Pooh has a band playing at the front. I've seen people clap and dance at your church.' Hilda got up and danced. Still singing, 'O Happy day.' Louise giggled.

'Not me, I don't dance and clap,' said William quickly. Louise walked over to him and patted his hand. She mouthed, 'not you.'

'Really?' said Pearl, turning to Louise. 'I didn't know your church was like that?'

'Yes, their church is quite lively. But the place I want to go is Gloria and Joy's Church. They tell me that is a place where they act like they've heard good news. Gloria said they sing and dance and jump and down. They even dance all around the building.' Hilda was spinning around the room now.

'I can't think of anything worse. You'd never get me there. We don't all wear our emotions on our sleeves, you know,' said William. He was staring at his mother as she spun around.

Hilda stopped dancing and looked at her son, and said, 'really? Who was it who went running down the hospital corridor shouting, "I have a son", after Josh was born, may I ask?'

'That's different,' said William. He blushed. Louise was smiling widely.

'You were happy and celebrating good news,' said Louise. She smiled and carried on helping Pearl.

William frowned and shook his head. 'The emotion overtook me.'

'Happiness does that,' said Hilda.

***

Later they all planned an afternoon film. Hilda and Louise made drinks, while William and Pearl found their seats. William chose his usual comfy chair in the corner. He planned to on having afternoon kip while the ladies watched a rom-com film. That was their normal Sunday afternoon treat. His seat had a parcel upon it. On moving it a sign inside dropped out. It read, 'Hilda and Pearl's Detective Agency.' William stared at it in astonishment. He wasn't the only one. This was obviously the first time Pearl had seen the sign.

Louise and Hilda brought through the tray of drinks and Louise stood staring at the sign alongside Pearl. Hilda spoke first, 'oh goodie, you've found my surprise.'

'Shock more like,' said William. 'Are you and Pearl setting up a detective agency?'

'First I've heard of it,' said Pearl. Merlin was obviously feeling left out. He rubbed himself along Louise's leg. She picked him up and stroked him.

'Not exactly a detective agency,' said Hilda.

'That's what the sign says.' Louise pointed at it.

'I thought it had a nice ring to it.'

'You might of mentioned it,' said Pearl.

'I just thought, given our success finding Ruby,' Pearl looked over the top of her glasses at Hilda. 'and solving the murders. Mind you, I'm not sure we have the right man there.'

'Hilda,' said Pearl. 'It's not up to us. The police are happy they have the right man. You remember how creepy he was when we met him?'

'I suppose you're right,' said Hilda.

'What about this detective agency?' asked Louise.

'It's more of a hobby really, a bit of fun.'

'If we put the sign up, people will start calling,' said Pearl.

'How about we just display it in the lounge?'

That compromise was agreed, and they all settled down to watch a film. William asleep in the corner and Merlin curled up on Louise's lap.

The White House, Washington DC, USA

On Hilda and Pearl's tour of the USA a year earlier, they had tracked down Pearl's twin sister, Ruby. She was working as The White House Chef. Pearl and Ruby's mother, Victoria Worth, had been forced to give them up at birth. A Mr & Mrs Parker adopted Pearl, they lived in Kilburn, London, next door to Hilda. They grew up as best friends from a young age. Even going to school together. Mr & Mrs Davies adopted Ruby. They emigrated to the Marlan, Ohio, in the USA soon after adopting her. They were farmers and owned the Big D farm.

Pearl's sister, Ruby, had been winding down towards retirement since her sister headed back to the UK a few months earlier. Her plan being to move to Florida. She had hoped that Pearl would join her. Then Hilda had sprung the tearoom idea, and all had changed. Ruby had a feeling that all could change soon. So, she continued her plans of moving to a two-bed condo in Florida. She knew nothing about Hilda's detective agency plans. Nor her doubts over the conviction of Orville Stanley for the murder of her parents.

People may well think that working at The White House is very glamorous. But working in the kitchen is not at all. Ruby tried to hand over more of the day to day running to her deputy, Zara. She had been training her up for a year. Many things still fell on her. That evening, there was a large banquet for foreign dignitaries. This was Zara's first major banquet. Ruby was tempted to let her run it alone and just observe from afar. But she still got more involved than she planned. By the time she headed to bed, she felt exhausted. She sat on her bed looking at the brochures on her retirement condo.

Marlan County Correctional, Marlan, Ohio, USA

At Marlan County Correctional, Orville Stanley was receiving a regular visitor. His lawyer Vance Jurgen. Orville was at the prison, on remand, awaiting trial for the murder of Ruby's parents in 1943 and Ellie in 1931. They were alone in a special room set aside for lawyers to talk with their clients. Orville asked, 'what are my chances?'

'They have DNA, physical evidence and eyewitnesses,' said Vance. 'You might do better to plead guilty and go for a shorter sentence.'

Orville's grey eyes focussed on his lawyer, then he said, 'but I didn't do it.'

'Most of the evidence says otherwise,' Vance shrugged and sorted his papers, 'except the fingerprints. The police claim that's a clerical error.'

Orville looked thoughtful, then cleared his throat. His lawyer looked up at him expectantly. Orville shook his head and stared at the table for a moment. Then he said, 'say the witnesses changed their mind, or just didn't turn up?'

'I don't know what you're suggesting,' said Vance, gathering his papers and stand, 'but I can't hear this.'

'Just sit down,' Orville sounded flat, defeated. Vance sat back down. 'I only meant if they decided not to testify or changed their testimony. It must happen.'

'Yeah, but...'

'Humour me.'

'The physical stuff alone is important... but jury's like to hear from people. They get confused by DNA. The physical evidence is old. We could show uncertainty about that too.'

Orville's grey eyes were looking at the wall. As if he was trying to see beyond it. Then he turned back to his lawyer. 'I have an idea,' he said.

Chapter Two

May 1998

State Forest, Marlan, Ohio, USA

Who knows what a victim feels facing certain death? We can't ask Sarah what she felt as she ran - her feet bleeding.

The first Sarah knew of him - the lights went out. Their fuse box in the outhouse. Stupid place, perhaps. She'd often told Jack that. A regret for her husband in later life. The night felt warm. Sarah ran into it barefoot.

Something had warned her – so she ran. Fast, desperate, scrabbling across gravel and mud. The house and its safety left behind. Sarah slowed, panting, sweating. Only her breathing and thumping heart filled her ears. Pine needles unfelt as she crouched in shadow. Safety - her house ahead. She'd run in a circle, the inky blackness fooling her senses.

Surprise in her blue eyes - then nothing. Two sets of dead eyes gazed at each other. No, his only appeared lifeless.

He stood above his victim, smiling in the darkness. His teeth like random peaks of yellow rock – sharp, ugly. After he departed, the moon shone brightly upon Sarah. Too late to guide her to safety. Laying among the wet leaves in blue ethereal light, a serene quality to the spectacle. At odds with the reality.

***

An early morning dog walker found her. Marlan is not a place known for murder. The last one in 1943, fifty-five years earlier. Before that, a shorter time gap to 1931. But the same man committed both those crimes and Marlan slept easily, knowing he was in the county jail, awaiting trial. True, it had taken fifty-five years and a couple of British pensioners to solve that murder. But the citizens of Marlan felt safe – but should they?

Hidden Garden Tearoom, Plympton-on-Sea, UK

Rev John Hanley turned up at the Hidden Garden Tearoom the day after the Shilton family visited his church. He had enquired after Hilda and found out where she lived. Having caused such a fuss the day before, one would assume Hilda might feel a small amount of guilt. Especially as the person she had embarrassed now stood before her. That is not how Hilda's brain worked. When Hilda saw the vicar in the tearoom, she assumed he was there to try their wares. Walking over to him she asked, 'what delicious treats can I tempt you with?'

'Ah, Mrs Shilton, I believe?' The good reverend bowed slightly. 'We met under... *unfortunate* circumstances yesterday.' He looked expectantly at Hilda.

Not understanding any cues for an apology, Hilda said, 'yes, very unfortunate. Can't be helped now though, I have already attended your rather boring service. Still, it's not beyond redemption. To use a term, you'll recognise. Are you having a drink or just here for idle chat? We do have paying customers, you know.'

'Oh, I, umm, can I have a pot of tea please?' said the vicar. His face flushed.

The café was crowded, and the nearest tables had noticed the vicar arrive. Most of that morning's customers were there because of the gossip about Sunday's service. Everyone went quiet and strained to hear the conversation between Hilda and Rev Hanley.

Hilda wrote on her pad and walked off, saying, 'one pot of tea coming up.'

'Now, umm, wait a moment,' said the vicar. He glanced at the many eyes focussed on him. 'I wanted to have a word while I was here.'

Hilda stopped turned back towards Rev Hanley. 'A word?'

'Yes, you see, St Marks has a long and illustrious history of worshipping God.' He wafted his hands in the air. 'I am merely the latest in a long line of incumbent Vicars.'

'Incompetence is nothing to be ashamed of, dear,' said Hilda. 'You can't help it.'

Rev Hanley took a step back and said, 'incumbent, not incompetence. It means the current vicar of this parish. The latest in a long and illustrious line.'

'Never mind,' said Hilda. She looked sympathetic. 'My pops always said it's hard to fill another man's slippers.'

'Slippers?' said the vicar. 'Oh... shoes.'

'Slippers, shoes, some footwear anyway. Now I must go and organise your drink,' said Hilda.

'If you can just wait a minute more, I, I have more to say,' said Rev Hanley. He sat down with a dramatic flourish. Wafting his jacket tails behind him. Then sitting straight, nose slightly upwards, he said. 'Now about yesterday...'

'I know, dear, as I said earlier. Dreadful, wasn't it? You can't expect to get it right straight away,' said Hilda. The other customers were moving their chairs a little closer. They were listening intently. You could have heard a pin drop in the café, apart from Hilda and Rev Hanley. A child sitting with his mother said, 'can I have a ...' His mother shushed him.

Rev Hanley's face turned a fetching shade of purple. He said, 'I have been here for five years!'

'Yes, that's a long time dear,' said Hilda, pursing her lips. 'Never mind. We can't all be quick learners.' She looked at him over her glasses.

Giggles and laughter came from around the room. The vicar breathed deeply. Then said, 'I have a *first* in theology and I received a *special mention* in my class at the ministerial training college.' He looked around at the customers. Many were his parishioners, head held high. The smiles and laughter caused him to look away.

'What a pity.' Hilda patted him on the shoulder.

'What do you mean, a pity?' said the reverend. He stared at her hand in horror, as if she had hit him.

'That you have fallen so far,' said Hilda. A gale of laughter erupted in the room. Some people doubled over, others laughing so loud that they could hardly catch their breath.

Rev Hanley shifted in his seat, and said, 'I came here to hold out an olive branch.'

'It's so good of you to realise you're in the wrong.' The gales of laughter in the room would have caused jealousy for a stand-up comedian. 'Now I really must fetch your order.

There are other customers waiting. We're very busy today for some unknown reason. It's not normally this full on a Monday morning.' Hilda walked off.

'I'm not in the...,' started the Vicar. But Hilda had already left. The customers gradually quietened down and went back to chatting. The consensus was one point to Hilda, nil to the Vicar. His head sunk forwards.

A few minutes later, Mrs Hanley, the vicar's wife, walked in, looking flustered. She was a woman you could easily miss. Mainly because she tried to be invisible. She came over to the table and spoke to her husband, 'Sssso sssssorry... I'm late... the queue.' She glanced around like a frightened bird.

'We're leaving.' Rev Hanley rose quickly.

'Oh... a, a, a drink?' asked Mrs Hanley. 'I, I, I thought...' she spoke to her husband's back as he headed to the door. She hastened after him.

Hilda was just walking across with a tray containing tea for one. She saw the vicar and his wife leave, and said, 'it looks like I have a spare pot of tea. Was anyone waiting on one?' A few hands went up.

May 1998

Sheriff's Office, Marlan, Ohio, USA

Sheriff Gerwin sat in his office, staring at two files. This was his first murder since he took office five years earlier. The one bit of evidence that CSI had collected on the murderer, and it made no sense. He called in his deputy, officer Coleman. They both looked at the results for ten minutes. 'You see, explain that?' Gerwin stood up and paced.

'It must be a mix-up at the lab,' Coleman was still reading the report.

It was DNA that matched a person in their database, Orville Stanley. But that was impossible. Orville Stanley was locked up on remand in the local prison, awaiting trial for two other murders. The only other murders that Marlan, Ohio, had known. They were way before Sheriff Gerwin's time, back in 1943 and 1931. He wasn't even born then.

'Yeah but look at that bit about degree of probability. They aren't even sure.' Gerwin stopped pacing and looked at Coleman.

'The covering notes say that's typical.'

'I'm gonna send it back and see what they say. I might have to call in someone.' Gerwin hated to admit it, but this whole thing was getting beyond him. First, the brutal murder of a young wife. It all seemed plain sailing, with plenty of physical evidence. Now the evidence itself made no sense. If only Hilda was privy to this information.

Marlan State Forest, Ohio, USA

A young couple were out walking their dog with purpose. Their purpose was sleuthing. The young couple, Annie, and Peter Cully were friends of Hilda and Pearl. They lived in Marlan, Ohio and first met Hilda and Pearl, the year before. The dog, for she is significant too, is called Kanga. Why was this couple out sleuthing? Murders fascinated Annie in general and, as they were so rare in her town, the latest one in particular. When Sarah was murdered, Annie had convinced Peter they should investigate. Then pass on what they found to Hilda. They knew that she loved to investigate and saw it as their job to help. After all, Hilda and Pearl had solved the previous two. Annie didn't lack faith in Sheriff Gerwin. It was just they remembered him from school. Little Johnny Gerwin had been in their class. Not the brightest spark. Everyone said he only got voted in as sheriff because the alternative was worse. Annie and Peter had no great expectations that he would solve the crime.

It was a warm day when Annie and Peter set off with Kanga into Marlan State Forest. They reached the area where Sarah's body had been discovered. No entry tape surrounded the area. Some of it had either blown down or ripped by curious onlookers. The investigators had long gone and any clues presumably discovered.

Kanga was interested in the area where the body had lain. No doubt because of the remaining scent of blood. Annie pulled her back and told her to stay away. Then Annie and Peter looked around the area. Standing for some time, wondering at the sadness of just how close Sarah had been to her home.

There was nothing of any obvious value and so they headed back to their car. As they trudged away, Peter's foot hit something. He stopped and picked it up. As he was about to throw it away, Annie stopped him. 'Wait, that may be a clue.'

'A lump of metal?' said Peter.

'You never know.'

'But if it is evidence. The Police would want it left exactly where I found it and no fingerprints.'

'Can you imagine going to Sheriff Gerwin about this?'

'Yeah, I know, but come on Annie.'

They took the clue with them. First, they took a photo of where it had lain, and a few shots of the surrounding area.

This was the 1990's, so they had to process the photos, two sets. Then post one set to Hilda. On arrival a week later, she looked at the images of a dark metal object on dark leaf covered ground and thought nothing of it. Perhaps Annie and Peter had a higher opinion of her sleuthing powers than were warranted. It is surprising how important a piece of old metal can be.

Plympton Playhouse, Plympton-on-Sea, UK

The Plympton Players amateur dramatics group met at the Plympton Playhouse, 7pm every Tuesday evening. The club had been struggling for some time before they lost their director. That was just the last straw. Posters sometimes used the initials PP at the PP, but locals found the alliteration annoying. They had started to find everything about the club irksome. It wasn't just the greater choice of entertainment available elsewhere, that kept people from the clubs shows. The club members were old and set in their ways. They did things as they always had. This included the style of acting, type of sets and even the costumes. These were ones left over from the theatre's original owners. Plays given The Plympton Player treatment could never be seen the same way again. Some of the townsfolk had read the leaflet about the theatre's demise and nodded in satisfaction. They talked of it being 'about time.' Fortunately for the future of the theatre, there was a silent majority who still loved it. Those who felt that all it needed was fresh blood. When these optimists heard of the old director's illness, they celebrated the chance of a new start and watched in eager anticipation.

***

The theatre building had been constructed in the 1930's by Sir Gerald Hustey OBE, a rich amateur theatre enthusiast. He and his wife Ethel used to host elaborate plays, followed by five course meals. They built an elaborate dining room on the premises, just for this purpose. Their friends, family, and business colleagues enjoyed the hospitality. What's not to enjoy? When Sir Gerald died, Ethel formed a charitable trust to run and manage the theatre. She lived and eventually died, hoping they would always use it as a place of entertainment. Unfortunately, she did not include a legacy to help pay for it. There was nothing in any of the legal papers to prevent the charitable trust selling the building and then ending the trust itself. So long as they used any proceeds for entertainment in Plympton-on-Sea. This was the situation the charitable trust was finding itself in. The building itself needed repair, inside and out. Add to that the lack of love for the theatre group using the premises. Things had not been going well.

***

The old dining room and kitchens from Sir Gerald's days were converted into a bar and meeting area. They used this in the intervals of plays and films. It was also a place for the Plympton Players to meet and rehearse their next productions.

A rag-tag and depressed looking group of people had gathered in the theatre dining area. It was 7pm on a Tuesday evening and time for their meeting. Looking at the elderly and dour group, it was easy to understand the town's opinion of them. Everything was about to change. Hilda breezed in, followed reluctantly by Pearl.

'You are all looking very sad.' Hilda smiled broadly. 'But don't worry, I'm here now, so everything will be alright.' All that was lacking was a fanfare. Pearl looked like a lieutenant with her captain.

If Hilda had expected a round of applause, smiles, or a warm welcome, it didn't come. The fifteen people in the room barely looked up at her. After the interruption, they looked back at the person who had been talking when Hilda and Pearl arrived. Lilly, for that is who had been talking, glanced at Hilda, and said, 'please take a seat and I will continue.'

Hilda and Pearl noisily found some chairs and, after much moving of people and furniture, settled in place. Pearl didn't look happy to be there. But Hilda could be very persuasive. 'Amateur dramatics are not my thing,' that's what she told Hilda. But as Hilda told her, 'You can always be backstage.'

'You can carry on now,' said Hilda. 'Then I will tell you all about me.' If she had not been sitting, she may have bowed.

'I don't know who you are.' Lilly peered over her glasses at Hilda.

'You won't until I tell you, dear,' said Hilda.

'Please, just be quiet and wait,' said Lilly. 'As most of you know, George has stepped down as director, for health reasons.'

'That's why I'm...,' started Hilda. Lilly put her finger on her lips and Hilda was quiet. It must have reminded her of school all those years earlier.

'The PTCT is...,' said Lilly.

Hilda cut in. 'What's the PCTC dear?'

'The PTCT is the Plympton Theatre Charitable Trust, and it's struggling. I know that a few of you are trustees, as am I,' said Lilly. She stared hard at Hilda, who was looking at her hands with great interest. 'The result of all this is that we are not sure what to do next and have called this meeting to ask for suggestions.'

'Can I speak now?' asked Hilda, looking at Lilly.

'Yes,' said Lilly. She leaned back and looked around the room.

'I would like to offer my services as a director of this club,' said Hilda. She looked at the club members as if she expected a cheer or shout of acclamation. There was an initial silence and Hilda felt disappointed. This group would not be easy to get motivated.

Lilly asked, 'are you qualified and or experienced?'

'I worked at the BBC in the 1930's,' said Hilda. She could not see Pearl's open mouth. 'I also appeared on Broadway.' Hilda sat up straight and felt very proud. The entire group stared at her wide eyed.

'Umm, you were a Broadway extra?' asked Lilly.

'No, I was the star,' said Hilda. She felt as if she ought to get up and bow, or perhaps curtsey.

'A star? On Broadway? What's your name?' said Lilly.

'Hilda Shilton.' Hilda got up and bowed. It seemed appropriate. Pearl put her head in her hands.

'I've never heard of you,' said Lilly. She looked at the other club members. All of them were shaking their heads.

'I think you need to explain about the accident,' said Pearl to Hilda. But that just made Hilda frown and shake her head.

'You had an accident?' said Lilly, her eyebrows lowered.

'No, no, I was the toast of Hollywood...' started Hilda.

'I thought you said Broadway,' interrupted Lilly.

'That's the one,' said Hilda, 'and the director wanted me to come back again. But I don't have an equality card,' said Hilda.

'Equity,' said Pearl, shaking her head.

'That too,' said Hilda.

'How did you get on Broadway without an equity card?' said Lilly.

'Never mind that now,' said Hilda, getting impatient. 'Shall we get on with voting me in as director?'

'Tell them what happened,' said Pearl. She waved her hand at the group.

Everyone looked at Hilda. Reluctantly, she started, 'it was last year; we were on the adventure of a lifetime in America. We'd been searching for Pearl's long-lost twin sister, hadn't we Pearl?' Pearl nodded.

Lilly said, 'hang on, what's this got to do with Broadway?'

'Give me a chance,' said Hilda. 'I'm getting there. You're very impatient. Now, where was I. Oh yes? We couldn't find Pearl's sister, and all seemed lost.' Hilda did a dramatic sweeping motion to one side and hid her head in her arms. Then she peeked out from under her arm. Everyone looked at her, puzzled. She sat upright and continued, 'to cheer ourselves up, we went to see a Broadway show. There you go. That didn't take long. Shall I mention Pappa de Luca's, Pearl?'

'That's not relevant.' Pearl shrugged her shoulders.

'Alright,' said Hilda. She screwed up her eyes. 'Let me think, we arrived at the Theatre and as I passed the stage door, it opened. You could have blown me down with a feather. This young man came rushing out and shouted, "you're a star!"'

'Hilda, really?' said Pearl.

'Alright, maybe he didn't use those exact words. But he was very relieved to see me. He said, "at last the person we've been waiting for, come this way." And he shuffled me into the stage door,' said Hilda.

'Why would he do that?' asked Lilly.

'Let me answer that,' said Pearl. Hilda looked crestfallen. 'Hilda wore the same clothes as the lead. Well, she always has. Add to that, the actual star of the show was extremely late.'

'Oh, I see, I think,' said Lilly. But she did not look as if she did. All the club members looked very puzzled, too.

'Yes, and he rushed me through. Saying thanks and you're wonderful, every two minutes. He could probably tell that I'm a natural star, you see,' said Hilda.

Pearl shook her head, then said, 'of course, I'd gone on ahead and wondered where Hilda was. I left her ticket at the ticket office and took my seat. Never in my life expecting to see her on stage.'

Lilly was sitting staring at Hilda and Pearl with wide-open eyes, on the edge of her seat.

'Yes, that's right Pearl, you were in your seat. Anyway, they took me to makeup, and I got ready. Do you know that the costume designer looked at me, huffed and walked off? Just because I was already in the right outfit. But the makeup artist was ever so nice. She said that he can be a drama queen,' said Hilda. She looked around at the club members and smiled.

'They seriously didn't realise that you were a different person?' asked Lilly.

'No, not at all, dear. I have star quality, you see,' Hilda posed. Lilly looked unconvinced. Hilda continued, 'Once I was ready, they took me to the wings. It was ever so exciting standing there, ready to enter on cue. Do you know it's very dark in the wings? I could hardly see the other actors waiting to go onto the stage.'

'Ah, that's why they didn't realise,' said Lilly. She nodded and looked around. 'One thing makes sense, anyway.'

Pearl said, 'I heard later that the actual actress arrived late and started banging on the stage door. Her taxi had broken down, and she had to walk the last block.'

'Don't keep jumping in, dear, it's rude. Where was I?' asked Hilda. She glanced at the ceiling, then continued. 'Ah yes. When I stepped out on that stage, I knew it was where I was meant to be. Everything was perfect.'

Lilly looked at Hilda open mouthed, and said, 'really, but how did you know the dance routines?'

'Let me explain,' said Pearl. Hilda frowned at her. 'It was a musical comedy, and Hilda knew the songs. As for the dancing... The opening number was... let's say complex. Hilda loves dancing, it's a great passion for her. But she is not Broadway standard.' Hilda looked shocked. Pearl said to Hilda, 'you're not.'

Hilda shook her head, and said, 'everyone loved it. I must have been good enough.'

'That's because you had a good go at copying your fellow dancers,' said Pearl. 'Not that the lead actress is meant to just copy the chorus. The chorus line dancers were waving and signaling to you like crazy. Trying to get you to go to your position. They even tried to show you a few moves.'

'I think I did marvelously,' said Hilda.

'You did,' said Pearl. 'The audience loved it. The whole effect to the audience was hilarious. It was a musical comedy, after all. The crescendo was brilliant. The semi-circle of fireworks behind you. You rising, spinning in the air on a wire, above a platform, during the final notes of the song. While the chorus line all turned towards you and waving flags. Although, I'd have to say that I was very shocked seeing you on stage. But you were fantastic.' Hilda looked pleased at Pearl's compliment. Lilly just looked amazed.

'As I was leaving, the press arrived. Full of praise at the brilliant new lead actress,' said Hilda. 'They asked me to stay on, of course.'

'Presumably, that's when he found out you were not equity members?' said Lilly.

'Tish, tish, minor details,' said Hilda. 'We were too busy looking for Ruby, anyway. Then there was that diamond thief.'

'Diamond thief?' said Lilly. Her mouth open wide.

'I think that will just add unnecessary confusion,' said Pearl.

'Perhaps you're right, dear. He was very confusing, especially when he drew that gun on me,' said Hilda.

'What!' said Lilly. She had turned quite pale.

'There's no need to worry,' said Pearl. 'It's all sorted out, and no one was hurt.'

Lilly didn't look convinced. She took a few deep breaths and then said, 'any other candidates?'

Lots of shaking heads. The club members decided, given the dire straits they were in and the great need of a director. Plus, the fact no one else was offering, they would give Hilda a chance. What did they have to lose? Perhaps a question they should have explored more fully. George, the previous director, had bought in scripts before he became ill. Which meant the club had everything ready to practise a new production. So, they all agreed to continue with that play. Hilda took the master script away, so that she could start planning parts and schedules. She would start auditions the next week. It may also have been an idea to look more thoroughly at George's choice of script. He had chosen it while feeling very unwell. Not the best choice he had ever made. It had been available cheaply. Mainly because no one else wanted to stage it. It had also been

George who kept choosing the wrong plays. Ones no one in town wanted to watch. If only they had examined all these things before deciding to continue with it. Not an auspicious start for Hilda's first production.

Hidden Garden Tearoom, Plympton-on-Sea, UK

The next afternoon, Hilda was just trying out a new dance move, whilst holding a full cup of coffee. She was trying to think about the murder case in America. The phone rang, just as she was trying a sprinkler move. This involved imitating a garden sprinkler rotating around. It was probably just as well she was interrupted, as her coffee was in danger of spilling. Hilda gave her usual full announcement of name place and number into the phone.

Ruby, Pearl's twin sister from the USA, said, 'Hilda, isn't that your old phone number?'

'Silly me, I am getting forgetful,' said Hilda.

'Aren't we all?' said Ruby. She was phoning from The White House. 'Is Pearl there too? I have information for you both.'

'Yes, she's just having a sit in the garden, while I dance around,' said Hilda.

'Can you fetch her?' asked Ruby. She sounded serious.

Interesting timing, considering Hilda's thoughts on the murder case. The reason Pearl phoned was to tell Hilda and Pearl that the trial was in six weeks' time. They would hold it in Marlan, Ohio. Ruby said she had rented a house for the duration of the trial. Hilda and Pearl could stay with her, as they were key witnesses. After Hilda hung up she smiled, maybe she would have an opportunity to put things right.

Chapter Three

May 1998

Fly-Away Travel Agents, Stoke Hind, UK

Pearl made simple work of preparing for their trip to the USA. As usual, Hilda didn't. She headed out in search of a travel agent. She soon discovered that Plympton-on-Sea didn't have one. So, she decided that as she wanted to visit her own bank in Stoke Hind, to sort out dollars, she would go to Stoke Hind. Hilda was unaware she could buy dollars in many places these days. Besides, there was a comfort in doing things the way you had always done them. Once Hilda arrived at Stoke Hind, she headed to the travel agents. Hilda burst in smiling and announced, 'I'm back. Did you miss me?'

'Ah, Mrs. Shilton, what a delight to see you again. We were so sorry to hear you'd moved. Weren't we?' Joyce wore a false smile and glanced around at her staff for confirmation. They all nodded in a very unconvincing way.

'How kind of you all,' Hilda, was oblivious to their insincerity. 'I have come back specially to seek your help. You were so wonderful on my last trip to America.'

'You're going again?' asked Joyce, her voice raised a pitch.

'I have a murderer to catch,' Hilda sat at Joyce's desk.

'A murderer?' Joyce was still standing behind her desk. 'I read about the diamond thief. Have they found that he committed murder?'

'Don't be a silly-Billy. No, this is the murderer of Ruby's parents, of course. Don't tell anyone, but I am quite a famous detective now. A positive Shylock Romes.'

'Of course,' Joyce looked confused. 'I assume your passport is still in order?'

'Yes indeed,' Hilda sat back and stretched. 'Although as good friends of The President, I wonder if I'll even need one.'

'Good friends of The US President? I heard about your visit to The White House and indeed Camp David, but...'

'Yes, yes, perhaps they'll send Air Farce One for me.'

'Farce? Is this a joke?' Joyce looked at her colleagues. They were all ignoring their clients and listening in. Which was just as well. Their clients were also fascinated by Hilda's stories.

'It's no joke. Hold on, I got it wrong.' There was a collective sigh in the room. 'Air Farce One is the plane Dougy flies in when he comes over here. It was Marry One that Pearl and I flew in. That big helicopter thingy.' Joyce did not seem any clearer with that explanation. But then, if Hilda had used the correct name, it may have helped.

A bit later, after sorting out the confusion and booking a normal commercial flight. Hilda headed out of the travel agents and off to the bank.

Barkeast Bank, Stoke Hind, UK

Mr Deville, the bank manager, was just leaving as Hilda arrived. She accosted him and asked, 'where are you going? I need to see you.'

'I'm off for my lunch. So, you'll either need to book an appointment or see someone else,' said Mr Deville.

'Are you allowed lunch?' asked Hilda.

'Of course I am. I need a break,' said Mr Deville. At that moment, Ms Wallace came hurrying out of the bank. 'I'm ready at last, Ricky.'

'Ricky?' said Hilda. She glanced between Ms Wallace and Mr Deville. 'How very familiar you are with your boss.'

'Ms Wallace and I both happen to be heading the same way,' explained Mr Deville.

'I see,' said Hilda, peering over her glasses at him.

'That's right,' said Ms Wallace. 'Rick... Mr Deville and I always have lunch together.' Mr. Deville screwed up his face.

'Do you indeed? Very nice, I'm sure. I bet Mrs Deville is happy about that too,' said Hilda. 'My detecting nose is twitching.'

Mr Deville coughed and spluttered, then said, 'it's a working lunch. Ms Wallace is my secretary; I check her figures while we eat.'

'Do you now?' said Hilda. Her eyes were wide. 'Before you go and carry out this important... work, if you could just sort out some dollars for me.'

Mr Deville hesitated for a moment and then said, 'I'll ask Joe to do it.' He opened the bank door and waved Hilda through.

Hilda headed inside, and as she passed him said, 'so long as you're sure Joe's capable.'

'He is the senior cashier,' said Mr Deville. Once inside, he walked up to the empty counter and called for Joe through the glass partition. He was sitting at his desk.

'Back from lunch already?' asked Joe. He smiled and looked over Mr Deville's shoulder. Hilda was behind him, and Ms Wallace was standing in the doorway.

'Can you please sort Mrs Shilton out with some dollars?' said Mr Deville. He then walked off.

'Aren't you going to check he does it right?' asked Hilda.

'I trust him,' said Mr Deville, walking rapidly towards Ms Wallace. They disappeared out of the door and up the street at speed.

Joe smiled at Hilda, and said, 'besides he has other priorities at lunchtimes.'

'You just concentrate on the job at hand, young Joe. I need some dollars,' said Hilda.

'Off to the USA again, eh? You're becoming a jet setter,' said Joe. He whistled.

***

All the naysayers who said that Hilda wasn't cut out for running a tea shop were right, she found it boring and hard work. Perhaps she just wanted it as a place to run a detective agency after all. If only her family and friends hadn't blocked the idea. Although no doubt there are many potential clients who may be glad that they did.

But having chosen to run a tearoom, Hilda was not someone to give up easily. Day after day, she slogged away. Night after night, she sank on the sofa, exhausted. Regular 9-5 work had never suited Hilda. She was a more spontaneous person. On a typical Saturday, Hilda was in the tearoom serving. Almost every table was full. Hilda flitted around in her usual disorganised fashion. Most of her time she spent talking to people. After all, her vision of being a tea shop owner had been sitting in a sunny English garden drinking tea, eating cake, and chatting to potential clients. She hadn't pictured the need to serve them tea. That part of the daydream was missing. But realism was never a part of Hilda's daydreams.

The White House, Washington DC, USA

Part way around the world, in the capital city of the USA, is Washington, DC. In that capital, is The White House, at 1600 Pennsylvania Ave NW. It's a building that has housed the US President since 1800. Within that famous building is an equally well-known room, the Oval Office. A room that Hilda sneaked into on her own visit to The White House. But let us not dwell on her misbehaviour. Currently, that room was occupied by the right person. Sitting at his impressive oak desk in a large leather chair, looking important, was Douglas Meyer. The President of the United States. He had just finished for the day and rose from his desk, then headed to the living quarters. He was in the middle of a convoy of security staff. Walking next to him, Hank, his chief of staff. Was in mid conversation, '... will get the most leverage.'

'What about opposition?' asked The President. Even though they were walking fast, he wasn't out of breath. The same wasn't true of Hank.

'We have all...' gasp, 'the support...' puff, 'we need....' gasp, 'Now you enjoy...' puff, 'your evening... Mr. President.' Hank finished.

'You have a good one too Hank,' said The President. They parted at the end of a corridor and Doug continued up to the residence at an even faster pace. He arrived to find his wife and children all in the sitting room. The TV playing cartoons.

'What rubbish is this?' asked Doug as he walked in. He checked for the TV remote.

Evelyn stared at 'The Leader of The Free World' and gave him a look to prevent further discussion. She was holding the remote. After a cursory greeting of his kids. Doug and Evelyn headed to the bedroom. They had to change, ready for a function that evening. Doug was adjusting his suit and Evelyn applying her make-up when Doug told his wife. 'We need to go to England.'

'What? When?' asked Evelyn. She stopped applying lipstick and turned around to face her husband.

'Three weeks,' said Doug. 'A bit last minute. Top secret stuff. Sorry, can't say more.' He looked away.

Evelyn sat for a moment, sighed, and said, 'that's OK, I'll bring Ruby and we can see her sister.'

'What about the kids?' asked Doug. He was struggling with some cufflinks. Evelyn got up and helped. Then she assisted him with his bow tie. He was never any good with those. Given a choice he would use a pre-tied one.

'I don't want them to miss school,' said Evelyn. She oversaw the children. She sat back down and finished her makeup. 'Do I look all right?'

'You look beautiful,' said Doug. He walked over and gave her a kiss.

'Mind my lipstick,' said Evelyn. She gazed into his eyes.

Stonehouse Manor, Upper Plympton, UK

Tucked away at the end of a narrow country lane stood a stately pile of faded grandeur and importance, Stonehouse Manor. An unknown parent, his mother had endowed Lord Leonard Russell with this down-at-heel mansion. His mother, whilst rich and powerful, didn't pass much wealth to Leonard. Just sufficient to be comfortable. He continued at Stonehouse Manor after marrying Mildred, a local councillor at Meedham County Council. Stonehouse Manor had once been the height of comfort and fashion. They had spent little money on it since. You might look tired and shabby after three hundred years.

Mildred had rushed into marrying Len. She was living to regret her haste. His titles and family crest were false and paid for by his mother to hide his true heritage. Mildred had tried over many months to uncover the identity of his parents; but failed. Len had never needed to work and lacked the drive to try. His mother had endowed him with enough money to be comfortable rather than rich. He had spent his days bumbling around in country pursuits until he met Mildred.

Mildred came across Len at a friend's shooting weekend. His title and apparent wealth enamoured her. He had caught her at that weak moment. That was her excuse. Len was showing an interest in her. She had asked about what he did. He explained he didn't need to work. Then he took her back to his mansion - money, and property. She fell head over heels in love with both; he was tolerable as well. It was night when she first saw the manor. It always looked good at night. One thing led to another. She wanted to land the fish before it got away.

After they were married, Mildred discovered they were not as well off as she wished. Len himself was a complete disappointment. Far too weak. Though many people may have considered the run-down manor house in which they lived an amazing luxury. It was not up to Mildred's high standards. No one would have guessed her lowly upbringing. But she had very high expectations.

A few months into their marriage, an international crime ring, The Conglomerate, contacted Mildred. They told her that their interests and hers aligned. Or at least they bribed her with promises of money and power. The Conglomerate allowed Mildred to handle their UK interests. Being an honest and upright public servant. She considered the proposition for thirty seconds before accepting it.

***

Saturday morning and Mildred was sitting in their drafty sitting room at the manor. The wallpaper peeling in one corner. Len walked in with a tea tray. He did all the menial tasks. Mildred had fired most of the staff Len had employed before their marriage to save money. Besides, Len did nothing all day. He may have argued that he no longer had time for fun. But his complaints fell on deaf ears.

'Tea love,' said Len. He smiled as he put the tray on a rickety table next to his wife.

'What are you smiling about?' Mildred glared at him.

'It's a beautiful, sunny day. I wondered if you might like a walk later?' said Len. He hesitated near his wife.

'There isn't time for that. I have calls to make,' said Mildred. She turned back to some papers she was studying.

'Not the Conglomerate again. Whoever they are, they seem so awful?' said Len, frowning.

Mildred stared at her husband and shook her head. 'Awful! You don't know what you are talking about. Nor how important The Conglomerate is. They'll save our bacon.'

'Are things really that bad?' asked Len. He looked seriously at Mildred.

'Just drink your tea,' said Mildred. She picked up her own cup.

After they finished silently drinking their tea and munching a couple of biscuits. Mildred sent Len off for his walk. She placed an international call.

William and Louise Shilton's House, Meedham, UK

William had been working late at the office most nights. But on Friday, he arrived back at the same time as Louise. Which was a shock for two reasons. First, because, as a teacher, she nearly always finished before him. Unless she had parents' evenings or other special events. Second, because he had never finished so early before. To top off the surprises, William was carrying a bunch of flowers.

Louise pulled up in the driveway. She leapt in her seat when William appeared at her car door. 'Oh my goodness, I thought you were a rapist,' she said.

'What? Carrying flowers,' said William.

'I don't know what they carry,' said Louise. She had her car door half open.

'Not flowers, surely. Anyway, you can see it's me now,' said William. He held out the flowers.

'Give me a moment to recover,' said Louise. She was puffing. William tried to both kiss Louise and hand her the flowers. All the while, she struggled to clamber out of the car.

Their neighbour, Ted, an older and unwell man, was in his garden. He had poor eyesight and could only see Louise struggling against a strange man. Ted knew it couldn't be her husband, William. He never returned home this early. Ted ran towards Louise and William, shouting, 'oi! I may be old, but I'm handy with me fists.' By the time he arrived, he was bent double, panting and wheezing. His asthma was playing up. That and the fact he was very unfit.

'Are you alright Ted?' asked Louise, putting an arm around his shoulders.

'I... am.... Fine.... Just.... Came.... To.... Help...' said Ted, between breaths.

'It's just me, Ted,' said William, waving at Ted. But Ted could hardly see because of the sweat running down his face. Just as well that no actual attack was underway.

'You'd better come in and have a sit down,' said Louise. She led Ted gently in the front door.

Inside the house, Louise had taken Ted to the sofa and went to get him a cup of tea. This left William standing looking at Ted, holding the flowers he had for Louise. Having regained his breath and wiped away the sweat, Ted said, 'nice flowers.'

'A gift for Louise,' said William. He started pacing.

'Does she like them?' said Ted.

'I don't know yet.' It probably came out sharper than he planned.

William's son, Josh, popped his head around the lounge door, and said, 'hi dad, oh and hi Ted. Where's mum?'

'In the kitchen, making tea,' said William. He had stopped pacing for a moment. 'You're here more than your own flat. Glad to see you still have your key.'

'Nice to be welcomed,' said Josh, laughing.

'Sorry, that came out wrong. It's always lovely to see you. I'm grumpy,' said William. He nodded towards Ted, who was distracted by reading William's golfing magazine.

Josh looked at the flowers in his dad's arms and Ted on the sofa, then said, 'ah, gotcha.'

'Yeah, well,' said William, shrugging. Ted glanced up from the magazine wide eyed and a blank faced.

'Pretty flowers, dad,' said Josh. He headed to the kitchen.

A short while later, Louise and Josh came through with tea and biscuits. William had sat down, his shoulders slumped. 'Are those flowers for me?' asked Louise.

'Yes,' said William. He sprang out of his seat. 'I have been working so late all this week. It's a special gift. Being Friday and all… date night.'

'What? Why? Eh?' said Ted. He looked at Louise and William.

'Come on Ted,' said Josh. He grabbed Ted's hands and led him out. He said to his parents, 'have a nice evening.'

William and Louise stared at their departing guests, then at each other. William whispered in Louise's ear. Louise smiled and gave William a kiss.

September 1930

Marlan, Ohio, USA

The two Stanley twins should have been identical, Orville and Wilbur. Biology made that true. But an accident meant Orville limped. Perhaps that should have made him tougher, harder. It often does with boys. Wilbur had a toughness, a hardness that came from nature, not nurture. He enjoyed teasing their pet dog. Tying sticks to its tail. He just plain enjoyed hurting living things. Never grew out of it. Probably just as well he never had the money for firecrackers.

Whether it was one too many sticks on Duke's tails or the constant teasing over the limp. Who knows what makes a gentle kid break? Some people just take it, over and again, then one day... enough is enough. They were down by the river and the weather was turning. Their ma had said not to hang around before supper. That day, the teasing became too much. Wilbur teased Orville about just how long it would take him to limp home. Wilbur laughed so loud at that one. Even threatened to eat Orville's supper. Maybe had he not kept kicking Orville on route and whacking Duke with that enormous stick. Or if he'd held back on throwing a stone at that bird's nest. Then stamping on the eggs. Was that the last straw?

Next thing the two of them were scrapping and rolling. Kicking and punching, shouting, and fighting for all they were worth. No one was there to stop them. The creek was nearby, and they ended up in it. Wilbur took the chance and had Orville pinned down good and proper. If their ma had not come looking for them, heaven knows what would have happened.

Everything changed after that. Wilbur, so near, drowned Orville. The murderous glint in Wilbur's eye. After that day, their ma decided Wilbur wasn't right in the head. What if he tried again? Or attacked another kid?

The creek where she caught them was fast flowing. Rocks so sharp folk had been cut up bad. Ma just acted blindly. Reported Wilbur, missing in that river. Told the sheriff he fell in, hit his head, went under. No, she'd not seen him surface. Sheriff called together everyone, and they searched. There was no trace. None could be found, nor would be found.

His own ma locked Wilbur up. Long enough that the coroner issued a death certificate. Orville was so mixed up by it all, he hardly knew what to think. Especially when his ma roped him into keeping an eye on his own brother. Like being a jailor, when there's been no trial or jury.

Early July 1998

Marlan, Ohio, USA

Two weeks had gone by since Ruby had phoned about Orville's pre-trial hearing. Hilda and Pearl had arrived a couple of days early to get over jet lag. Hilda popped round to visit Annie and Peter while Pearl was still recovering. After all, it was only a short walk, about three miles from the rental house Ruby had organised.

Hilda was sitting in her favourite chair at Annie and Peter's. Kanga had taken up position at her feet, looking up suspiciously at her. As if to say, 'you look vaguely familiar.' Since her last visit, Annie had bought in some British style tea bags. Peter was brewing a cup for Hilda, following some earlier instructions. Once everyone was seated with drinks, Annie asked, 'did you ever make any sense of that piece of metal?'

'What piece of metal, dear?' asked Hilda.

'The metal in the photos we sent,' said Peter. He glanced at Annie. She rummaged in her bag for the piece of metal and handed it to Hilda.

'Oh, yes,' said Hilda. She sat forward in her seat and took the object. 'Mind you, it looks very different from the photo you posted to me.' In truth, Hilda had spent little time looking at the photo they'd sent.

Annie said, 'photos can be deceptive. What do you think, Hilda?'

Hilda stared closely at the item. She screwed up her eyes. Then she lifted her glasses and looked again. Shaking her head, she put her glasses on again, and said, 'it looks like nothing I've ever seen before. Except that time...' She stared at the ceiling.

'What time?' said Peter.

'Oh, of course dear, you weren't there,' said Hilda, screwing up her eyes. 'Now let me think. It's like Winnie the Pooh, isn't it?'

Annie looked at the object, and said, 'is it?'

Peter was also looking at the photo, shaking his head.

'No, not the thingy me jig,' said Hilda. 'I mean thinking. Think, think, think. I feel like my head is full of fluff. I need to stand up to think.' Hilda didn't just stand, she started to tap dance on the wooden floor. Then sang a little ditty in time to her dance.

'Does that help,' asked Annie.

'Yes,' said Hilda, nodding. 'I must move around for my brain to work. I can't think sitting still.'

After watching Hilda dance around for a while, Peter said, 'the object, any ideas where you saw it?'

'It's coming back to me.' Hilda stomped and did a grand ending with jazz hands, then sat down.

Annie waved her hand to encourage further information. Hilda stared at her hand, mesmerized. Then, as if she had seen a vision, she said, 'Orville, that nasty man. He had it. Played with it in his hands.' Then she sat back and relaxed.

Marlan County Correctional, Ohio, USA

A couple of days later, Pearl, Ruby, and Hilda pulled up in a large parking lot. Then entered the drab and uninspiring one level building. The search for contraband was thorough and caused a few complaints from Hilda. Orville Stanley's lawyer, Vance Jurgen, met them in the waiting area and took them to a private room. Their meeting with Orville would come under the client privilege confidentiality rules granted to his lawyer.

Orville stood and looked at the three ladies for a while. Then he sat down. They were all staying at a distance along the back wall. Prison guards monitored the meeting through glass panels. Vance suggested the ladies sit down. Eventually they did, on chairs by the wall. Orville said, 'thank you for coming. I know it must be hard.'

'I don't know what you hope to gain,' said Ruby. 'I saw you that day, walking away from the well. Covered in blood and dirt. I know you killed Ellie. Hilda and Pearl say that you know things about my parents only the murderer could know. You're a double murderer. I don't know why we came.'

Orville rested his hands on the table. 'This is going to be complicated to explain. You might not believe me.' He took a deep breath. 'I have a twin, Wilbur.' Ruby began shaking her head. Hilda nodded and looked at Pearl.

'He named us after the Wright brothers. Our pa's only contribution to our life. That and the junkyard of a house we lived in. He left just after we were born.'

'You had a twin. He died when you were young,' said Ruby firmly.

'Please listen, I'll get to that. It's a big part of all this,' said Orville, I know this sounds crazy. Ruby shrugged and sat silently.

Orville continued, 'no one knew how our ma would make ends meet. Cash wasn't exactly free flowing. But she kept me well dressed for school. The welfare officer never had no cause to visit.'

'Only time I ever saw your brother Wilbur at school. He was in trouble,' said Ruby in a distant, quiet voice.

'Yeah, he was a different case that's for sure,' said Orville. He stared at the table. 'Ma was always dressed in rags, too. I never understood it. Nor why folks said she stank. Used to tease me bout it.'

Ruby kept her focus on the floor. She had joined the teasing about his ma at school.

Orville sat staring at the ladies. Then he took a deep breath and said, 'Wilbur tried to kill me...'

Ruby leaped from her seat, as if propelled by an unknown hand. She said, 'No, no, no, you're twisting things, it's, it's, you, you're the murderer.' She turned to Hilda and Pearl. 'Come on, I'm not listening to any more of this.' She was hyperventilating. She walked towards the door.

Hilda stood up quickly and took hold of Ruby's hand. She said, 'this isn't the man we saw. Hear him out.' Ruby searched Hilda's eyes and her breathing slowed. She turned towards

Orville and said, 'explain, but if I...' her words petered out. Her shoulders sagged.

Orville said, 'Wilbur was... maybe is a monster. Ma realized it that day he tried to kill me. He was teasing bout me limp.... we got into a fight, down by the crick.' He stopped and stared at the table.

'But what about the drowning?' asked Ruby.

Orville glanced up at her, then back at the table. He said, 'was me who nearly drowned. Some nights, I wake choking, remembering.' The words seemed to echo around the room.

'Then why did we all hear it was Wilbur?' asked Ruby. Her eyes searched his.

No one spoke for a few minutes. An air conditioning fan hummed. As Ruby opened her mouth, Orville said, 'Ma didn't want him out of her sight... after what he did. Guess it scared her he'd do it again. Kill someone next time.'

Ruby's mouth was still open, she slowly closed it. Orville fixed his gaze upon her. His eyes were watering as he said, 'ma yanked me outta the crick, near enuf dead.' Orville breathed hard, closed his eyes, yet tears still found their way in rivulets down his cheeks. 'I don't recollect much a whiles after.' He opened his bloodshot eyes and stared at Ruby. 'Ma locked Wilbur up. Told the sheriff he'd drowned.' Orville had a haunted appearance. Like someone living in the past. 'Didn't work long. Wilbur broke a window. Ma fetched him back. He'd git out again.' Orville's eyes closed, and he seemed to be asleep. The only lie to that being the constant tears. Hilda broke the spell, asked if he needed a drink. His eyes sprung open in surprise. The rest of his story came even slower. As if it were so painful, he had shoved it away deep inside. But he continued, 'the time Wilbur pushed Ellie down the well, ma was ill.... I was ment to be lookin out fer him.' Orville's words came out through tears. 'When we both got older, she got me to swear I'd help. But you've met him.' Orville stared wildly at Hilda and Pearl, fear in his watery eyes. 'I'm not strong. What could I do?' He slumped back in his chair.

'Where's your ma now?' asked Hilda gently.

Orville shook his head. Tears ran free. They could just make out the words, 'gone.' When Hilda asked, 'do you mean, dead?' He just nodded.

Hilda asked if he suspected Wilbur had a hand in that. Orville shrank back in his seat and all the remaining colour disappeared from his face.

Ruby's eyes had softened as she listened to the harrowing tale. At the Pearl took hold of Ruby's hand, then said to Orville, 'I can't imagine having a twin like that. If it's Wilbur, we met. Then he is very scary.' Hilda agreed.

Ruby looked into Pearl's eyes, grasping her hand tightly. Then she reached across and took Orville's hand. He looked up at Pearl and Ruby in shock and sobbed louder.

Hilda walked over to the table and sat in a chair opposite Orville. She gazed at the scene, Ruby, Pearl, and Orville all grasping hands. Not a dry eye between them. Then she glanced at the object in her hand and said to Orville, 'I've just realised this is Wilbur's.' She placed the metal object in front of Orville. Security had let her bring it in, as it had no sharp edges.

'Where'd you git it?' asked Orville. He wiped his eyes on his sleeve and picked up the metal piece.

'A friend found it next to the place of the latest murder. But what is it dear?' asked Hilda. I last saw Wilbur holding it.

Orville turned the metal over in his hands. It was about the size of a medium egg. Light brown and uneven. It had been worn smooth by handling. There was an indentation in it that looked like the shape of a wolfs head if you had an excellent imagination. One of the security guards banged on the glass window. He put it down again and said, 'Wilbur's lucky wolf iron. He got it near an old coal mine. Dared me to follow him. I did a short ways; got scared and headed out. After bout half hour he comes out bold as brass. Holding that lump of iron above his head like a trophy. Howling and a hollering. He always carried it ever since. Most times in his hand, rubbing it, fondling it, like some lucky charm. It started sharp, he wore it smooth over the years. He must be fit to burst having lost that. I bet he spent a time looking after he realised it was gone. I never liked to cross him. He'll be angrier than a bull on heat bout losing it.'

Vance jumped in, and said, 'that murder is the one with the DNA that could either of you. This bit of metal is evidence Wilbur committed it. Your friends should have left it at the murder scene; it's vital evidence.'

'They took photos of where it was. They were telling me your sheriff is not very good at murders,' said Hilda.

'Sheriff Gerwin would not be my choice to investigate this. But some of his staff are OK,' said Vance. He took all the details and the lump of metal from the table.

Hilda got up ready to leave, and said, 'let's hope we don't run into Wilbur again, if he's such a crosspatch.'

Pearl said, 'the question is, where is Wilbur now?'

'It's something I have been trying to find out,' said Vance. 'It looks like he may have been at their homestead. There's evidence that someone has been there.'

'If my brother's still around. You'd all best be careful,' said Orville.

Chapter Four

June 1998

Outside Marlan County Correctional, Ohio, USA

Wilbur ears must have been burning, as he sat outside the prison. He would have an idea why Orville would want to see the three ladies. His dark demeanour suggested it did not make him happy. He headed back to the homestead that he had indeed been using. Whenever he saw Vance heading towards it, he had hidden. On route he bought some more knives. You can never have too many knives. Guns were not things he had experience with. Perhaps just as well for the three ladies. With a knife, he needed to be close.

Rental House, Marlan, Ohio, USA

When the three ladies returned to the rental property, they were still processing everything. Ruby phoned her friend Chad. He worked for the Secret Service as part of the president's protection detail. She asked him what to do about the danger from Wilbur. He told her he would make a few calls and call her back.

They locked all the doors and windows and stayed inside while they waited. Chad had given them instructions not to answer the door to anyone. Which was just as well.

A heavily disguised Wilbur turned up at their door. He rang and knocked. Looking out of the window, they saw what appeared to be a police officer. It was tempting to answer the door. But they could see no police car nearby and he was alone. As he walked around the building that the ladies got scared. They saw his face at a window. Grey dead eyes peered in; they recognised him. They all huddled in a corner. It was getting late, and no lights were on. He obviously could not see them because he left.

Chad called back and after hearing of the incident, he headed to the ladies himself. He arranged a week's emergency leave. He had already sorted out a few friends who lived locally to form an ad hoc security detail. The ladies had a code word check in place. His friends arrived first. Hilda loved the idea of code words. It reminded her of James Bond. When Chad's friends arrived and knocked on the door, Hilda tried out her version of the code, and said, 'it's cold in here.'

Pearl said, 'you were meant to wait for them to say, "it's cold in Little Rock." Then we say, "not as cold as in here." Now you've confused things.'

The security guards outside were chatting among themselves about what to respond. Then one had an idea, and said, 'umm, it's cold in Little Rock?'

'It certainly is,' Hilda responded. Pearl sighed and called out, 'sorry guys, she meant, not as cold as in here.' Then Pearl opened the door. Much to Hilda's disgust.

The team of four heavily armed guards walked in. They checked out the house. Beefed up the security and organised a rota and defensive positions. The ladies felt much safer. Especially once Chad arrived the next morning. Wilbur returned the next day. But on seeing an armed guard patrolling out front, he retreated. Not what he expected from three old ladies.

Marlan County Courthouse, Ohio, USA

A few days later, the remand hearing began. The court room was crowded with locals and media. Orville Stanley was a local celebrity criminal. If there is such a thing. The headlines varied from, 'Ogre of Ohio.' To 'Marlan's Murdering Monster.' They seemed to like alliteration.

Hilda, Pearl, and Ruby were sitting just behind Orville and his legal team. One of their security guards was sitting next to them. Even unarmed, he was formidable. The others were outside, patrolling the grounds. The judge called order, and the proceedings began. At least they would have done, had Hilda not jumped up and strode to the front. It all happened so fast that the judge hardly had time to react. She spoke boldly and clearly, saying, 'your highness, or is it your worship... no, I mean your honour. I am a bit of an expert in crime and I declare that there is no case to answer. I am satisfied that all evidence is... mistaken. DMA is misleading and witnesses have... recounted. The whole thing is a miss-dial. Throw the case out.'

The only thing that the judge threatened to throw out was Hilda. If she didn't sit down and be quiet. Normally, he would have thrown her out immediately. But she seemed like a harmless old lady. Hilda returned to her seat, grumbling about the unfairness of it all. As she passed Vance, she shrugged. It was all down to him now. Looking at him, she was unsure he was up to the task at hand. He got up, apologised to the judge, and explained the fresh evidence. Witnesses were called who had seen Wilbur and Orville together after Wilbur had supposedly died. Then Pearl and Hilda were called one by one to give testimony. When Hilda was on the stand, the judge looked at her suspiciously. She smiled and nodded at him. Vance asked her, 'is the man you met at Big D's Farm, Mill Lane, in this courtroom?'

'Big D's what dear?' asked Hilda.

'The house where Ruby grew up and her parents were murdered,' said Vance.

'Why didn't you say,' said Hilda. She looked at the judge and shook her head. 'People can be so confusing. Would you mind if I got up for a quick two-step? It helps me think.'

'Just answer the question,' said the judge, rather sharply.

'No need to be a crosspatch dear. Well... that man there, Orville, looks just like him. But it isn't him. Does that make sense?' The judge looked red faced.

'Can you explain?' asked Vance.

'Well, the man we met didn't limp and this man limps, and...' said Hilda. She stared at the ceiling. 'Well, my pops used to say that some people made your skin crawl. The other man made my skin crawl. Orville doesn't do that. He is nice dear. You will like him, your worshipfulness.'

Fingerprint evidence was also given, and a few other people testified more lucidly about Orville. Vance also pointed out that the latest murder, of Sarah Howes, could also not have been committed by Orville. There was plenty of evidence that he was in the county jail at the time of the murder. This added to the proof that a genetically identical twin existed. The judge agreed Wilbur must still be alive and there was sufficient evidence he was the murderer rather than Orville. He dismissed the case against Orville and suggested that the sheriff concentrate his efforts on finding Wilbur. Hilda pointed out that she had asked for that at the beginning.

Flight back to UK

On the flight back to the UK, Hilda was effusive and said, 'well, I'm glad that's all behind us.'

'What do you mean?' asked Hilda.

'Justice put right and all that,' said Pearl.

'You don't seem to realise,' said Hilda. 'The actual murderer, Wilbur, is still out there.'

'Oh yes, I'd forgotten that. What with the judge saying, "case dismissed" and Orville going free.'

'That was the case against Orville. His twin brother, Wilbur, murdered someone just a few months ago. Things are most definitely not sorted. I am worried about your sister, Ruby. She is retiring soon. That means she won't be protected in the White House.'

Hilda had just cause to be worried. Wilbur had followed Pearl and Hilda to the airport and Ruby to the White House. Only their bodyguards on route had protected them from his interference. He had no passport to travel to the UK, and no means to access The White House. For now, the ladies were safe. He returned to Marlan, Ohio. Perhaps he was thinking a reunion with his twin brother was overdue.

Sheriff's Office, Marlan, Ohio, USA

Sheriff Gerwin and his deputy, Officer Coleman, were standing at the front of a crowded room. 'Well?' said Sheriff Gerwin. 'Any ideas at all?'

One of the eight officers present stuck her hand up. Gerwin stared at her, and said, 'you're not at school, Lynne, out with it.'

Lynne's neck flushed red, she said, 'well, what about a stakeout?'

'You've been watching too many films,' said Gerwin sharply.

'She may have a point,' said Coleman. He was studying the ceiling tiles. 'After all, there is evidence he's using the Stanley homestead. Well volunteered Lynne.'

'Oh, umm, I, I, I meant,' said Lynne.

'Yes, well, you suggested it, so you can do it,' said Gerwin.

'Will I have backup?' said Lynne.

'Just call it in if he turns up,' said Gerwin.

Plympton-on-Sea, UK

Two of The Plympton Players long-term members, Garry, and Caz Hilkins had been working nights when Hilda became the new director. Neither of them usually worked nights. But Gary's work had an opportunity open for extra pay working at night. They both signed up. They were saving for a new extension. Six weeks of working nights gave them a boost to their savings.

Gary knew nothing of Hilda being voted as the replacement of George. He just heard the sad but opportunistic news. The Plympton Players was in financial trouble and George had stepped down as director. Gary was the assistant director. George had always relied on him and would be nothing without him. That's what Gary told everyone. Yet oddly, no one thought of him when the old director retired.

Plympton Playhouse, Plympton-on-Sea, UK

Hilda and Pearl were back in Plympton, having been away for two weeks. They arrived home on a Saturday and after a couple of days getting over jetlag; they had the Plympton Players meeting. The friends arrived at the theatre forty minutes early and set about arranging the room ready for the rehearsals. Hilda was keen to set out a mock-up of the stage. But Pearl and common sense won through. They arranged all the tables together in the middle in a long row. Hilda sat at the head with Pearl beside her, taking notes. This first evening would only be a read through. After all the furniture moving, they were both feeling hot. The evening was warm. They threw the doors and windows open wide.

The members of the Plympton Players arrived in small groups. The conversation muted. A common complaint on arrival was about the draft. The windows were never open and certainly not wide. As for propping open the doors - never. Few of the club members made eye contact with Hilda, even though she greeted each one cheerily. They grumbled to each other. Lilly arrived part way through and came to check that everything was ready. On seeing the open windows and doors, she immediately closed them. Then she walked up to Hilda to check that everything was ready. Hilda said, 'everything is ship shape and... umm everything is ship shaped.'

'Bristol fashion?' said Lilly.

Hilda looked at Lilly and frowned and said, 'I think we'll get on with the practice tonight. Maybe look at fashion shows another time.'

Lilly opened her mouth, but then saw Pearl shaking her head. So, she walked over and found a seat. Hilda looked around the room and asked if that was everyone. Lilly told her that was probably all they would get. To get everyone moving, laughing, and sharing. A state Hilda considered essential to life and most certainly necessary for a theatre group. She planned to use ice breakers. They were something she had been reading about in the magazine, 'Theatre Director Monthly.' A publication she decided she must read as a new theatre director. The local newsagent had got a copy for her and ordered it monthly. It was full of wonderful suggestions for getting the best from your cast and crew. Although aimed at the professional theatre industry, Hilda found much to inspire her. In future weeks she would set out goals and do group pep talks. Carry out one-to-one encouragement, recognising and rewarding her best people, and seeing if she needed to let anyone go. Pearl tried to tell her that was all far too professional an approach for this group. But changing Hilda's mind was like trying to stop the tide. Pearl understood how King Canute must have felt.

Hilda's first ice breaker was the teeth game. You had to hide your teeth and say a person's name. But each person had to give themselves an add on to their first name. So that Hilda became Hilda Honey and Pearl became Pearl Pear. Lilly became Lilly Lemon, Mark became Mark Mango, and Sarah became Sarah Sausage, and so on it went. You then went around the group, introducing yourself by your full, silly name and addressing the other person by their silly name. No one could show their teeth in this process. Hilda gave them a test run. Once the group got the hang of saying, 'Lilly Lemon to Sarah Sausage,' without smiling and showing their teeth, the game could start. But, of course, they smiled and laughed quickly, which was the idea. It broke the ice and a group of sour faced and miserable people transformed into a friendly laughing melee.

After the success of her first icebreaker, Hilda tried two more. The idea being to help people relax and get to know each other. As the group already knew each other, just Hilda and Pearl needed the ice breakers. But the group sorely needed to cheer up. At the end everyone was chatting happily and looking impressed with Hilda. The success of the ice breakers convinced Hilda that all the ideas in 'The Theatre Director Monthly' would work. Pearl wasn't so sure; she just handed out the scripts. Hilda announced that this week they were going to do a read through and then people could decide what to audition for. She was tempted her to do an initial pep talk, but then Pearl pointed out the time.

After someone had handed the scripts out, Gary Hilkins barged through the doors, ready to take charge. He was not paying any attention to the activities happening in the room. Storming up to the table, he stood there authoritatively. All the assembled group stared at him. He looked at Hilda and asked, 'who are you?'

'I was wondering the same thing, dear,' said Hilda. She stared at him over the top of her glasses. 'Are you wanting to join the group? I think we have a spare script.' She glanced at Pearl for confirmation. Pearl nodded and handed one towards Gary. He just stared at the proffered script.

Gary glanced at Hilda and said, 'I don't understand. What's happening? I'm here to direct the next show.'

'That's all sorted,' said Hilda. 'I'm the new director. Nice to meet you, Mr...' She awaited a name.

'You?' said Gary. He took a step back.

Hilda said, 'yes me, as my pops always said, a stitch in time…' She didn't finish the sentence.

'Saves nine,' said Gary, distractedly.

'Nine what?' said Hilda. She raised an eyebrow.

'The saying,' said Gary, shrugging. Everyone was staring at him.

'What are you saying?' said Hilda. She looked around at the gathered members.

'Can we get on?' said Lilly. She stood up and walked over to Hilda.

'That's what I want,' said Hilda. She was impatient to start.

Gary had to take a script and join in. His wife Caz had taken time parking the car. When she walked in, she stood for a moment, taking in the scene. Hilda stood at the front, explaining dramatically how the play was to be staged. She was giving a one-woman performance of it in short form. She wished that she had set up a mock-up of the stage as she originally planned. Everyone was watching her. Some in fascination, some in boredom. Gary looked pinched. Caz walked over to her husband and whispered into his ear, 'what's happening?' He just shook his head. She sat down next to him and watched the evening unfold.

At the end of the night Hilda said, 'read the script thoroughly. After all, you can't expect to know it from one performance. However good I was.' Hilda seemed to hesitate, awaiting an applause that never came. She shrugged and told them to come along the next week, ready to audition. She suggested they chose two or three parts they liked. Just in case they didn't get their first choice.

Gary had gradually changed in his demeanour as the evening wore on. He was obviously not concentrating on anything Hilda did. But it appeared his brain was working. By the time he left with Caz, he was smiling. Caz looked at him oddly. Perhaps she thought he had lost his reason. Maybe he had.

Hidden Garden Tearoom, Plympton-on-Sea, UK

The next morning, as Hilda was opening the doors of the tearoom, she was bustled out of the way. Two burly secret service agents had been waiting outside for her to unlock. The moment she did, they bundled her inside and re-locked the door. She stood by the hallway wall, panting. It took a while before Hilda recognised one of them as Chad. He was the Secret Service agent she had met first at Camp David. That is the country retreat of The President of the United States. Hilda and Pearl had ended up there the year before, on their trip across America. They were guests of The First Lady. Hilda has a knack of ending up in some incredible places.

Hilda hit Chad on the shoulder and said, 'you scared me half to death.'

'Sorry ma'am,' said Chad.

'Don't start that ma'am stuff again,' said Hilda.

'Sorry Hilda, we are the advanced party for The First Lady,' said Chad. He was looking around all the time. This was his job. Checking security and threats.

Hilda followed Chad's gaze. 'Are you expecting my coat and scarf to attack you?'

'I'm just checking my immediate environment,' said Chad.

'Honestly, I think my hallway is safe. Let's go upstairs to the flat,' said Hilda. They ascended her stairs and were soon in the main room. Chad and his fellow agent checked it for security risks. Chad stopped at the detective agency sign. 'You're running a detective agency?'

'I was planning on, but everyone else thought it was a bad idea,' said Hilda.

Chad nodded and moved on. He covered the opposite side of the room to his colleague.

'That China ornament looks safe to me,' said Hilda. 'Now you were saying about Evelyn visiting.'

'That's right,' said Chad. He was still scanning her room for threats and kept glancing at the detective agency sign.

The news about Evelyn visiting made Hilda feel like jumping and clapping. Evelyn employed Ruby, Pearl's twin sister, as her personal chef at the White House. Hilda considered Evelyn a friend. It would also be good to see Ruby again. See what was happening about Orville and Wilbur. It had only been a week since they were over in America. But things could have changed. Hilda had been thinking and dancing about the case, not necessarily in that order.

'The President is here next week. He's on a top-secret visit. The First Lady is with him. You mustn't tell anyone.' Chad stared at Hilda seriously. Why anyone would trust Hilda with top secret information is a mystery. But in this instance, they may have been safe.

'Guides Honour,' said Hilda. She held up a few fingers and crossed her heart. She couldn't remember the proper sign.

'Really Hilda, only Pearl can know,' said Chad. He looked at her sternly.

'Of course,' said Hilda. She was still trying various hand signs. 'Just the family.'

'No!' said Chad loudly. 'Only you and Pearl.'

'But William and Louise will be so sad to miss out,' said Hilda, pouting. 'They know Evelyn and LOTUS too.'

'You mean POTUS. I'll ask if they can be told,' said Chad. He walked to one side and spoke into his radio. A few minutes later, he had exciting news. 'You can tell your son and his wife. But absolutely no one else. They must be clear on that as well.'

'How exciting! Josh will be so pleased to hear about it,' said Hilda. She jiggled and danced.

'Not Josh,' said Chad. He was looking red faced. 'Just you, Pearl, William and Louise.'

'Why ever not, dear?' said Hilda. She stopped jiggling. 'Josh is hardly a security risk. Remember, he took photos at Camp David.'

Chad pursed his lips, then let out an enormous sigh, and said, 'this is the final list. You, Pearl, William, Louise, and Josh.'

'But not Gloria and Joy?' asked Hilda.

Chad looked like he would explode. He drew himself to his full height and pushed back his shoulders.

'That's fine, not Gloria, Joy... or the Rev Pugh. Oh, I've just thought,' said Hilda. Chad looked like he might draw his gun. 'Ruby is coming too?' asked Hilda. 'We need to catch up.'

Chad let out a big breath, and said, 'yes, she's in the entourage.'

'Oh, and one more thing,' said Hilda. Chad scowled. 'Thank you so much for keeping us safe the other week from that murderer, Wilbur. Chad smiled and said, 'you're very welcome. I couldn't have him harm my best ladies.'

'I'm your best lady?' asked Hilda, sighing.

'You three ladies are among my best.' Chad winked. Hilda danced around the room. Then she ran off to tell Pearl. She was in the garden sorting out the tables. Once Pearl came up to see Chad, he reiterated the need for secrecy, for security reasons. The visit was to be the next week. The President would not be with them. Chad double checked Hilda had no Nerf water guns planned. Which she thought was a silly thing to check. Anyone who remembered Hilda squirting a Nerf gun towards the President in Washington DC, may not think it a silly question. Chad took Pearl to one side and asked her to double check for any such toys. Hilda found the reminder of a Nerf gun, merely acted as a prompt to consider a second try. Fortunately for everyone, she forgot soon afterwards.

Stanley Homestead, Marlan, Ohio, USA

Officer Lynne Walker was regretting suggesting a stake out. She had not meant just one person and certainly not only her. Lynne had positioned her car in an elevated position at a distance from Orville and Wilbur's homestead. Her view partially obscured, but she didn't want to be any closer. As the evening drew on, she would see any lights inside. She also had a view of cars entering the roadway up to the property.

Wilbur had been cautious ever since he saw a police car near his home a few days earlier. Now he always parked in a clearing nearby and walked the last part. As he crossed the highway, he caught sight of the reflective stickers on the police vehicle. Ducking back into the treeline, he made his way up to the rear of the car. A lone female police officer inside - interesting.

Chapter Five

Mid-July 1998

Harbour, Plympton-on-Sea, UK

Plympton-on-Sea, the seaside town where Hilda and Pearl had their tearoom, was once a thriving fishing village. Like many along the South coast of England, its days as a working harbour were past. It was now mainly a tourist attraction. Pleasure boats and the occasional fishing boat to hire tied up alongside it. The one remaining fishing industry was lobster and crab fishing. A handful of boats plied their trade, selling locally and sending their best catch up to London. They piled their lobster and crab pots around the harbour. Tourists found these many coloured baskets a photogenic delight. They set off the sweeping majesty of the stone harbour. It's high walls, cobbled walkways, and sunlight glistening on the blue enclosed water.

One brisk and breezy Friday morning. Unusually cold for a July day. Karl Dansk was standing at the edge of Plympton harbour looking out to sea. There was a small semi-circular pinnacle at the end of the harbour wall. It stood by the opening and commanded unobstructed views of boats entering and leaving the harbour. Karl stood in his usual vantage point. His black beret, a hangover from WWII, was keeping his bald head warm. He felt out of place, uncomfortable, like a Victorian clock in a space rocket. No longer the fashionable composer, world renown. Respected and admired. Now either ignored or a subject of children's comments, 'what's that man got on his head?'

The Plympton Princess pleasure boat was heading out to sea. A few hardy visitors braced for a tour of the bay. Karl had a tear in his eye, not only from the chill breeze. He had first seen that boat with his wife, Lillian, when they retired to Plympton twenty years earlier. Their working life had been one of globetrotting. A few years in California, USA. Karl's fame and his many concerts and appearances meant the city had suited him well. As they grew older, England was the place they wanted to settle. Plympton a childhood favourite, warm memories of sun and the pebbled beach. They found an old fisherman's cottage on the harbour and settled into an idyllic life. Twelve years later, Lillian had died.

Friends had asked Karl why he stayed in Plympton after Lillian's death. His answer was always the same. Twelve years of memories in a place made him feel close to her there. As time passed, friends stopped asking, stopped calling. Perhaps he became morose, reclusive. The last eight years on his own had not improved his sociability. Lillian was always the sociable, friendly one. Karl turned and trudged home along the harbour wall. He stopped and stared; a strange and yet familiar sight caught his eye.

Hilda and Pearl tap danced along the harbour wall. Hilda was teaching Pearl a move that she had accidentally discovered at a doctor's surgery in America. Although Pearl found the connection with medicine hard to follow. Hilda watched Pearl's feet to make sure she kept in time, and they danced right past Karl without noticing him. Not really a surprise. He was much changed, and they were concentrating on the dance. As they danced on, they left a trail of staring faces all along the harbour wall.

Karl stared at Hilda as she passed. Recognition flickering in his eyes. He opened his mouth to speak, but then stopped. Continuing his walk home, he looked thoughtful.

***

Gary and Caz Hilkins House, Plympton-on-Sea, UK

Gary Hilkins was sitting in the front room of his semi-detached council house. His football team was on TV and winning. He looked at the screen, but his face was blank. Caz walked in with beers and snacks and asked, 'how we doing?'

Gary glanced at his wife and said, 'what? Oh.' He checked the score on the screen. 'Winning, one nil.'

'Brilliant,' said Caz. She put the snacks down and handed Gary a beer. 'You don't look happy.'

'It's that woman,' said Gary. His face matched their red leather sofa.

'Not the club again. Can't we just forget it tonight and enjoy the match?' Caz grabbed a handful of crisps and sat next to her husband.

'I've got to stop her,' Gary stared at Caz. 'I should be director. I've waited so long.'

Their team scored another goal. Caz leapt up and danced around. Then stared at her immobile husband. 'We scored... again.'

'Oh... right,' said Gary. His eyes were blank - beer untouched.

'You really are in a mess. After the game, we'll think about it. What about the idea you had the other night at the club?' asked Caz.

'When I thought it through, it wouldn't work.' Gary studied the carpet. The game was in a lull, players seemed to kick the ball around with little purpose. It matched the mood in the room. Then came half-time.

'I might have an idea,' said Caz as she headed out of the room.

'A way for me to take over?' Gary's shoulders lifted.

'Yes,' Caz's words were feint and echoed. Just as well, the downstairs toilet had a thin door. 'At least I think so.'

Gary smiled. His dentist had often asked that he visit. Perhaps it was for moments like that toothy smile. Still, it didn't last long. After the half-time, the other team scored two goals in the last ten minutes. It was going to be a penalty shoot-out. His team was useless at penalties. Then Caz shared her idea. It was as useless as his. They both agreed to think about how to overcome the problem. On that unhappy thought, they went to bed.

Gary woke in the middle of the night and said, 'I've got it.' Caz dragged herself from sleep and asked, 'got what?'

'The answer,' said Gary. 'How I can get to be director.'

After Gary had told Caz his idea, she argued it was very mean. But he would not be dissuaded and so they went back to sleep after planning.

***

Orville & Wilbur Stanley Homestead, Marlan, Ohio, USA

It was getting late, and Lynne called in to base. She wanted to know how long they expected her to keep watch. Back at base, officer Coleman manned the radio. He had not been happy to be countermanded by his boss over Lynne's suggestion. Hearing her call in, he bristled. In annoyance, he told her to cover until midnight.

Lynne had already been sitting in the car for ages. She checked the time, three more hours. A comfort break was in order. Just as well she had brought food and drink. But what goes in…

Wilbur saw the police vehicle door open, and the officer get out. He hid behind a tree. Then watched Lynne squat in the bushes. She looked vulnerable; weakness always appealed to him. He reached into his right pocket and took out a knife. His left hand came out of his pocket empty. No lucky wolf iron: he grimaced, remembering. Slowly, he made his way towards the unsuspecting officer, licking his lips in anticipation.

Multicoloured blue and white lights flashed briefly. A spotlight highlighted Lynne. 'Whoa! What you up to, officer Walker?' said Ted.

'Turn that off, Ted,' shouted Lynne. She covered herself up.

Unseen by either Lynne or Wilbur, officer Ted Pearson had decided to surprise his fellow officer, Lynne. Wilbur slipped away, disappointed. The lack of his lucky wolf iron was causing him problems. Ted hung around, chatting to Lynne until midnight. The stake out failed and was not repeated. Gerwin decided Wilbur would not be foolish enough to return to his homestead. In fact, he returned there every night.

***

Harbourside Cottage, Plympton-on-Sea, UK

On the day Karl Dansk had seen Hilda and Pearl on the harbour, he returned home. He sat by the fire in his 17th Century fisherman's cottage, nestled in Plympton harbour. It had once been three cottages. A clever architect and builder had converted them into a cosy seaside home. Karl's harbourside home held constant memories for him. The small front yard, with a low wall, had a stone bench that Lillian had bought when they moved in. She wanted to sit there and greet passing strangers. Something Karl had never done. Lillian had designed and planted the back garden. Hedges enclosed it on two sides. There was a rocky outcrop at the back. Karl had a gardener keep its borders and beds neat. But he never sat in it. Even looking out at it from the kitchen or dining room gave him a virtual punch. He saw Lillian crouched over the beds, weeding.

In the mornings he sat in the front of the house. It acted as a lounge. From his leather chair by the fire, he could see out of the multi-paned sash windows to the busy harbour. He had never upgraded to double glazing. He preferred the old wood frames.

Karl patted the arm of a second, empty chair, also setup by the fire. 'Busy day out there, my love.' He spoke gently to the memory of his wife, Lillian. On an intellectual level he knew she wasn't there. Emotionally, he spoke to her and even heard her reply. He sighed, a deep, guttural sigh. When she was alive, there would be few times she had sat still. She always rushed around, so full of energy and life. Karl looked around the room. Logs crackled on the fire, a small piece of burning wood jumped onto the hearth and gradually its light dimmed. He stared at its fading light and a tear ran down his face.

The lounge had an eclectic mix of furniture. Ranging from antiques so old they looked more suited to a museum. Those were Karl's choices, many inherited from his family. To plastic and chrome pieces from their days in the States during the 1960's. Lillian had chosen those. On the walls were old masters, alongside modern daubs, as Karl described them, and framed manuscripts of music. Every wall crammed with certificates of excellence in music. Platinum records, paintings or photographs of Karl and Lillian with the great and the good. From Presidents to stars of stage and screen. In a beautiful oak corner cabinet, there were awards and plaques. Karl got up and walked over to a mahogany desk bureau. He opened a drawer and took out an ivory-coloured album. It had 'Wedding,' written on it in silver cursive letters. Turning a few pages in, he stared at a page with a photograph of himself,

Lillian, and a close friend. He nodded. The women in the photo bore an uncanny resemblance to a younger version of Hilda. Had the photograph been colour rather than black and white, then her red curly hair, now dyed, and green eyes, still shining bright, might have confirmed it. After replacing the album in the drawer, he sat back in his chair by the fire. He turned to the empty chair and said, 'she hasn't changed.' He laughed, a hollow laugh, nodding, 'yes, and she's still dancing.'

***

Hidden Gardens Tearoom, Plympton-on-Sea, UK

A few days later, at the tearoom, Hilda and Pearl were getting ready for their important visitor. William, Louise, and Josh had joined them after hearing about the visit. They were sitting on some makeshift chairs. Hilda had insisted they leave the sofa and comfy chairs for Evelyn and Ruby. The tearoom was closed for the day. Chad recommended it. William pointed out, 'it feels like a royal visit, the way you're behaving.'

'She is a very important person,' said Hilda. She was laying out tea plates on a coffee table.

'I don't think you needed to borrow silver cutlery though gran,' said Josh. He stared at the table, with its fancy plates, silver cutlery, and napkins. A small crystal vase with a rose stood in the centre. Pearl had dissuaded Hilda from having banners made.

'As my mother always said, always put your best foot in your mouth,' said Hilda. She looked around the room, feeling proud.

'You certainly do that,' said William, laughing.

'Honestly, don't be rude to your mother,' said Louise. She frowned at William. Then said to Hilda, 'you meant put your best foot forward, didn't you?' Louise got up. She had noticed a plate was out of alignment and went to adjust it.

'Do I?' said Hilda, brushing imaginary dust off the arm of a chair.

Pearl brought through the cups and saucers and put them on the table, and said, 'I'm ever so excited about seeing Ruby again. But it's making me nervous.'

'Don't you worry about anything dear,' said Hilda. She beamed. 'I'm here.' Pearl stopped, looked at Hilda, and gulped.

'That might be why she's worried,' said William under his breath. Louise stared at her husband. Josh giggled.

The limousine drew up outside at 10:30am, along with three other vehicles with security and ancillary staff. Plus, a couple of UK police cars. The First Lady didn't travel lightly. If the President had been coming, they would have filled the whole town with security vehicles and the air filled with helicopters. Not exactly a secret.

Neighbours and passers-by noticed the US flag on the long black car. They watched as figures in black suits leapt out of vehicles and created a cordon around the limo. Chad and a couple of other security agents entered the tearoom first. They checked inside the shop, outside in the garden, and upstairs in the flat. Hilda, Pearl, William, Louise, and Josh watched as the security team ran around them. They were patted down for weapons. Hilda was the last to be checked.

'You can take your hands off those, young man,' said Hilda.

The agent was patting Hilda's hips. He looked up in surprise from his part bent position. Being tall, he had to bend to reach. Normally, the security detail would have included several women. But only two were available that day and both were in the car with the first lady. This meant that a man was having to pat down the ladies present. Not a standard procedure. Also, not one Hilda was happy about. He apologised and explained he must continue. For some inexplicable reason. The agent was doing the pat down from the bottom upwards. He had asked Hilda to hold her arms in the air. Having already been told off for touching her hips, as he rose higher, he received a slap in the face. The agent nearly retaliated until Chad stepped in and smoothed things over. Hilda continued to mumble about, 'being manhandled at my age. My mother would have a pink fit. I know about people like you.'

Chad swapped the offending agent with another and cleared Hilda as free of weapons. Her tongue obviously didn't count.

As the agents continued checking the flat, Josh told one of them, 'I think the teapot is safe,' after watching him check inside it. The agent glared at Josh, who was then silent. Josh had spotted that the agent's jacket had a bulge where he carried a gun.

Once Chad was sure that all was safe, he double checked the placement of the guards in the cordon and allowed The First Lady to leave the limo. As she got out, she noted to Chad, 'that took a long time.'

'Mrs Shilton,' those two words were all the explanation Evelyn needed. She nodded and headed towards the flat.

Two of the UK police officers accompanying the convoy had just qualified. This was their first official duty. It had been a mix-up by the duty sergeant. One she would pay for later.

Officers Hugh and Lore had the same initials as another pair of officers with far more experience. Officers Hugh and Lore were eager to jump into their initiation of policing; if a little daunted. They had expected to be put on traffic duty. Or kept in the office, making tea. To be out on such an important assignment was a surprise; to everyone.

Officers Hugh and Lore stood for a few moments with their fellow UK police officers. Then both decided that they were not playing enough of a part. Stepping forward, they tried to join the line of black suited security personnel. As always, the security service staff were keeping an eye out in every direction. Especially as The First Lady had moved. As officers Hugh and Lore stepped forward, a security services agent grabbed Hugh, while his colleague grabbed Lore.

'What are you doing?' said the agent. The one recently sent down after searching Hilda. He patted Hugh down, checking for weapons. This time patting from the top downwards. Finding the baton and taser, he removed them.

'I might well ask you the same question,' said Hugh, trying to prevent the agent from taking his equipment. He said, 'I am a member of her majesty's constabulary.' The more experienced UK officers were shaking their heads. One or two were smiling.

'You are not authorised to get near The First Lady,' said the agent. 'Especially not with any weapons.' he pointed at the items he had removed. Hugh continued to argue with him.

Lore was having a similar contra-temp with his captor. After checking their ID, they were told to join their colleagues further back and had their equipment returned. Hugh and Lore were red faced and asked one of the older officers what was the point of them being there. They wanted to lodge an official complaint about their treatment. But older, wiser heads talked of politics and jurisdiction. Technically, the UK police were in charge. In reality, they just stood back and let their American cousins get on with it. Hugh and Lore were told to forget about the incident. They were not pleased. Once they had received a reprimand from their superior officer back at the station, they were even less happy.

Meanwhile, Evelyn Meyer, The First Lady, entered the tearoom. Hilda was ready to rush up and give Evelyn a hug. She restrained herself. Just as well, or the agents may have restrained her. Instead, she said, 'how lovely to see you again dear.' She bowed.

'Hilda... Pearl, it's a delight to see you both,' said Evelyn. 'No need to bow.' Then noticing William and Louise. 'What a delight to meet you both again... I don't think we've met.' She was looking at Josh.

'Our son Josh,' William, was waving towards Josh.

'As in Josh Shilton, the photographer?' asked Evelyn, frowning.

'You've heard of me?' Josh looked pleased.

'You photographed Camp David,' said Evelyn. She sounded frosty. Unknown to Josh, she was not pleased with him. When he had taken the interior shots at Camp David, he had moved the furniture. In his eyes to improve the shot. Unfortunately, those interiors were designed and dressed by Evelyn. Interior design was previously her job and now her hobby. Hilda had added insult to injury by moving the furniture while staying there.

The people who knew all about this were Ruby and Pearl, whom Evelyn had told afterwards. Pearl leapt into action to prevent a scene. 'Ruby!' said Pearl. As she saw her sister enter the room. 'It feels longer that eight days.'

Evelyn heard the commotion and turned around. She went over to share in the joy. The media well knew Evelyn as someone who loved sentimental reunions. They left Josh thinking he had missed out on praise from The First Lady. Whereas they had spared him a reprimand.

Hilda joined Evelyn and asked, 'are the children not with you?'

'School is more important than trips abroad, or so I tell them,' said Evelyn. She noticed the table. 'This looks a treat, such fine China and delicious looking food.'

'Why don't we have it in the garden?' said Louise. 'We can move everything out there.'

'What a lovely idea, tea in an English garden. I feel like I'm entering a novel,' said Evelyn.

'Let's hope you don't get stung by a wasp, or any ants in your pants dear,' said Hilda, screwing up her face.

Evelyn looked horrified; her security guards reached for their guns. Pearl shook her head, and said, 'don't be like that Hilda, you know wasps don't cause problems this early and we don't have any ants near our tables.'

'I was just joking,' said Hilda. 'I remember how you like a laugh, Evelyn.'

Evelyn and her guards didn't look like they enjoyed a laugh. They looked as if they hadn't laughed in a long time. But Evelyn smiled politely. They all headed outside. Pearl and Ruby managed to get some time to catch up on the latest with Orville and Wilbur.

***

The day after the visit from The First Lady, Hilda was happily serving people in a crowded tearoom. Everyone had heard of the important visitors from the day before. Few people receive visits from The First Lady of the United States. When Hilda and Pearl had moved to Plympton, there were rumours of their illustrious connections. But no one believed it; until now. Even the vicar turned up in the tearoom, ready to forgive and forget. Maybe, as a Christian, that should be his usual stance, without famous friends as a motivation.

Hilda was loving the attention she received. Every time she went to take an order, the customers asked how she was. If they hoped that would prompt an answer about the visit the day before, they were disappointed. At one table Hilda regaled the occupants with tales of her poor night's sleep. Another heard of her impending dental trip. One group from the local WI, had to sit through tales of Hilda's stomach problems. The vicar heard tales of woe about her knees. It took a young lad of six, off sick from school, but somehow able to manage the café, to ask the right question. His mum started the ball rolling. She asked Hilda, 'how are you?' Then the little lad said to his mother, 'mum, you said she saw the Presidents' mistress.'

The mother turned bright red and apologised for her son. They should have all thanked the little boy. As it switched the conversation to The First Lady. But the young lad wasn't happy as he didn't get to hear about the Presidents' mistress.

They pulled chairs into a circle, with Hilda at the centre. She was in her element. What had been a brief visit from The First Lady became very dramatic indeed. By the end of Hilda's retelling, Pearl wondered if she had been present at the same event. In Hilda's version, the security agents were waving sub-machine guns. One had even been carrying the nuclear trigger. Another had indecently groped her. Pearl jumped in to explain that he was just searching her for weapons. Hilda huffed and continued her tale of an averted terrorist attack in which they had all been rushed to an underground bunker. Pearl could only shake her head in wonder. According to Hilda, The First Lady had granted special status to the tearoom. Which sounded like a royal warrant or an equivalent to a Michelin Star. Apparently, it was because Ruby, a six-star chef, worked for Evelyn. Someone questioned the existence of six Michelin Star awards. Hilda pointed out that 'everything is bigger in America.' That shut them up. Pearl had no memory of these things. But let Hilda tell her tall tales, anyway. Hilda's imagination was running wild. It was a wonder she stopped before suggesting The President of the United States had secretly turned up. Maybe that would have followed.

The Hidden Garden Tearoom became a unique venue after that. Hilda became an honoured member of the community. The mayor talked to her about opening the new civic centre - she agreed. Pearl would have preferred if Hilda had done more serving and less talking.

***

Stonehouse Manor, Upper Plympton, UK

Lord Leonard Russell was standing in the courtyard of his home, Stonehouse Manor. He looked puzzled, as well he might. Just a few minutes earlier, his wife, Mildred, had instructed him to leave. She shouted at him and told him to go for a walk. She was often terse with him. Today he looked more shaken than usual. It was their anniversary, and he had arranged a surprise. A special meal at a local restaurant, one Mildred had often commented upon. The venue was booked up weeks in advance, so gaining a table there had been hard work. He looked at his watch, then at the front door. Their booking time was in half an hour. Having taken a few hesitant steps, he opened the heavy door and crossed the dark hallway. He crept towards Mildred's office and peeked through the doorway. Standing in the darkness, he would be invisible to her, in her sunny office.

Mildred was still sitting at her desk, talking on the phone. 'Len doesn't know about any of this,' she said, listening and nodding. Len stood in the gloomy hallway. Mildred continued her call. 'We can move forward with the next stage.' She nodded and mumbled. 'Perfect, I'll get that done.' Then she hung up.

Len crept outside. He tripped several times on his walk. On returning he asked Mildred about the phone call. She just stared at him and then shook her head, saying, 'you must have misheard.'

'You said I do not know of something,' said Len.

'It's easy to get the wrong end of the stick if you hear half a conversation,' said Mildred, shrugging.

Len studied his wife. Years of practice as a liar made her very convincing. He frowned and said, 'I guess you're right.'

'While you're here, I need you to sign a document,' said Mildred. She passed some papers to him.

Len was about to read it when Mildred said, 'don't you trust me?' He hesitated, looked from the document to her and then signed it. He pointed out that it needed a witness. She just waved that away and explained she would sort it later with her secretary. While he was in the next room, Mildred signed the witness section. Although she signed it as Karen Jones, Secretary. The address of the witness, if checked, was not traceable. She was relying on the fact that it would not be checked.

***

A cheap hotel, Marlan, Ohio, USA

On release from prison, Orville stayed away from his homestead. His lawyer had discovered evidence that his twin brother Wilbur was using it. He had no wish to see him. Staying instead at a local hotel for safety. Not that it deserved the name hotel. It desperately needed repairs. Orville funded his stay by acting as an odd-job man. He was sure that the amount of work he did should have paid for a suite at some swanky place. But the owner grumbled about even including food.

Wilbur had been waiting for Orville for a few days at their home. He knew they had released him; he grew impatient. Finally, he realised he must have made alternative sleeping arrangements, so he started searching. A few days later, completely by chance, Wilbur saw his brother unloading a truck of lumber outside a hotel. Wilbur waited till night-time, watching, and waiting. The townsfolk of Marlan had placed a very handy bench across the street.

Orville liked to get out of his cramped room and get some fresh air most evenings. As he rounded a corner, he got a shock to see his brother. 'What the hell are you doing here?' said Orville.

'Is that any way to greet your brother?' said Wilbur.

'You gave me a shock, is all,' said Orville.

Wilbur glanced around. The street was quiet. 'You been saying things about me. That ain't nice.'

Orville took a step back from his brother, and said, 'no, no, I.... no, I...'

'What's the matter? You look nervous. I'd never hurt my brother.' Wilbur stepped very close to Orville and held his shoulders. They were face to face.

'I... I would never... say or....' started Orville.

'Orville is that you?' asked Vance, walking towards them with a small group of friends. Wilbur let go and disappeared before they reached them.

'I'm well glad you came along,' said Orville. He was shaking.

'Was that Wilbur with you? It's dark,' said Vance.

'Yes, and I don't know what he'd have done if you hadn't come along,' said Orville.

Chapter Six

July 1998

TSU Plc, Meedham, UK

Harold had seen a potential in William from the day he started as an office junior many years earlier. He had nurtured him, treating William as the son he and his wife Dorothy had never had. Harold encouraged William to further education. He excelled in his exams and at work. William rose rapidly from office junior to accountant to senior manager. Whilst some at TSU, saw Williams rise in the company to senior department manager as favouritism, everyone in the know realised it was merit. When Dorothy had died the year before. William and Louise were the people Harold turned to for support.

One Monday morning, Harold Styles called for one of his favourite managers, William Shilton. His secretary phoned through to him. William headed up to Harold's office. He always enjoyed going to see Harold. As he entered Harold's office, the opulence and grandeur of it again struck him, combined with warmth and cosiness. That summed up Harold as a person.

William had a spring in his step. Harold looked up from some papers, and said 'morning, you look very bright this morning. Good weekend?'

'Oh, umm...,' said William. His face took on a beetroot hue.

Harold had a crinkly smile. He lent back in his high-backed leather chair and swung it to the right, pointing to a chair next to him. Harold was not one for power games. Sitting behind a large desk with his 'juniors' seated on a smaller chair on the opposite side was not his style.

'I've had some figures back from the branches in America,' said Harold. He studied his sheet of paper. 'Obviously it's early days. They have only been going a short while. But the initial results are excellent, especially New York.'

'That was my favourite branch,' said William. He sat up straight.

'Well done,' said Harold. He beamed at William as he would a son.

'You know that ever since Dorothy died, I am easing up here?' said Harold.

'Yes,' said William. He looked at Harold, concern in his eyes.

'I've always seen you as my replacement for the future. So, I keep gently pushing that idea with the board. It's best if one of them suggests you as a director. Then hopefully you will become CEO in the long term,' said Harold. He lent forward.

'Thank you, I...' said William.

Harold cut him off, saying, 'don't thank me, being a director is hard enough. If you end up as CEO. That's a whole other thing. You'd the need board to vote you in.'

'We're a long way from retiring anyway, I'm sure,' said William. He shifted a bit in his seat.

'Maybe not. Two things have happened recently. First, your work in the US has been noticed by the board. It hasn't hurt that you impressed my friend Larry. As you know, he's now CEO over there. The fact he's the First Lady's father went down well with the board. On that front, your visit to The White House was also commented on, positively. Anyone who hob-nobs with Presidents must be a cut above. The other thing is not such cheerful news. I have some major heart problems. A replacement would be the only answer and at my age, well, you know?' said Harold. Instinctively, he rubbed his chest.

'No!' said William. He looked desperately at his friend and father figure.

'They don't know how long I can go on. But the medics certainly want me to slow down. I'm going to start off by reducing my working week to three days. I've already whispered the idea of you as a director into the right ear. Next, I'm going to lean on you a lot as I ease up. I hope that by the time I step down completely, the board will vote for you as CEO,' said Harold. He stopped rubbing his chest, and turning to his desk, he slapped it. It seemed as if he was saying, 'meeting over.' So, William got up and thanked him again.

William and Louise Shilton's House, Meedham, UK

That evening, William had a lot to process and tell Louise. They agreed it was hard to be happy about the promotion when they were both so worried about Harold. Louise was concerned that he was eating enough and looking after himself properly. He got caught up in work and forgetting to eat. Not something William suffered from.

Louise went out into the hall and phoned Harold to invite him over for the coming weekend. She told him, 'We haven't seen you for ages. The weather forecast is looking good. Fancy a barbeque?'

'You know I love barbeques, count me in,' Harold sounded pleased. Ever since he got back from the office, he had just been sitting in his work suit, staring out the window. Once he put the phone down, he smiled and stood up.

Louise started planning for the weekend, writing shopping lists, and then she walked through to find William. He was sitting reading his paper when she walked in. She told him to find the barbeque grill and clean it.

'It's only Monday,' he said, looking up from the sofa. 'Besides, it's dark out.'

'There's a light in the garage. You might find that the barbeque doesn't work, then you'd need to fix it or buy a new one,' said Louise.

William leapt up as if a spring had propelled him, and said, 'I'll get it working. No need to squander money on a new one.'

They had forgotten that weekend Hilda was already visiting. Harold found her a lot of fun. But William was always on edge that his mother would embarrass him with his boss. There was time for them to remember that detail and get anxious.

***

At the weekend William was trying to light a barbeque in the garden. Hilda was standing next to him on one side and

Harold on the other. Perhaps they felt it would give him support. By the look on William's face, they just added to his stress. Louise brought the meat and other bits out from the kitchen and placed them on a nearby table. She surveyed the scene and asked, 'everything going well?'

'Fine,' said William. He didn't look up. Louise shrugged and headed back inside.

Hilda watched William for a while and then said, 'are you sure you're doing it right dear?'

'Of course, I am. I have done thousands of barbeques,' said William. At that moment, Louise was walking back out with some utensils. She looked at her husband and her eyebrows raised. 'Lots of barbeques,' said William. He looked at his wife with his own eyebrows raised.

Harold laughed, and said, 'I love being here.' He walked over to the table where the food and drink were laid out.

'It'll be going in a minute and then we'll get the meat on,' said William. He was still trying to get the coals alight.

'I am just enjoying the company and the wine,' said Harold. He picked up a glass of wine and walked over to a chair where he sat down. He leaned back and closed his eyes.

'Where's my wine?' said Hilda, looking at her empty hands.

'You didn't want any,' said Louise. She sorted a few more things on the table next to William.

'That doesn't sound like me,' said Hilda.

'Quite!' said William. He blew on the charcoal a bit more. It was smoking a lot, but not yet glowing.

Harold opened his eyes and sat forward, then said, 'I'll fetch you a drink, my dear lady.' He stood up and bowed to Hilda as he headed to the drinks table.

'Ooo, you're my Argos, dear,' said Hilda. She wafted herself with her hand.

'That's a shop,' said Harold, looking oddly at Hilda.

'Really? My memory isn't what it once was. I meant you're looking out for me. I found this delightful book in a charity shop,' said Hilda. She took out a small dictionary of unusual words from her bag and handed it to Harold. Looking through it, he couldn't find Argos, but he found argus, and said 'here's the word you meant, it means, one who is ever vigilant; an ever-watchful guardian. How kind of you. I will endeavour to live up to that moniker.'

'I haven't gone ga-ga just yet then,' said Hilda. She giggled.

'Of course, you haven't. Now, what apéritif may I obtain for you?' said Harold. He made a sweeping gesture with his hand. As if it were a knight's cloak.

'Oh, I don't want any teeth. I have all my own, you know. A few missing here and there,' said Hilda. She opened her mouth wide to show. Pointing into her mouth at the gaping holes. 'I was at the dentist the other day, you know. I like to look after my teeth.'

Louise's own mouth was open almost as wide. Her eyes were also quite wide. She had often had to convince Hilda to see the dentist. Harold was averting his eyes rather than looking into Hilda's gaping mouth.

'Mother! What are you doing?' said William. 'Close your mouth. Harold doesn't want to see your teeth.'

'That's... alright,' said Harold. He was looking a little peaky.

'You asked about my teeth,' said Hilda. She wondered at people sometimes. They were very puzzling.

Later, after the BBQ was eventually lit, and they had eaten. William came out from helping Louise clear up. Hilda was sitting next to Harold. He heard the end of Hilda's comment. She was saying, '...my little boy, a director of your company? Whatever next.' Then they both laughed loudly.

William walked back inside and said to Louise, 'I think my mother has just ruined my chances of becoming a director.'

'Don't be silly, Harold's a sensible man. He won't be that easily swayed,' said Louise. She looked out of the kitchen window. Hilda had just spilt her red wine on Harold's white shirt. He was looking at her oddly. Louise looked at William, then back outside. She shook her head and pursed her lips. 'No... I'm sure it will be fine. Just fine.'

Plympton-on-Sea, UK

At the Plympton Playhouse, everything was ready for auditions. Hilda was in full director mode, calling out, 'OK luvies.'

Pearl looked at her oddly. Hilda just assumed this was the correct way for directors to talk. A director on TV had used that expression. What Hilda had missed was the irony. No one was listening to Hilda, anyway. Pearl clapped her hands and shouted for order. The gathered club members, including Gary and Caz, quietened down. Pearl got them to line up while Hilda, Lilly, the club secretary, and herself sat at a table. One by one the potential actors came forward to audition. Pearl took their names, and what part they wanted to audition for.

After each audition, the three of them had a brief chat, made notes and then Pearl called, 'next.' They were struggling to find the right cast.

The play that the retired director had chosen was what is sometimes called a 'bedroom farce.' Set in the 1970's - maybe it should have stayed there. Hilda and the others had to choose two main couples, some hotel staff, and a few others for the play. Everyone else would work backstage or 'front of house.' Given the range of people available in the club and the descriptions in the script, matching them proved difficult. At the rate they were going, most of the club would end up 'front of house.'

The play involved two couples, and the humour revolved around a mix up at a hotel one weekend. The first couple were Mr and Mrs J Lions, a middle-aged and conventional pair. It described them as average looking, whatever that meant. At least the club had plenty of candidates for these two. The other couple comprised a young man, John Lions, planning a weekend away with his girlfriend, Trudy. Because of the hotel policy, he booked the room in the name of Mr and Mrs Lions. It described John Lions as 'ruggedly handsome' and Trudy as 'a bit of a stunner.' It had further descriptions that we'll miss out. Whoever wrote the script had a strange turn of phrase. As Hilda and her co auditioners looked at the potentials for these roles, no one in the club was an obvious fit for those descriptions.

Typical of these types of 1970's bedroom farces, the plot revolved around a confusion over people and rooms. The couples with the same names, Mr and Mrs Lions, booked in for the same weekend. This created a perfect setup for a weekend of confusion. Because it was a bedroom farce, there had to be more than one pretty woman running around looking sexy. The play, therefore, also featured a sexy maid. Keep in mind the play dated from the 1970's. It described her as 'a pretty young thing,' with the added description, 'early twenties, fantastic figure.' Except it didn't use the words 'fantastic figure.' The maid was a part that Hilda had seen for herself after reading the script. She was reading the original description. It was not an apt description of Hilda, even in her younger days. Not that such things as facts would stop her.

The play began with the hotel manager having an affair with his pretty young maid. There were several close misses between his wife, the maid, and the manager.

The two Mr Lion's arrive before their respective 'other halves' and get sent up to their rooms. Which, of course, given the type of play, have adjoining doors. A door that the maid forgets to lock. Again, a perfect setup for a bedroom farce. They rely on mix ups and confusions. People walking in on each other in various stages of undress and compromising situations. Overacting, standing on stage in frilly underwear with hands in the air in mock surprise. You know the kind of thing.

The hotel had sea views and the two rooms had balconies next to each other. The setup starts with the two men arriving and being sent up to their rooms. Next, Mrs Lions, the older, more traditional one, arrives and is sent to the wrong room. The younger John Lions is in the bathroom, preparing for the arrival of his young lady. Mrs Lions unpacks and then heads down to the restaurant. Coming out of the bathroom, John sees cases on the bed and thinks Trudy has arrived. He puts the case away in the wardrobe and is shocked at how old-fashioned her underclothes are. Not the style he has seen her in before. Let us not dwell on the how and when of that. Glancing in the chest of drawers, he holds up a pair of bloomers in horror. The weekend does not look set to go as he expected.

Meanwhile, young Trudy arrives and is also sent up to the wrong room. The older and married Mr Jonathan Lions' room. He is asleep on the bed, tired after the journey. Well, he would be. That's the kind of character he's playing. The curtains are closed, and the room is dark. Trudy sees the figure on the bed and, being a fun-loving sort of girl, she surprises him. It certainly has that effect when a scantily clad young lady gets into his bed. His unexpected reaction causes Trudy to rush from the room thinking John has gone off her.

The weekend continues with many such misunderstandings. The adjoining door gets a lot of use, being mistaken as a cupboard. At the end, the older, mature, and married, Mr and Mrs Lions have a livelier weekend than expected. Young Trudy discovers John Lions' true nature and leaves. The hotel manager and his wife are reconciled. The hotel maid finds true love with the bellboy.

This kind of play only works when timing, props, and lighting all go smoothly. The humour relies on what the audience can and cannot see at just the right time. It also needs appropriate, believable actors playing the parts. They need to arrive and move around on cue. None of these things were easy to achieve. Whilst it was an outdated and sexist play, it could still be funny, if done right. But the biggest problem for the Plympton Players would be finding the right actors. The club had shrunk over the years and those remaining were older, and not the best actors.

As Hilda, Pearl and Lilly worked through the auditions, the problem became very apparent. Mr and Mrs Jonathan Lions were easily cast. But the club totally lacked suitable candidates for the younger and better-looking couple, John Lions and Trudy. As for the maid... In the end, it was a compromise. The description of Trudy as, 'a bit of a stunner.' With added notes saying, 'early twenties, pretty, and attractive figure,' went to someone best described as, 'could pass as late thirties, average looking at a distance on stage. Let's not talk about her figure.' John Lions, who described as in the cast list as 'ruggedly handsome.' With added notes of, 'late twenties, looks like he works out,' went to a man who could be charitably described as, 'late fifties, overweight, keep the lighting low.'

Things were not looking good. The retired director had chosen an outdated style of play. They couldn't even do it justice because of the cast. Still, as Pearl said, 'it's a very sexist way of describing women. So maybe having some genuine women won't be a problem.' She certainly got her wish when Hilda played the maid.

The rest of the cast were chosen. Oddly, Gary and Caz didn't audition for parts. They opted to be backstage. Gary on lighting and Caz on the scenery. Two crucial roles for the smooth running of the play.

Plympton-on-Sea, UK

Rev John Hanley turned up one Saturday evening at Hilda and Pearl's door. Hilda's first comment was to tell him that the café was closed, and they were resting. He explained he was visiting as their local vicar. After all, they were his parishioners. Hilda stared at him wide eyed and asked, 'are we?'

'Oh yes, anyone in my parish is my parishioner,' said the reverend. He stood looking beyond Hilda, up the stairs. As if expecting to be invited in.

'What if we don't want to be dear?' asked Hilda. 'Or if we're atheists?' She was blocking the door.

'Are you an atheist?' asked Rev Hanley.

'Well, no, of course not. I just wondered,' said Hilda.

'Can I come in then?' asked the reverend. He was hopping from foot to foot. Hilda wondered if he was trying out a dance.

'I suppose so. Hopefully, Pearl is decent. It is our time off, you know?' said Hilda. She still stood in the doorway. If the vicar was dancing, she was unimpressed.

'Oh, I don't want to intrude,' said the vicar, stepping forward. Hilda finally led him upstairs. As they got near the upstairs door she shouted, 'are you decent dear?'

'What's that?' shouted Pearl from inside the flat.

'Are you dressed? Or are you in your naky shaggy? We have a visitor,' said Hilda. She stood by the upstairs flat door, with her hand on the doorknob. Without waiting for a reply to Pearl's level of clothing, Hilda burst through the door and led the vicar in. He had a hand over his eyes, not knowing what to expect. Which caused him to trip as he entered. Pearl was perfectly decent, sitting on the sofa, watching TV.

'Oh, Rev Hanley,' said Pearl, as she witnessed him flying into the room. 'Are you alright?'

The vicar recovered his feet and accepted an offered seat. Hilda asked if she should put the kettle on and then stood by the kitchen chatting. Pearl kept saying, 'were you going to put the kettle on?' Then, just as Hilda turned to do so, another part of the conversation grabbed her attention and she got distracted. The vicar also got distracted, but for him it was the detective agency sign that caused his problems.

'You're gumshoes,' said the vicar, a fan of classic American detective movies.

Hilda lifted her slipper, 'have I, maybe Merlin brought something sticky in.'

Pearl stared at Hilda aghast and said, 'no he didn't.' Then calling to Merlin she said. 'Don't you listen to her, come here my darling.' Merlin was stretched out on the carpet. He opened his eye's part way, lifted his head a short way, then lay back down, ignoring the world.

'Gumshoes is an old name for detectives,' said the vicar.

'Are you suggesting I'm old.' Hilda placed both hands on her hips.

'Oh no, of course not.

'I should hope not, I'm only seventy-eight you know. But I realise that I look much younger.'

The vicar stared at Hilda. She looked expectantly at him. He said nothing. She huffed and headed into the kitchen to finally make the drinks.

***

Although the vicar spoke a lot, he didn't say much. Just local gossip. Miss Honey had lost her cat. After an extensive search they discovered it had moved next door. Apparently, it preferred the neighbour's selection of cat food. Mr Hardy had celebrated his 96th birthday. He still lived at home and had all his own faculties. Hilda begged to differ on that score. She told the vicar that he had turned up in the tearoom and mistaken her for his daughter. It wouldn't have been so bad, but he kept asking why she wasn't at school and threatening to withhold her pocket money.

The vicar made the mistake of mentioning Mrs Cushla, one of his parishioners, on an extended stay in hospital following major surgery. They had limited her to bed for a couple of weeks, which she found boring. Then the vicar regaled them all with the story of Mrs Mossop, a recent widow. Everyone knew how often Rev Hanley visited her. The vicar told them of all the problems she was having with her house. How he had been needed, morning, noon, and night. Hilda and Pearl winked at each other. They had heard of his night-time visits. Mrs Mossop seemed the unluckiest of people. Mice in the pantry, fused electrics, falling shelves, and flooding washing machines.

When Hilda asked why a handy man or indeed a plumber couldn't be called upon for some of these unfortunate incidences. The vicar blushed and said, 'Mrs Mossop wasn't left well provided for.'

When Hilda said, 'we know who to call on if our washing machine breaks then dear.'

The vicar looked flushed and said, 'ah, now... I didn't mean to suggest...'

'That's fine vicar, we will only call you about burst pipes,' said Hilda, laughing. 'Anyway, here's your hat. What's your hurry?'

'Hat, what do you mean?' said the vicar.

Hilda was on her feet shooing Rev Hanley out of the room. He said, 'oh, I see, time for me to go. Goodnight, ladies.'

'Yes, yes, goodbye dear,' said Hilda. She had the vicar down the stairs and out of the door.

'Hopefully see you on...,' started the reverend. But Hilda had already closed the front door on him before he finished. He realised he had not given them a notice sheet and so popped one through the door. Hilda saw the sheet come through the letterbox. She read the list of services at St Marks, then filed it in the round filing cabinet with all the other rubbish. When Pearl first heard Hilda say she was going to file a piece of paper in the round filing cabinet, she was puzzled. Then she saw her throw it in the bin and laughed.

Rev Hanley knew nothing of Hilda's treatment of his notice sheet. He already looked dejected enough as he walked off, shoulders slumped. Perhaps his visit with the local celebrity had not gone as planned.

Hidden Garden Tearoom, Plympton-on-Sea, UK

Post comes in many shapes and sizes. We often leave bills till last. Whilst a personal letter gets immediate attention. A stiff, high-quality envelope, from a solicitor, that arrives by registered post, is always mysterious. It causes a mixture of anxiety and excitement. Are we being summoned to court over an issue we know nothing about? Or has some long-lost relative died in a distant country and left us a gold mine? The morning post held such a letter and Hilda held up an envelope addressed to her from Messrs Kerridge, Lister, and Jingle Solicitors. It was an embossed cream coloured envelope. She admired the quality for a while and then called Pearl over. With anything official, it's best to have Pearl involved. Once Pearl had joined her, Hilda ripped open the letter and read it out loud. They looked at each other. Pearl took the letter and read it a few more times. Then said to Hilda, 'have you ever seen a letter demanding ground rent?'

'No,' said Hilda, which was telling the absolute truth.

Councillor Mildred Russell had illegally intercepted all letters about ground rent. Tim, a close friend of hers, worked at the solicitors handling the ground rent for the tearoom and flat. Mildred had arranged that Tim allow her to 'hand deliver' the letter each month. But she made it clear to Tim that if asked, he say that he posted the letter. Tim agreed, but then, ever since school, he would do anything for Mildred. Just one look from her made his day. She promised so much from that look. Yet, nothing more than a look and a kind word had come his way. Whenever she visited the solicitor's office, which was also her legal advisors. Tim's eyes never left her; he was like a lovesick puppy.

Pearl phoned the solicitors and spoke to Tim. He sounded flustered when he received the phone call. Tim told her that the solicitor was out, but he could explain the basics. He said that the reminder letters had gone out each month, and they were now in arrears. As per the letter, the leaseholder was starting action to take possession of The Hidden Garden Tearoom. When Pearl exclaimed at the unfairness of a firm being able to take possession of a property worth hundreds of thousands over a debt of a few hundred pounds. Tim remained silent. Afterwards, he phoned Mildred to tell her about the call. She told him to hold his nerve and say nothing.

When Pearl had hung up from calling Tim, she looked at Hilda, who was expectant.

'It's genuine. We need to fight this. Or you'll lose this tearoom in a few months,' said Pearl.

'As my pops always said, there's no use crying over spilt jam,' said Hilda. She looked far more relaxed than she ought.

Pearl looked at Hilda and sighed.

Chapter Seven

July 1998

Plympton Civic Centre, Plympton-on-Sea, UK

The next day at the new Civic Centre opening ceremony Hilda looked her normal self. No one would have guessed that the threat of closure hung over her tearoom. Nor that the home and business she had put her reward money into would all be lost. Instead, Hilda beamed from ear to ear. As Councillor Mildred Russell looked at her, she may well have doubted the information Tim had given her. Could the letter really have been received? Did they phone him? All her machinations, on behalf of 'B,' seemed to have worked. But looking at Hilda's radiant face, that could not be true. She needed to check. She walked over to Pearl and stood near her. Then casually dropped into conversation that a friend at the solicitor's office had mentioned a problem they were having, but no details. Pearl looked at Mildred and said, 'isn't that confidential?'

'He just mentioned that as a friend of Hilda's I ought to know you have some legal problems. He thought I could help?' said Mildred.

Pearl softened and told Mildred about the ground rent problem. Mildred held a fixed look of concern on her face the whole time. Then turning away momentarily; she smiled. She turned back to Pearl, and said, 'I'm really sorry, there's nothing I can do.'

While this was happening, up on the platform at the front, the mayor was chatting with Hilda. Preparing her for the coming task. It would usually be his job to open such things. But he looked happy to hand it onto this local celebrity. A friend of the US President. Hilda was getting more and more eager to start on the ribbon cutting. She had seen them in movies and on the news many times. Her only disappointment was not having a button to press as well. Everything else was exceeding her expectations. There were banners, a platform to stand on, a good-sized crowd, a band playing stirring music and reporters from the TV and newspapers. She also had a giant pair of scissors. Everything was fantastic. She waved the scissors around.

Hindsight is a wonderful thing, and we are all incredibly wise with its use. If we could see the future, no doubt we would be wise in the present. We may suggest that anyone knowing Hilda would have been able to foresee the future. Certainly, William and Louise, who were at the event, were a little concerned. Perhaps you have already jumped into the future and seen the dangers ahead?

Hilda did none of the things people feared at the ribbon ceremony. William watched as she cut the ribbon with the giant scissors and announced the new Civic Centre open. He breathed a sigh of relief. She put the scissors down without incident. Well, she waved them around dangerously quite a lot first. Louise patted William's shoulder, and said, 'see, nothing to worry about.'

'I suppose so,' William, looked up at his mother. Hilda was bowing and waving at the crowd.

The mayor was looking at his perfect celebrity and no doubt planning where to use her next. Then Hilda reverted to her usual self. She tapped the microphone to get everyone's attention and said, 'I was talking to the Civic Centre manager earlier. She was telling me they will be running exercise classes every day. Looking at you lot, I'd say you need more exercise.' She looked sternly over her glasses at the crowd. 'Yes, you in particular.' She stared hard at a man in the crowd, and said, 'put that hot dog down. You as well put that ice cream in the bin. Have you seen yourself in a mirror?' The two people highlighted went bright red and rushed off. 'I'm going to get things started now. Up you come.' A group of people of varying ages came onto the stage. They wore multi coloured leotards. After shoving the mayor to one side they filled the stage. He looked shocked and said, 'hang on.'

'Right, maestro, hit it,' said Hilda. She was centre front of the stage.

The band master had obviously been primed. The band played lively aerobics music and the people on stage leapt about as if they were on fire. Well, Hilda tried. Many in the crowd, including Louise, joined in. Others, like William, slunk to the sides. The reporters filmed, scribbled, and flashed their cameras. The mayor looked at his ceremony and shook his head. They did not invite Hilda to open anything else. The reports in the local news were mixed. One ran an article on the two people Hilda had highlighted as being unfit. They talked of their embarrassment and shame. Other papers and the local

TV focussed on Healthy Hilda and had photos and videos of the impromptu aerobics.

After talking to Mildred, Pearl headed back to the tearoom. She lost interest in the ribbon cutting, so she missed all the excitement. As the tearoom had few people, she left the two staff to carry on managing alone and headed up to the flat. She made a phone call to her sister Ruby, who was still in London with The President of the USA and family. After she hung up, she looked far more relaxed. Her sister had promised to chat with The First Lady. Pearl knew Evelyn had some useful contacts.

TSU Plc Board Room, Meedham, UK

William's first experience of a board meeting was when he was called in on a Tuesday morning. Harold had asked the board to meet him. This was William's chance to impress. He was wearing the suit, which Louise had convinced him to buy for their visit to The White House the previous year.

The boardroom at the TSU offices was plush. Situated on the top floor, it had windows on three sides. It had views across the municipal car park in one direction and the disused canal in another. Harold was on a committee trying to secure funding to clean it up and create a beautiful natural space in the centre of Meedham. Anything would be preferable to the half drained muddy puddles filled with old shopping trolleys and car tyres. From the last window, a vista across the High Street treated any viewer. Being higher than the building opposite afforded the board members the treat of viewing rusting air conditioning units. They could also see the poorly maintained roof on the bingo hall. Hot days had an added delight. The caretakers and cleaners from the bingo hall sunbathing in their tatty underwear. For all these reasons, the board members had opted to fit blinds across windows. They lit the interior with a mixture of crystal wall lights and chandeliers. These gave a pleasing warmth to the wood panelling.

Sitting around the large oak table, in leather seats, was a selection of men and women, perhaps surprisingly, for such an archaic company. One of the two female directors was Miss Jennings. She had worked for TSU since the early days. Now in her seventies, she still had a razor like mind and did not suffer fools easily. She managed the human resource part of the company. She still called it payroll. The other was younger, a more recent addition. There were four other board members. Plus, the CEO, Harold Styles, and his secretary. Two other board members, Mr Tibbert and Mr Unbridge, had retired the previous year.

William walked in hesitantly and looked at the seven people sitting around the table. He felt like a schoolboy going in front of the headteacher. All that was lacking was a school cap to scrunch up in his hand.

'Take a seat,' said Harold. He pointed to a chair at the opposite end to himself. This put William in a very exposed position. Three people on each side of the table and Harold, at some distance, sitting at the head of the table.

'Tell us about yourself,' said Miss Jennings'. Her voice was matter of fact. William jumped a little and glanced towards her. She was acting in her role as head of HR.

'Right... yes... umm...' he said.

'A little more concise would be helpful,' said Mr Tate. Cutting William off. He was a corpulent man who would make an excellent Father Christmas. He made others feel foolish. Although his own abilities were limited. He was an old school friend of Mr Tibbert and had gained his position out of favour, not merit. Harold had plans to retire him as soon as possible.

'Yes, of course,' said William. He looked at Harold, who was smiling at him. 'I have worked here since I left school...'

'School, not university?' said Mr Dailies. He had a narrow face and angular features. Despite his seventy years, his hair was dark. Perhaps hair dye could be thanked for that. He valued education highly as he had graduated top in his class. But his memory and faculties were failing.

William looked at Mr Dailies, and said, 'yes, that's right. I started at the bottom, an office boy.' A few of the board members sniffed and huffed. Mr Dailies seemed to have lost interest. Or have nodded off. The other directors just looked on with interest.

Mr Tate reached down to his bag, which was not the expected Santa's sack. He drew out a file from his case and glanced at it. Then said, 'You worked for me, for a time.' He raised his eyebrows. The figures he was reading showed that when William worked for him, his department had been at its most productive.

'That's right Mr Tate,' said William.

Mr Tate nodded. His fat rosy, red cheeks and white hair just lacking the red hat with a white bobble.

'I remember when you started here,' said Miss Jennings. She had a clear and commanding voice. 'You were always a bright lad, wasted as a filing clerk.' Everything on her paperwork showed William as a positive asset.

'Thank you,' said William. His face a shade of red. 'I went to night school.' He looked at Harold, who nodded. 'Mr Styles encouraged me.' There were other nods around the room.

'I could see potential in him as well,' said Mr Tate.

'I agree,' said Miss Jennings. She peered over her glasses at William. 'I said so then.' Mr Tate and Harold both nodded.

'I worked my way up to department manager,' said William.

'Not before time,' said Miss Jennings. 'You're a hard worker. A well-deserved promotion.' She looked at Harold. It had been she who insisted on the promotion.

William smiled at her. Her face was hard. She looked down at her notes, then back up. 'Have you all seen these figures for the US branches?'

One or two board members seemed to start a little, as if woken from sleep. There were mumbled sounds, grunts, and acknowledgements. Then Harold said, 'William has worked hard since his first day here. He is conscientious and efficient. His staff have respect and a high regard for him. His department is among the most reliable and profitable we have. I sent him to the USA as our ambassador to set up our new branches, because I trust him. I can't say higher than that. He proved worthy of that trust. Now I am asking you to vote him onto the board. We need some fresh blood now that Mr Tibbert and Mr Unbridge have retired.'

'We need time to discuss it in private,' said Mr Dailies. He sat up straight. They gave general assent to the idea around the table.

'Fine,' said Harold. He then said to William, 'if you could wait outside a while.'

Hidden Gardens Tearoom, Plympton-on-Sea, UK

It had taken a couple of weeks, but at last Ruby made it for one last visit to see Pearl and Hilda before her return to the US. She arrived early evening. The weather was gorgeous, so they sat in a cosy corner of the garden. Hilda went to make a pot of tea and rustle up some snacks while the sisters chatted.

Ruby and Pearl got up to stretch their legs and have a walk around. Ruby loved flowers and wanted to inhale their scent and enjoy their beauty. They were standing by a flower bed with a deep yellow rose. A bee was visiting the flowers. Merlin was watching the bee with interest. He kept batting at it with his paws. Fortunately, it didn't sting. The church bells rang out; this was the night they practiced. The fragrance of flowers filled the air. Ruby breathed in the scent and said, 'this is such an amazing place, the garden is so beautiful. I can see why it would be so awful if she lost it.'

Pearl took in the garden's beauty and said, 'it's charming alright. But Hilda's acting as if nothing's wrong. I guess that's her way.'

'I've had a word with Evelyn, and she has spoken to a friend. One who knows The Duchess of Devonshire,' said Ruby.

'She's such a wonderful lady. I hope she can help,' said Pearl.

'You'll miss it here,' said Ruby. She searched her sisters' eyes.

'I'll miss Hilda and the place,' said Pearl. She looked down at the crazy paving. Wildflowers and grasses pushed up between the cracks. Merlin had given up on the bee and found a warm area of paving to lay on.

'You've not told her you coming to the USA?' said Ruby.

'Not yet,' said Pearl. She glanced at Ruby and sighed. 'I don't want to tip things over the edge for her. Like I said, she acts like all is fine...' She shrugged.

Ruby nodded and said, 'I understand. You think hearing you're leaving might be the last straw?'

Pearl watched a bee land on a rose. She opened her mouth to speak, then heard Hilda say, 'I thought the kettle would never

boil. Well, as my mother always said, "watch cup never toils."'
Pearl laughed.

'Before I go, Chad tells me that the local sheriff still hasn't caught Wilbur. Orville had an unpleasant run in with him the other week. So, he is still out to cause trouble,' said Ruby.

'You take care,' said Pearl.

'Don't worry, I will,' said Ruby. They all hugged.

Let's hope that care is enough to keep her safe. Ruby was due to retire and move to Florida on her return to America. No more protection from the Whitehouse security.

William and Louise Shilton's house, Meedham, UK

Louise had a feeling of Déjà vu as she pulled up in her car. Ted was once again in his front garden, kneeling and weeding. Louise saw a figure in her peripheral vision. She reacted blindly. William had been standing in the shade of their driveway hedge. Ted heard Louise scream. But this time, William shouted to him as he stepped towards the car, 'it's just me Ted.' If only Ted had better eyesight and hearing.

Louise had not heard William identify himself either. Her radio played loudly. She enjoyed singing in the car at the top of her voice. Nor had she seen him step from the shadows into the sunlight. If only it had not been such a sunny evening. Louise just saw a dark shadow in her peripheral vision. She acted on instinct. Looking over her left shoulder, away from William, she rapidly reversed out of the drive. Leaving William standing alone. Yet again holding a bunch of flowers, but this time he also had a bottle of champagne. As he headed to the front door, he muttered, 'not again.'

It wouldn't have been so bad had it not been for Ted. He had heard Louise scream; she was deafening. By the time he got up, he was just in time to see the back of a strange man entering William and Louise's house. His knees were not as good as they once were. Getting up took a long time these days. His eyesight was not clear enough to recognise William at such a distance. Ted's suspicions, once raised, needed investigation. He set off at his fastest speed to check what was happening. He gasped and panted his way towards the house.

Sometimes things seem to conspire to cause problems. Ted knew William didn't get home this early. Louise should be back by now, and he'd heard her scream. Yet her car was missing. Ted knew this was all very peculiar and most likely urgent. For a moment, he considered knocking on the door and challenging the strange man. As he bent double, gasping and sweating, common sense took over. He headed back home and phoned the police; this warranted an emergency 999 call.

Meanwhile, Louise had stopped at a nearby call box and phoned 999. A stranger in her driveway. This was an urgent police matter. The police received two calls about a stranger at Louise's home address and despatched a unit to investigate. Fortunately, one was nearby. Or was that fortunate?

Meanwhile, William, the unwitting cause of all this distress, sat in the front room of his house. Still wearing his suit jacket, flowers in one hand, bottle of champagne in the other. He looked from the flowers to the champagne. A siren blared outside. He glanced at the window, wondering where they were heading.

A police car pulled up on the street, and two officers got out. They meet up with Ted; he had walked back to the end of William and Louise's driveway. Just as they started hearing the details from him, Louise arrived back. She had been told by the emergency call handler to wait five minutes, then meet the police at her home. The officers discussed the situation with Louise and Ted. Having found out all the facts, however wrong they were, one officer fetched a megaphone. He spoke into it, 'this is the police. We have you surrounded.' A bit of an overstatement, with two officers, both standing next to each other at the front of the house. 'Come out peacefully. We don't want to come in there.' That bit was true. On a Friday evening, at the end of their shift. They were ready to head home. Already this would cause a lot of extra paperwork.

Inside the house, William stared at the switched off television. Where were the voices coming from? He put down the flowers, picked up the remote with his free hand, and pressed it. The TV switched on. He turned it off again, then walked over to the radio and checked it was also off. The radio was on a table by the front window. William stood staring at the radio, scratching his head. The officer outside his house said, 'this is the Police. Please come out... this is your last warning.' He sounded desperate.

William pulled the net curtain aside and saw two police officers standing next to Louise and Ted. He opened the net curtain further and waved with the hand holding the champagne bottle.

'Is that a gun?' shouted an officer. 'Get down.' Diving onto the tarmac driveway.

The other officer copied him and then called into his radio from his prostrate position, saying, 'possible shooter. Armed response needed.'

Louise glanced between the two prone officers and her husband, behind the net curtains. She waved back. He waved again. She waved, he waved. Then Ted waved and said, 'that looks like William.' He was standing close enough to see, even with Ted's poor eyesight. Getting onto the ground had not appealed to him. Even with the risk of a gun.

One officer looked up at Ted from his position on the ground, and asked, 'is William a known local felon?'

'He always seemed a decent chap. I suppose you never can tell,' said Ted. 'Although, he shouted at me once.'

The officer spoke into his radio, saying, 'possible known local felon, name of William. History of violence.'

'William Shilton,' added Ted, helpfully.

'Additional info, surname Shilton, please advise,' said the officer. He adjusted his legs and arms. He looked uncomfortable.

'Don't be silly. It's my husband. Ted, you're no help. He only shouted because you couldn't hear him over the mower,' said Louise. She walked towards the house.

'Husband?' said the officer. He glanced up at Louise as she headed to the front door. Then spoke into his radio, 'could be a setup. Husband and wife may be in it together. Please advise. The informant is heading into the premises to join possible armed intruder. She is now at the door. Suspect is opening the door. The suspect is at the door with a possible weapon... wait one... um... is it too late to cancel armed response? Right, OK, got that. Best be safe.... Possible mix up though.'

Later, after the armed response unit had arrived. When William was 'disarmed' of his Champagne. Once he had it inspected and returned. After the ARU had complained at having their time wasted. Following the two officers' reprimands at mistaking a bottle of Champagne for a gun. When all the explanations had been made and apologies given. After all the police had then left in a noisy convoy of vehicles. When Ted had eventually gone home, following a cup of tea and biscuits.

Louise and William were finally alone and sitting on the sofa, sipping Champagne. Louise smiled, and William looked at her seriously. The police had blamed him, which seemed most unfair. Even though he had not made either of the two emergency calls. After two glasses of champagne, he looked more relaxed. William eventually told Louise his good news about becoming a director. Louise asked, 'will that mean a pay rise?'

'Yes, but I don't have amounts yet. Harold told me we would sort out specifics later,' said William. He lay his head back on the sofa and let out a long breath.

Louise gave William a hug, and said, 'well done you. Quite an achievement.' William smiled and hugged Louise back.

Promenade, Plympton-On-Sea, UK

Lord Leonard and his wife Councillor Mildred Russell were walking along the promenade at Plympton. Every so often, someone would stop Councillor Russell to chat about a local issue. She pretended to be interested in their worries, then promptly forgot about it after leaving them. Her husband walked one step behind her.

Hilda danced towards them. Not an unusual occurrence on several counts. This was a Sunday afternoon, so the tearoom was closed. Dancing was Hilda's usual means of movement and the only way she could think properly. She had a lot to think about. What was unusual was to see Hilda without Pearl. Had Mildred asked, she would have found that Pearl was in her bed, suffering from a headache. Which was what Pearl had told Hilda. She was merely enjoying a bit of peace and quiet on her own. Every so often she needed a time quietly reading. This was such a day.

As Hilda drew level with Len and Mildred, she stopped. Not completely stopped, of course. A slight rhythmic swaying and some tapping of her toes continued. Hilda tried to look serious, for she had an important question to ask. She said, 'ah, hello dear.' That wasn't the important question. But Hilda wanted to ease into it. 'I have a problem.' Often when Hilda started with that line, people were treated to a list of her ailments. Not that she had more ailments than a person of her age should expect. In fact, she probably had fewer than a person half her age could ever wish for. I am not suggesting people wish for their ailments. Hilda just shared things a bit too freely. It had all begun when people started saying, 'how are you?' rather than, 'hello.' Whilst most people understood that to be an innocuous greeting, Hilda saw it as an excuse to explain her innermost feelings. Well, if people must give Hilda an opening, then they must expect her to take it.

Back to Hilda's important question. Mildred was staring at Hilda, waiting for her to elucidate her problem. She had already learnt not to ask how she was, through bitter experience. Instead, Mildred merely raised her eyebrows. Hilda noted this action and said, 'are you alright? Your face seems a little odd. I saw a poster about strokes. Do you think you could be having one? Let me think, they had an easy way to remember. A sort of test.'

'FAST,' said Mildred.

'Don't be impatient, let me think. The first letter was F, I think,' said Hilda.

'I know it was F. The acronym was FAST,' said Mildred, tapping her toes.

'Acronym,' said Hilda. She screwed up her face. 'I don't think it was one of those. I am talking about a stroke.'

'Look, I am not having a stroke,' said Mildred. 'So, let's forget it. I think I already know your problem.'

'Really?' said Hilda. She stopped dancing and stared at Mildred. 'Are you a mind reader, dear?'

'No, but Pearl talked to me at the ribbon cutting,' said Mildred.

'Well, I never, of course. This could be something different,' said Hilda.

'Yes, I suppose so. What is the problem?' said Mildred sharply.

'Ah yes, dear, my problem. Now what was it? Oh, hello there Len. You were a long way back. Are you out for a walk as well?' said Hilda. 'You always seem to keep a few steps back from your wife.'

'Oh, hello Mrs Shilton,' said Len. He bowed a little to Hilda.

Mildred frowned at him and then stared at Hilda.

'Right, I've remembered. It's about my tearoom. A solicitor has sent me a letter about a lease or something. Pearl says they will end up owning it. All because of a small amount I owe for some rent or other,' said Hilda. 'I don't suppose you can help?'

Len looked at his wife, puzzled. She looked away from him and said to Hilda, 'that is the same thing Pearl mentioned. I told her there's nothing I can do.'

Len stared at his wife, and said, 'really?'

Mildred frowned at her husband. Then turned ready to go, saying, 'of course, I can't, well, we must be going. Come on, Lenny.' Len stood for a moment, staring sadly at Hilda, and then plodded along after his wife. Hilda shook her head and danced on her way. She glanced behind her after a while and noticed Len was still a few steps behind Mildred, 'strange,' she thought.

CHAPTER EIGHT

July 1998

The Vicarage, Plympton-on-Sea, UK

The Rev Hanley had only one visit planned on Tuesday morning. A visit to Hilda Shilton. Whilst seated at breakfast, the vicar told his wife that today he would win Hilda over. He had heard of her troubles with the ground rent on her café. Gossip travels fast. If only useful information travelled as fast as gossip, things in the world would run a lot smoother. Rev Hanley told his wife that he wanted to lend a listening ear. In doing so, Hilda would see that she needed his council and turn to him for aid and comfort. His wife may well have found such thoughts at odds with her views on her husband. He didn't spend a lot of time comforting her or indeed being with her at all. Being shy and retiring, she was not the sort of person to challenge him. She hid away, quietly at the vicarage. Let's hope he occasionally lent her a listening ear. Or some comfort and solace.

As the holy vicar decreed his plans, his wife meekly agreed. She then passed him his plate of bacon and eggs. Two slices of toast, buttered properly as he liked it. She was about to sit down and eat her porridge when he frowned. She asked what the problem was. He shook his head and reminded her he was still awaiting his morning coffee, freshly ground, one sugar. Leaving her porridge to get cold, she sorted out her husband's needs. As they ate, he continued to inform her of his plans. She listened and nodded occasionally. He spoke in a commanding voice, saying, 'I may have failed so far, but as you know, the needs of others are a foremost priority for me. Hard work and application are ever my watchwords. Could I have another slice of toast, please?'

His wife leapt up from her now stone-cold porridge and fetched his toast. 'Yes, the needs of others are paramount,' said the thoughtful vicar. Nodding firmly, he rose and left the table for his wife to clear up. He had the important job ahead of dressing appropriately.

Ministers of the Church of England wear a variety of garments. Their selection depends on how high the church is. Theologically, not physically. Though presumably if the church were physically very high, that would also affect their apparel. Mostly, it was the duties being performed that decided the accoutrement. As Rev John Hanley robed himself that morning, he was dressing in a sombre fashion as befit his mission.

Hilda herself was unaware of all the attention she was about to receive. Had she known, she would have been most surprised. She may even have stayed in to receive the vicar's visit. Being oblivious of all the Rev Hanley's hard work, she had other plans that morning.

When Rev Hanley finished his robing preparations. Which just involved putting on a dark woollen suit and his usual white collar. He requested and received his wife's seal of approval.

It's unlikely that she would dare refuse it. He then strode off towards the tearoom. He would win today. On arrival, he heard Hilda had headed into Meedham by bus just five minutes earlier. He sped after her. As the bus stop came into his sight, the bus was already appearing around the corner. The vicar ran. Sweat dripped down his back. He was not a fit man. A dark, heavy wool suit did not work well as a running outfit on a hot, sunny day.

Rev Hanley reached the bus stop just in time to see the bus set off. From within the bus, Hilda noticed him running along the road and waved to him. He stood, or rather bent double, at the bus stop, gasping for breath. Sweat dripped down his face. He looked deathlike, his hand on his chest. A voice called to him. It was not the call of a heavenly angel. He had not died. One of the parish council members had been driving past on their way into Meedham and seen him at the bus stop. They offered him a lift, which he accepted.

The drive was long enough for Rev Hanley to recover his breath and composure. Once in Meedham, the vicar headed to Hilda's favourite café, The Coffee House. He had heard gossip it was her favourite café. He always stored away such information for future reference. On entering The Coffee House, he stood in the doorway like a portent of doom, in his black suit with a dark expression. The Coffee House customers stared at the vicar and absolute silence fell upon the room. No doubt they assumed that someone had died, and he was there to administer the last rites. Or carry them away on the wings of ravens. Having glanced around and reassured themselves that all was well. People resumed their conversation. Perhaps a little quieter than before. Rev Hanley looked around and could see no sign of Hilda. He continued his search outside The Coffee House.

Meanwhile, on the high street, a traffic warden glanced left and right as she walked purposefully along. A crowd was gathered around a street trader, Baz. Hilda walked along the high street and saw the stall. Curious, she stopped to watch.

'You there, young lady,' said Baz. He pointed at Hilda. 'I bet you can't solve this impossible puzzle?'

It took Hilda aback being singled out from the crowd, but it pleased her he recognised her youthful energy.

'What puzzle, dear?' asked Hilda. She stepped forward to look.

'It's rather tricky and has baffled the minds of many,' said Baz. He waved his arms dramatically. 'In this very street, four people have tried and gone away empty-handed.'

'Oh well, I had better not try then,' said Hilda. She started to leave. Other people who had gathered when they heard Baz call also lost interest and continued to walk on.

'Ah!' said Baz. 'When I said impossible, I meant for ordinary mortals. You seem to me exceptionally clever.'

Hilda stopped and turned around. She said, 'you must be a very poor judge of character. My son always says I am exceptionally bad at puzzles. Mind you, I think he can be a bit rude.' Some other people also stopped and formed a crowd.

'Absolutely, young lady, and if I may say so, you look too young to have a grown-up son,' said Baz.

Hilda preened herself, and said, 'you may indeed.' She looked at the people, who were forming a circle around her and Baz.

'I think you would do very well at this puzzle,' said Baz. He stepped around the table towards Hilda.

'But isn't it very hard?' asked Hilda. She stepped away from the table.

'Yes, it is very hard indeed. I just think you have the brainpower to solve it,' said Baz. He was trying to usher Hilda towards the table.

In the gathered crowd there was a young lady, with her baby son sleeping in his pushchair. She had stopped to watch out of curiosity. Now she looked interested. A group of teenagers stood a little way off, half watching, half chatting to each other. They were curious. A middle-aged couple stood hand in hand; they had met through an online dating agency. The man was smiling. The lady pulled his hand. He gazed into her eyes. She grimaced. Hilda's repartee with the street trader caused the lady to look around and relax.

'Do you really think I could solve a hard puzzle?' said Hilda, looking back at Baz.

'Yes, of course, that's why I suggested it,' said Baz. He was getting into his stride. He had a fish on the hook.

'But you were shouting out that it was impossible. If it's impossible, then no one can do it,' said Hilda.

'Just a figure of speech. Not impossible for you, young lady,' said Baz. His smile was getting very broad. He looked very much like a tiger with its prey.

'Well, I think you should make your mind up. Is it impossible or not?' asked Hilda, getting impatient.

'It's not impossible for a clever lady like you,' said Baz, bowing to her.

'How do you know I can do it? Could I try it out first?' asked Hilda, innocently.

'Ah! Now these games have a cost, only a tiny one. Just to cover my expenses, you understand. I can't afford to stand out here all day and not charge anything,' said Baz. He made it all sound very reasonable.

'A cost? Money, you mean. Oh, dear, I'm not rich, you know. I'm a pensioner,' said Hilda. She glanced around at the growing crowd. 'You won't believe it, but I'm 78.' There were no surprised faces, but one or two nods of encouragement.

'Tell you what, I will give you the special Tuesday pensioner's rate. How would that be?'

Hilda looked at the crowd for support. There were pursed lips and shaking heads.

'These people don't seem convinced,' said Hilda. She pointed at the crowd.

Baz made a point of ignoring them and focussed on Hilda. Then he said, 'they are just jealous because you are getting a special rate. They know that if you solve this puzzle, you will win…' Baz thought for a moment, '£100!' The crowd clapped. They could see the sign that read in big letters: 'Solve the puzzle and win £50.'

'I suppose that is a lot of money, but how much do I have to pay to win it?' asked Hilda. She made her eyes go wide.

'It's just £1,' said Baz.

'£1! That's an awful lot of money. I don't think I can afford that,' said Hilda. She got her purse out and peered into it as if it contained her last penny in the world. She pushed the notes out of sight.

Baz frowned and said, 'OK lovely lady, just for you, 50p.' The crowd clapped again. He looked pleased with the response.

In the crowd, the middle-aged man put his arm around his date. She gave him a withering stare. However, instead of causing him to let go, it had the opposite effect. He cuddled her tighter. A shout from the crowd distracted her.

'25p!' said an anonymous voice.

'No... Now come on folks, I have doubled the reward and halved the stake. I can't make it any cheaper,' said Baz, sweating.

'So, all I need to do is guess this number?' said Hilda. She had walked to the table and was picking up papers.

'Hold on a second,' said Baz. He looked desperate. He was juggling the crowd and an unruly pensioner.

'Oh, I see, most of these are the same,' said Hilda. She turned over several sheets of paper at once.

'I haven't explained the rules. I meant them to be the same. You must...,' said Baz. But Hilda interrupted him.

'It's OK, I think I have it now,' said Hilda. She had turned all the sheets over and was opening every box on the table.

Baz desperately tried to stop her, but it was like herding cats. The crowd was cheering, laughing, and clapping. Even the group of teenagers, who until that point had feigned disinterest, were laughing out loud and moving closer. The lady on the date became so engrossed in Hilda's antics she was ignoring the arm around her. The young mum missed her baby wake up in all the hubbub. The baby looked around, obviously wondering what all the noise was about.

'This is not what you do,' said Baz, trying to be heard over the crowd.

'32,' said Hilda, loudly.

'I bet she's right,' called a voice from the crowd.

'No, she isn't,' lied Baz.

'Oh, what is the answer?' asked Hilda.

'I am not continuing this; you have not played by the rules,' said Baz, sulkily.

'Answer, answer, answer!' chanted the crowd.

'Alright, it's 30,' lied Baz.

'But this is the answer card,' said Hilda. She held up the answer card. Written clearly on it, the number 32.

'You cheated,' said Baz, pathetically.

'Liar, liar, liar!' chanted the crowd.

'But, but, but... she cheated,' said Baz. He turned to the crowd; arms outstretched.

'Give her the money,' shouted a voice from the crowd.

'Money, money, money,' followed the chant.

'It's alright, if you don't think I deserve it,' said Hilda. She looked frail as she stared at the ground.

'Money, money, money,' continued the crowd.

'OK, OK,' said Baz. He obviously decided retreat was the better part of valour. He got out £100 and held it aloft. Then slowly, ever so slowly, handed it to Hilda. She snatched it and popped it in her purse. Then Baz looked at his empty stake money pot. Hilda had not even given him the 50p stake money. Baz was completely defeated. Today was meant to make him money. Instead, he was £100 out of pocket.

'Thank you dear,' said Hilda, smiling. The crowd broke up.

The lady on a date turned to move and found a firm grip around her waist. She said,

'Get off me!' Her date let go.

The middle-aged man said to her back, 'can we meet up again?' He obviously felt it had been a very successful date. She ignored him and walked away.

The teenagers all agreed that it had been the best afternoon for ages. They hoped that man and the odd lady would be back the next day. Unfortunately for them, that wish was not granted.

A community police officer walked up and said, 'whose table is this?' Hilda pointed at Baz.

Baz had to pay a fine for not having a licence. It had been an expensive day. Baz would never return to Meedham again. So perhaps Hilda had done the citizens of that town a favour.

It was as Hilda was walking away from a sorrowful Baz that she saw Rev Hanley. She said, 'hello dear, I saw you running after the bus.'

'Yes, I fancied a day in town,' said the Vicar. He was being less than truthful. An odd habit for a man of God. 'I'm glad to see you. I wanted to condole.'

'Oh,' said Hilda. 'Will you be able to?'

'Able to what?' said Rev Hanley.

'Condole,' said Hilda, walking away.

The vicar kept pace with Hilda, and said, 'I hope so. I am here to do it with you.'

Hilda stopped and turned towards the vicar, saying, 'with me? I am 78, you know, dear, and I have never done it before. Isn't it a bit late to start now?'

The vicar stared straight at Hilda, and said, 'I have no wish to cause any perturbation.'

'Will I need to do that as well? Is it difficult?' said Hilda. She screwed up her face.

'I can see that I am causing some perplexity,' said the vicar.

'Really? My son has just had his windows changed to those,' said Hilda. She shook her head.

'Perplexity in his windows?' said Rev Hanley, scratching his head.

'I think so dear, at least it sounded very much like it,' said Hilda. She walked again.

Rev Hanley stood and stared at Hilda's back, his head to one side. Then his face lit up, and he rushed to catch her, and said, 'are you thinking of Perspex? Or perhaps uPVC?'

Hilda glanced at the vicar, and said, 'oh, you are clever. You ought to be a teacher rather than a vicar.'

The vicar was having difficulty keeping up with Hilda. He was sweating and panting. He said, 'let me... get back... to why... I was... wanting to... meet with... you.'

'A dance or a song, was it?' said Hilda. She stopped and let the vicar catch up and catch his breath.

'No, I want to condole with you,' said the vicar. He had to breathe deeply. He was not at all fit.

'So, you said, whatever that means,' said Hilda. She stared at the vicar, gasping for breath.

'Share in your sorrow and show you how much I care,' said Rev Hanley. He put on his best caring face. But the sweating and redness spoiled it.

'Sorrow? You do look sorry for yourself. Are you quite alright?' asked Hilda. 'I have no sorrow.'

The vicar stared at Hilda. Then said, 'I must have been misinformed? I heard you are going to lose your home and business.' He almost smiled.

'Oh that, don't let that worry you. Things will work out. You just go on the dole with someone who needs it,' said Hilda. With that parting comment, Hilda waved and walked off. Rev Hanley stood in the High St. dripping with sweat and still very red faced. Perhaps he needed to enrol in the new Civic Centre aerobics classes.

Stonehouse Manor, Upper Plympton, UK

Mildred and Len sat at their kitchen table, eating lunch. There seemed to be an atmosphere between them. Len's plate was untouched. He put down his utensils and stared at his wife. Then asked, 'is this your doing?'

'Is what my doing, the meal? You made that,' said Mildred. She glanced at him before taking another mouthful.

'Not the meal. The lease issues on Mrs Shilton's tearoom,' said Len. He was uncharacteristically sharp.

'You have no idea, do you? It's all up to me,' said Mildred. She got up and headed to the sideboard. Clicked on the kettle, put a tea bag in a cup.

'What exactly have you done?' asked Len.

Mildred glanced at her husband and said, 'I'm tempted to tell you.'

'Tell me what?' said Len. He walked over to his wife and stood in front of her.

Mildred turned away from him, and said, 'never mind.'

'Whatever it is, you can't force an old lady out of her home,' Len said sternly.

'You be as noble as you like. You're too late. If you cause any trouble, just remember, you signed the papers too,' said Mildred. The kettle boiled; she poured water in one cup.

'You never told me what they were,' said Len. His eyes glanced at his own empty cup.

'You didn't ask,' said Mildred. She flicked her hair and walked to the fridge to fetch the milk.

'I feel like I don't know you,' said Len, staring at his wife.

Mildred brought the milk back and poured it in her cup. Then, still holding the bottle waved it at Len as she said, 'there's a lot you don't know. You're just too soft. Had it too easy. You don't live in the real world.'

Len looked at the anger and bitterness on Mildred's face, and said, 'if your world is the real one. I am glad that I don't live in it.' He walked out and left Mildred drinking her tea.

Chapter Nine

August 1998

Sunset Time Resort, Florida, USA

Pearl's twin sister, Ruby, retired from her job as The White House chef with as little fuss as she could manage. Her boss and friend, The First Lady, Evelyn Meyer, threw a party. A mere hundred people attended. Ruby had paired the list down from two hundred. She made sure no media attended. Her hope being not to tip off Wilbur about her retirement and leaving the safety of The Whitehouse.

Ruby arrived at her new condo in Florida to a welcoming committee. Maybe not so much a committee as two people. Josie and Ange liked to greet all newcomers to the Sunset Time Resort. They were inside Ruby's condo. 'Welcome to your new...' is as far as Josie got, before Ruby screamed. With the expectation of a murderer looking for her, she didn't need surprises.

After Josie and Ange explained they were not burglars, and they ran the residents' committee. Comprising two people. Ruby asked, 'how on earth did you get into my home?'

'Ferdy's a friend,' was all the explanation Ange offered. Later, Ruby met Ferdy, or rather Ferdinand, the caretaker, security, and grounds person. She changed her locks after that meeting and didn't give him a copy.

Ruby had chosen the Sunset Time Resort for its supposed security. A gated community with full-time guards. She now discovered security was not as great as expected. The full-time guards comprised three in total. They worked ten hours on, ten hours off. Only one guard per day. They were all as useless as Ferdy. In theory, Wilbur didn't know where Ruby had moved. She had a two-bed condo, ready for when Pearl could join her. If she ever got up the courage to tell Hilda that she was leaving.

Plympton Playhouse, Plympton-on-Sea, UK

There's a well-known expression in stage life, 'break a leg.' The idea is to wish a performer well. But it sounds like you have a desire to see them in a splint. Its origins are much less easy to pin down than you might think. There are fifty-seven roots to the expression. All they can agree on is that it's positive.

What a pity that sayings and helpful wishes alone are not enough. As Hilda gathered her performers and backstage crew together for a pre performance pep talk, they needed good luck. It's said that a poor dress rehearsal is a positive sign. Which should mean a perfect first performance. No one standing in front of Hilda that night looked convinced of that. So many things had gone wrong in the dress rehearsal. It was difficult to see how the live performance could be anything but a failure. Unbeknown to Hilda, Gary and Caz Hilkins had enacted none of their plans to mess up the show. Everything that went wrong in the dress rehearsal was to do with bad acting and poor timing. If the club members had known that they were in for a whole raft of fresh problems, no one would have bothered to turn up on the opening night. Hilda, the eternal optimist, was in charge and she was full of smiles. The show went forward with her expectation that it would be wonderful.

In the audience for this first performance were William, Louise, and Josh. They had front row seats. Just behind them sat a row of local and even national reporters. Having a celebrity like Hilda direct the show made it of national interest. After all, she was a friend of the US President. Further back in the theatre sat Karl Dansk, the retired composer and one-time best friend of Hilda's. He had yet to remake her acquaintance. The time for that meeting lay in the future. Just as the time they were last close lay fifty years in the past and many miles away, in London.

Karl first met Hilda when he was performing at the BBC, and she worked as head chef. Hilda was a breath of fresh air. Her husband Arthur was more down to earth. But he became Karl's great friend. When Arthur died, soon after William was born, Karl and Lillian aimed to help. But they were such jetsetters, so busy with his work, that their visits to Hilda became further apart and eventually stopped. As Karl sat in the Plympton Playhouse, remembering the past, he looked sad. He was about to get up and leave when the lights dimmed, and the curtain rose.

Act One

In a play, timing is key, especially a comedy. Gary and Caz had been planning the downfall of Hilda's play for a while. As Gary sat in the lighting booth, he grinned and rubbed his hands. The timing and lighting on this play would be anything but perfect. The script, with all its lighting cues and notes from the dress rehearsal, lay in front of him. As the curtain came up on a Hotel Lobby, Gary checked the notes. The lights on stage came up exactly as they should. All started better than the dress rehearsal. His wife, Caz, stood in her place backstage. She operated the scenery flats and organised the props. Anything physical on stage, other than an actor, she operated it. A small crew of helpers acted on her orders. If anyone could have chosen two worse people to handle the major backstage roles in the play, it's hard to see who they could have selected.

On stage, an actor playing a doorman stood near the fancy wooden doors with pretend glass. He was looking out through the 'glass' onto a painted backdrop of a street beyond. Noises of distant cars and people added to the exterior effect. An actor playing the hotel receptionist stood behind a semi-circular desk in the opposite corner. He answered a ringing phone, saying, 'Hotel Splendid, how can I be of assistance?' he listened. 'A double?... Sea views?... And the name?... Mr and Mrs J Lions. We look forward to welcoming you tomorrow.' He wrote in the register with a flourish. He managed this much better than in dress rehearsal. At the rehearsal, he'd got the names wrong, dropped the pen and fallen flat on his face trying to pick it up.

'Oh, Henry darling,' said a woman's voice offstage. She sounded very much like Hilda. 'Please help me. My duster's stuck.'

'Just coming,' said Henry. He quickly exited through a door behind the reception desk. It opened without incident this time. They had applied a lot of oil to it after the squeaky hinges of the run-through. After the actor playing Henry exits through the doors, giggling and muffled sounds are heard offstage.

The phone rings again. Henry shouts from offstage. 'Fred, could you please get that? I am... busy.' More giggling offstage.

'If I must,' said Fred. He huffs and puffs as he trudges towards the phone. It stops ringing. He hobbles back towards the door. It rings again. He huffs and puffs again as he struggles towards the phone. It stops ringing. This happens once more; Fred moves towards it faster this time and says into the phone, 'Hotel Splendid, can I help?' He listens... 'Let me check.' He calls to Henry. 'Have we got anymore sea view doubles left?'

'Look in the register,' shouts Henry from the other room. He sounds muffled and exasperated.

Fred checks the register, grinning. Then says into the phone, 'yes, we have one available. How many nights?... Just the weekend... and the name? J Lions, is that Mr and Mrs?' His voice seemed to rise at the end. 'Alright, goodbye.' He hangs up and writes the details in the register carefully. There are still noises from offstage. He keeps looking towards the door behind him. From which the noises emanate.

Fred then struggles back to his post. As he arrives at the hotel door, Mrs Henry Faring, the receptionist's wife, is walking up to it. Fred opens it for her and welcomes her to the Hotel Splendid.

'Alright Fred,' said Mrs Faring. 'You can save all that for the paying customers.' She looks at the empty reception desk and asks, 'where's Henry?'

To understand the next bit, a few things need explaining. The woman offstage didn't just sound like Hilda. It is indeed the lady herself. She had ignored the requirement that the maid be a 'pretty young thing.' She wanted the part, and she would have it. Besides the club was not attracting any younger members of any sex. The next thing to understand is that the set rotated. At the appropriate point, the audience would see both Mrs Faring approaching the reception and Mr Fairing in a clinch with the maid on the other side. The idea being that Mrs Faring would catch Mr Fairing in a compromising position with the maid, dishabille, partially dressed to you and me.

All very 1970's and sexist. Not that Hilda seemed to mind being a sex object. If she could be called that. The last thing to know is that as the set rotated, spotlights would highlight parts for the audience to watch.

Gary rubbed his hands together as he looked at the upcoming scene in the play. He glanced at the switch marked 'Scene 1 rot/sec/light.' This was the switch that would light up the area where the maid, Hilda to you and me, and Henry were in a compromising situation. Caz was ready on cue backstage. She controlled the rotation set rotation. She should have been holding the lever ready to operate the mechanism. Instead, she stood staring at the stage. On stage, Mrs Faring headed towards the reception desk. At this point, critical to the humour, the audience needed to see Henry in a clinch with Hilda on the other side of the door. Mrs Faring was fast approaching that door. The set did not rotate and the lights on the part of the stage containing Hilda, or rather, the maid and Henry, stayed dark. It may have been a blessing for the audience if it had stayed that way.

As Hilda was the director, no one had been able to talk any sense into her about her outfit. She was playing the maid and being a 1970's bedroom farce; they dressed the maid in a non-typical way for a real maid. At this point in their clinch, the housemaid was supposed to be only wearing a lacy bodice, stockings, and suspenders. 'I am not some Parisian hussy,' was Hilda's response to that suggestion. After much argument that the play called for the actor to be in her underwear at this point. Hilda agreed to a compromise for the actual play, not the dress rehearsal. The first everyone saw of this compromise was opening night. Hilda wore big white bloomers, on top of a pair of thick brown tights. The tights were so thick and woolly they could have doubled as trousers. She had on a rather large and sensible white bra. It didn't really deserve the term undergarment, as it was extremely sensible and modest. All this was on top of a very large black, all in one swimming suit. She assumed the shocked looks from her fellow thespians were looks of appreciation. They just didn't know what to say to their leader. So perhaps keeping the lights off and stage stationary was not a bad thing.

Mrs Faring had reached the point where the set should have rotated. She hesitated, not knowing what to do. Then continued to walk towards the door to the back room. This was not in the script; the stage should have moved before she reached this point. She didn't want to open the door before the set had rotated. The set was still stationary, so she walked over to the reception desk and improvising turned back towards Fred, the doorman and said, 'how are bookings Fred?'

'Oh, um... very good, Jean, I mean, Mrs Faring,' said Fred. He glanced at the silent audience.

Backstage, Caz saw Hilda for the first time and realised that the audience must see her as well. She had an intercom to call

Gary and updated him. She said, 'put the lights on Gary. Hilda looks a fright, I'm gonna rotate the stage. This will work better than our original plan.'

The stage rotated so that Hilda and Henry came into full, spot lit view. Some of the audience giggled, a few gasped, a couple of snorted. Then Henry said his line, 'you're such a ravishing beauty. I just want to....' Henry couldn't finish the line because of the hoots, shouts, and catcalls from the audience.

'Where're you looking, mate?' Shouted a voice from the audience.

'Get your eyes tested,' said another.

Other, even less kind, comments were also shouted out. Hilda only heard the laughter. It was a comedy, after all. In her mind, that meant success. By the end of the first act, she was feeling very proud of her work. The other actors wanted to pack it in and not bother with the rest of the play.

Things went from bad to worse. In the scene where Trudy walked in on Mr Jonathan Lions, asleep in a darkened room. Gary left all the lighting on full. She was meant to get undressed and slip into his bed in the dark, wearing only some skimpy underwear. Then run across the stage in the said underwear after discovering her mistake. In the original play, that actress was a young beauty. Thus, the stage directions were that Trudy ran across the front of the stage where the lights were a little brighter. The audience could enjoy a thrill of excitement at this sight. As the Plympton Players had no such beauty to play the part of Trudy. They had changed the stage directions. Gary's notes instructed him to: 'keep the lights low, extremely low.' Trudy was told to keep well back on the stage. There would be no thrill to be had, seeing their Trudy run across the stage. More likely a few shocked gasps. Gary ignored the stage directions and put on the full lights over the whole stage. The audience was treated to a version of the play never before seen. The actress playing Trudy, having been told they would not see fully her, chose a strange outfit. Her version of a sexy corset and stockings gave a new meaning to that description. Perhaps in Victorian times, when a glimpse of stocking was looked on as something shocking, it may have been a sight to behold. In the 1990's it just looked, at best, quaint, at worst funny and old. When she ran across the stage in the bright lights, there was stunned silence. Then shouts that do not bear repeating. It was also obvious that it was the wrong man in the bed. Trudy's feigned surprise looked ludicrous. Her reason for getting into bed in the first place had no rhyme or reason. Trudy was meant to run across the stage and out of the room door. But Caz made the door stick. Thus, Trudy was left rattling at the door in her. We can't call them 'scanties.' Probably best describe them as 'amples,' or 'plentifuls.' She ended up leaving the stage via the audience, going down the front steps and out of the emergency exit. Throughout the play, Caz caused the adjoining door to stick when it should open and stay open when it should be closed.

In the scene, when Trudy was in the shower and Mr Jonathan Lions walked in. The room was meant to be full of steam and Trudy discreetly hidden by it. Caz blew the steam straight out and Gary turned the lights up. So, the audience could see Jonathan wolf whistling at Trudy wearing a bright pink body-coloured track suit. His line, 'you look in the pink.' Had a completely different meaning.

After much coercion the actors finished the play. A play described in the best review as, 'The worst play I have ever seen in my life.'

No one seemed to realise that the major issues came from lighting and scenery, cues being missed or deliberately changed. But then it is often said that the leader is ultimately responsible for their team. A captain sails a ship, even when not holding the wheel. The CEO takes the blame when a company loses money. A Prime Minister... well, let's not get carried away. The principle has been established.

Hilda sat in the dressing room after the show. Pearl had gone home. She was tired and needed an early night. The cast members had left one by one. A few grumbled complaints and sniffs directed at Hilda as they departed. The actor who played Trudy was perhaps understandably, the most upset. She talked of never being able to show her face in town again.

Lilly spent a long time talking to Hilda. She outlined her reasons for trusting Hilda. The desperate need that the club and indeed the Plympton Playhouse had for that play to succeed. She gave Hilda a blow-by-blow account of her arguments with customers in the foyer, wanting their money back. The ticket office phone never stopped ringing with people cancelling tickets for the rest of the week. A local supermarket owner, who was in the audience and had contributed a large amount towards the show, had said he was not happy. He had used words that Lilly did not want to repeat. He had demanded his money back. Only Lilly's pleading had rescued that further disaster.

Hilda was unusually subdued as she listened to Lilly. Then she got up and said, 'you can't make an egg without breaking pans.'

'What?' said Lilly, as she sank into a seat, exhausted.

'It was my mother's favourite saying, mind you, she did make a lot of noise around the kitchen. Especially when pops was late back from work,' said Hilda.

'Have you heard anything I said?' asked Lilly. She closed her eyes and held her head.

'Oh yes, dear. We need to do better tomorrow. I totally agree. Miss Kerns did a very poor job,' said Hilda.

Lilly opened her eyes and sat on the edge of her seat. Then said, 'never mind what Miss Kerns did. You have not grasped what I'm saying at all. The plays off. Finished!'

'Yes, I know that. I'm about to go home and have a rest. I think you should, too. If you don't mind me saying, you're looking a little frazzled, dear,' said Hilda.

'Don't you understand? The play is no more, finished, stopped, cancelled. It was no good. The audience has cancelled for the rest of the run,' said Lilly. She sank back again into the seat, mouth and eyes open wide.

Hilda looked at Lilly, blinked, then laughed, then said, 'you're a hoot, I suppose this is one of those local customs to welcome a new director.' She almost skipped towards the door. As she left, she waved cheerily and shouted. 'See you tomorrow.'

Lilly leant forward, putting her head in her hands, and sobbed.

Hidden Gardens Tearoom, Plympton-on-Sea, UK

Next morning in the garden, whilst they ate breakfast, Pearl approached the subject of the night before. She said, 'it's a shame the play was a flop.'

Hilda looked at Pearl across the table, and said, 'whatever do you mean dear? The audience loved it.'

'The play failed, it went wrong, it was a flop,' said Pearl. She'd put down her cup of coffee and was staring intently at Hilda.

Hilda laughed and stood up, heading inside to fetch some more toast, and said, 'ah, I see, you're in with Lilly. Playing a joke on me.'

Pearl got up and followed Hilda. She said, 'no, wait, I'm not joking. Neither was Lilly. The play was really a failure. People have cancelled their tickets for the rest of the week. The club members are refusing to act anymore. Poor Miss Kerns has locked herself in her house.'

'I'm not surprised dear, if she wanted to play such a young part as Trudy. She should have dressed the appropriately,' said Hilda.

Pearl opened her mouth. It looked as if she may be about to say something. Then she shook her head. Hilda had reached the back door of the tearoom. She stopped and turned around. Then said, 'but all the laughter, people obviously enjoyed it.'

'They were laughing at things going wrong,' said Pearl. She looked like she wanted to say more.

'Most of the actors weren't very good. Not up to my standard,' said Hilda. She stared off into space.

Pearl raised her eyebrows, and said, 'I guess so. Well, it puts the Plympton Playhouse in a tricky situation.'

'Yes, yes, I'm sure, I'm sure,' said Hilda. She wandered into the kitchen area of the tearoom and put some toast in. She looked distracted. Once the toast was ready, she headed back out to the table they had set up for breakfast. Pearl followed her.

Once they were both sat, and Hilda was munching on her toast. Pearl said, 'are you alright?'

Hilda looked at Pearl and said, 'I'm just fine.' Fine was never a helpful situation for Hilda. It was the nearest she got to upset.

William and Louise came round to Hilda and Pearl's flat that evening. Louise walked over to her mother-in-law, arms wide, and hugged her. She said, 'I'm so sorry the play didn't work out.'

'Never mind dear, there is always tomorrow,' said Hilda.

Typical of Hilda, she did not mope about or act sad about the failure. Anyone seeing her would assume she had directed a success. Hilda didn't seem at all upset about the play. That is, to people who didn't know the signs. She wasn't dancing or singing, so something was wrong. With Hilda, time was a great healer. She bounced back faster than most. Her family knew that her bouncy self wouldn't be in hiding for long.

Louise told them about William's promotion to director. The evening would have turned into a celebration of William's new job. But Pearl let slip about the ground rent problem. William and Louise were far more worried than Hilda. Pearl said that her sister was going to bring it up with some legal experts she knew. Which was odd, as the only experts she knew were American. But no one queried it.

During all their chatter, Louise thought she heard a knock at the door. No one ever seemed to use the doorbell. They all stopped talking and listened. There was another bang. Hilda went down to answer the door and her squeals of delight told them all it was Josh. Once he was upstairs and sitting with them all, he shared some news. A magazine had hired him to shoot some photos in Transylvania, a region in Romania.

'Isn't that where Dracula lives?' said Hilda, eyes wide. She considered fetching a crucifix, but wasn't sure that she had one.

'He's not real,' said Josh.

'You say that now,' said Hilda. She nodded sagely and looked around the room. 'Maybe I have a crucifix in the drawer unit.' She got up and walked over.

'I say that because it's true. He's a fictional character. In fact, that is why the magazine want the photos. For a Dracula themed tour. They are going to have actors there for me to shoot,' said Josh.

'Just make sure you take some garlic and a wooden stake, dear,' said Hilda. She rummaged in the top drawer of the unit. 'Don't forget to pack a crucifix.' She pulled out a cross and chain and presented it to Josh as if it was a magic charm. 'I think I have some garlic.' She headed to the kitchen.

'Gran, honestly, those are myths about a fictional character,' said Josh. He laughed, putting the cross on a nearby table.

Everyone else was looking on, smiling. Pearl got up to make some drinks. William said, 'has your gran told you about the lease problem?'

'Yes,' said Josh, frowning. 'The other day. I suggested a solicitor.'

'I thought she'd tell you first,' said William. He looked accusingly at Hilda, who was rummaging in the kitchen, trying to find the garlic.

***

The next day, Hilda and Pearl were rushed off their feet in the tearoom. It seemed like the whole town had turned up. They had to organise a queueing system outside in the street. It stretched so far down the street that people were standing in front of the post office and general store. Much to the chagrin of the owner. He kept coming out and asking people to keep his doorway clear. He wouldn't have minded if a few of them came in and bought something.

Everyone was keen to see Hilda's reaction to the dreadful play. Those who had seen it wanted to see her face after the fiasco. Those who had only heard of it second-hand wanted to get in on the action. Then there were those who just happened to be passing and saw a queue. We all get drawn into a queue. There must be something good if everyone wants to go. The queue grew longer as the day went on. Had Hilda and Pearl been better businesswomen, they would have put up their prices for the day. Supply and demand, the basis of capitalism. Fortunately for all those waiting, that did not happen. The tearoom ran out of cakes. So, the last people in the shop could only buy drinks. But then they were only there for the gossip. Much tastier than any cake.

It disappointed people as they sat looking at Hilda. Rather than a broken woman. They saw her breeze around, singing, skipping, and taking orders. She was being true to her normal resilient character. She had bounced back after the temporary low of the night before. The bolder ones asked her about the play. Perhaps they thought that would reduce her to tears.

'Oh, some actors were terrible dear,' said Hilda. She resisted naming names.

'But weren't you one of the actors?' asked one lady.

'That's true, I lifted the quality a bit,' said Hilda. 'But even my talents could not rescue the whole play.' A man who had been present stifled a laugh.

'How are you doing?' said one rather foolish woman. Hilda then treated her and everyone in earshot to a list of her ailments and troubles. They shunned the questioner from polite society for a couple of weeks after that.

Many people tried different approaches to question Hilda. They all received similar responses. The failings of others. Hilda's heroic efforts. A lack of interest in theatre these days.

Gradually the queue went down, and the tearoom emptied. The Hidden Gardens Tearoom had their best takings ever that day. They placed orders for extra cake the next day. They would not be needed. The town of Plympton had decided that there was no fun to be had in viewing Hilda's grief. She was not in distress. Quite the contrary, she seemed to enjoy life to the full. Those who had also heard a whisper that she was going to lose her home and the tearoom doubted that information as well. Surely, if that was true, she would look at least a little sad. They did not understand Hilda.

***

Early on that Saturday morning, the phone woke Hilda. It took a few rings before it fully roused her from her dream. She picked it up and said, 'hello, who is it?' The lack of her normal greeting was no doubt a result of her tiredness and confusion.

'This is Vance Jurgen, Orville's lawyer.'

'Who dear?' said Hilda. She was not fully awake.

'From the USA, the lawyer you met, who was defending Orville Stanley. You helped have him freed,' said Vance.

'Now I remember, you're that funny little man with the beard,' said Hilda.

'Oh, well, I do have a beard,' said Vance.

'Orville, the good twin, I remember,' said Hilda.

'Yes, he's the good twin. His brother, Wilbur, is the bad lot,' said Vance.

'I never had a brother, but if I did, I'm sure he would have been good, like me,' said Hilda.

'Anyway, the reason I called was that Orville has disappeared.'

'Like a magician?'

'A magician?'

'Yes, in a puff of smoke.'

'No, I mean he has gone, can't be found.'

Hilda muttered under her breath about magicians doing just that.

'I didn't catch that, Hilda. But what I was saying was that last I saw him, his brother accosted him, the bad one. Then next I know he's gone.'

'How very shocking, but how does that affect us?'

'The thing is, I heard that Pearl's sister Ruby had retired. Now she has left the protection of The White House, she'll be vulnerable. I wondered if it was linked?' said Vance.

'Oh, my goodness...' Hilda dropped the phone and ran to Pearl's bedroom, almost tripping over Merlin on route, 'Pearl, Pearl, we have to warn Ruby straight away.'

Meanwhile, Vance was saying, 'hello, are you still there?'

Chapter Ten

August 1998

1062 Street West, Marlan, Ohio, USA

Wilbur walked out of a phone booth, smiling. In his car he picked up a road map and traced his finger down to Florida. As he started his engine, in a distant part of town, sirens had started up.

Marlan State Forest, Ohio, USA

Orville opened his eyes and closed them again just as fast, the pain too great. He re-opened them, grimacing. Everything was murky. Trees above and around him. Something cold and hard filled his right hand; it shone in the half-light — a knife. He dropped it and tried to stand. He grasped for something to hold on to. A heap of clothes beside him. Scrambling backwards and unsteadily to his feet, he looked down. Gradually, it resolved into the body of a young woman. Her clothes had dark patches. Was that blood?

Flashing blue and red lights burst through the darkness. The main road was just a few feet away. Within minutes, police officers surrounded him. Beams of powerful flashlights lit up the scene. Orville stood above the corpse of a woman. His hands and clothes were covered in her blood. A knife lay at his feet, where he'd dropped it moments before.

'I didn't do it,' said Orville, weakly.

Sunset Time Resort, Florida, USA

Ruby had just finished chatting with Pearl on the phone. She was sat out on the front porch. Josie ran by on her early morning exercise, followed a minute later by Ang. After sitting thinking for a few minutes Ruby headed back inside and phoned a friend. Security at Sunset Time needed improvement.

Harbourside Cottage, Plympton-on-Sea, UK

Having not seen Karl Dansk for fifty years, it seemed unlikely Hilda would recognise him easily. He'd already passed her a few times without her recognising him. Once in the audience at the play. During the intermission, she'd popped out into the bar area to chat with her family, and they'd stood next to each other.

Karl was an altered man. For fifteen years, he had not written or conducted any music. His agent no longer called, unless checking on royalties. He was almost forgotten, apart from the occasional quiz show or a documentary about the music greats. Now he lived off his royalties. His looks were much changed. Having grown a beard and gone bald and grey over the years. No one ever recognised him.

He had watched Hilda's play with sadness and now sat at home looking deep in thought. He turned to the empty chair next to him and spoke to the memory of his wife, Lillian. 'Hilda needs our help, my love. What can we do?' He stared at the chair, nodding, as if hearing an answer. Then he seemed to brighten. 'Of course.' He stood up. 'Are you ready for a walk, my love?'

Karl locked his front door, then headed across his small front yard, onto the harbour. He stopped and took a deep breath of sea air. The fishing boats had piled lobster pots everywhere. In some places they were taller than him. As he rounded one pile, he bumped into the back of Hilda.

'I'm sorry, why ever were you walking backwards?' said Karl.

'Well, you might ask,' said Hilda. 'It's the only way to do this dance move.'

'But why do a dance move on a harbour?' asked Karl.

'To live is to dance,' said Hilda, 'and it helps me think.' She danced more steps in demonstration. Then on across the harbour.

Karl rushed after her and said, 'what is life without music and dance? It is the very breath of life, pulsing through our veins.'

Hilda stopped and turned around. She peered at Karl through narrowed eyes. Then decided the sun was in the wrong place, so she grabbed his shoulders and moved him. Then she put a hand over his beard. A smile broke out on her face. 'Karl Dansk, well I never. Where's Lillian?' She glanced behind him.

Karl's face darkened, and he said, 'she died eight years ago.'

Hilda gave him such a warm hug that he just cried. Since Lillian had died, no one had hugged him. He had no friends left close enough for that. At the funeral it had all been platitudes and handshakes. Hilda's warmth was genuine. She kept hold of him while he cried. He clung onto her like a life raft in a sea of despair. Pearl had been chatting to someone a short distance away. When she caught up with Hilda and saw her hugging what appeared to be a strange man, she looked away. Then went off for a short walk. When she returned fifteen minutes later, Karl was just letting go. His eyes and nose the matched the sign advertising lobsters. His beard was a mess, as was Hilda's shoulder. But Hilda seemed unconcerned. Karl got out his hanky, a large cotton one, and cleaned himself up. They noticed Pearl and Hilda introduced him, saying, 'you remember Karl Dansk?'

Pearl stared at him blankly, then a minute later her eyes opened wide, and she said, 'Karl! Well, I never. How have you been? Where have you been? What have you been doing? Didn't you have a wife, Lana, or something?'

'Lillian, she died,' said Karl. His eyes misted again.

'Oh, I am sorry, me and my big mouth,' said Pearl.

They found a bench, and all sat chatting. Pearl had only known Karl at the beginning. So, there was less catching up with her. For Hilda there was much more catching up.

Sunset Time Resort, Florida, USA

Wilbur had driven for hours from Marlan. Only stopping twice for gas and food. Gated communities feel safe for their residents. A false security, as Ruby had already decided. Wilbur had already found his way inside. He had considered hopping over the ridiculously low fence that surrounded the compound. Then decided that the security guard on the gate presented the easiest access point.

Driving up to the main gate with a pizza box, Wilbur told the guard, Ferdy, he had a delivery for Ruby Davies. Ferdy made no confirmation call. He just waved Wilbur through. 'If she's out, I'll have it,' said Ferdy. He did one thing right, making a note of the pizza delivery driver's plate number in his daily logbook.

Wilbur had forced Ruby's address from Orville. She gave it to him in case he needed to contact her. Wilbur parked a short distance away and watched the property. Being mid-day and hot, the street was empty. Ruby's blinds were down.

As Wilbur inched through Ruby's backyard, he knocked over a bottle. It clinked and a nearby cat squalled and ran away. He listened, no sound from inside. The only sound outside was the departing cat. Reaching for his knife, he wielded it and gave it a practice swish and jab. His face set hard when he felt his empty pocket. He missed his lucky wolf iron. He'd hoped Orville would have it. Now he knew the police had it. Ruby's back door gave Wilbur no trouble. Lock picking was a skill he learnt early in life. He explored the condo. Each room was empty.

Ferdy checked his watch. Not yet lunchtime. His tummy was rumbling. Must be seeing that pizza twice in a row. As the delivery van drove away, Ferdy remembered something important. Ruby was away at a friend's house. 'Why would she order pizza? That's strange.' His shift replacement interrupted his deep thoughts, and he never took them any further. He headed off to have his lunch at the local Pizza Palace.

Wilbur drove off with a sour look. He had no way to know when Ruby would return and had no wish to wait around indefinitely. He headed back to Marlan. If he'd stayed, it would have been a long wait. Ruby had called Evelyn and asked if she could spend some time back at The White House. Explaining the threat, she was under, Evelyn was happy to help.

Lilly's House, Plympton-on-Sea, UK

Gary and Caz Hilkins called on Lilly. She did not look pleased to see them, but invited them in. Her natural politeness overcoming her dislike.

Once seated, they started on the reason for their visit. They had found a sponsor willing to pay for a production of a play at The Plympton Theatre. On the understanding that they directed and produced it. Also, Hilda must have no part in it. Lilly cross questioned them on a few details. Which she found were surprisingly vague. She agreed to think about it and get back to them. She was desperate to save the theatre.

***

The Plympton Theatre Charitable Trust was meeting at The Plympton Playhouse. Their six-monthly business meeting was a subdued and unhappy event. After much discussion and argument, they agreed they had to go ahead with their plan to sell the building. Hilda's failed production was the last straw. Lilly, a long-time member and advocate of the theatre, had been thinking about Gary and Caz Hilkins' suggestion. She asked the members what the latest date was that they had to put the property up for sale. The treasurer did some calculations, and they agreed that if they could find a sponsor for one last production. They could wait six or seven months before putting the building up for sale. Lilly knew that was a tight schedule to find a sponsor, decide on a play, rehearse, and stage it. But Gary and Caz had told her they had everything in place to put on a full production in three months. The Trust agreed to proceed with Gary and Caz as directors and producers of one last play.

Lilly called them that night to break the news. After she hung up, Gary turned to Caz and said, 'now we'd better find a sponsor.'

'I told you we should have found one first,' Caz huffed.

***

Next day, Gary and Caz both took an emergency holiday off work. Neither of their employers were happy. But as they took it as a holiday, it was agreed. They headed around all the businesses in Plympton and Meedham. At each, they pleaded the case for sponsoring the play. At each, they were turned away. They were not popular people. Nor were they skilled in their approach. By the end of the day, they were both tired and despondent.

Sitting on the sofa after their evening meal, Gary said, 'I have an idea.'

'Not another one. It's your ideas that got us nowhere so far,' said Caz.

'Listen to it all, don't jump at the beginning,' said Gary. He sat on the edge of the sofa.

'What is it?' asked Caz. She picked up her glass of wine.

'You know we have savings?' said Gary.

'No! Absolutely not,' shouted Caz. Spilling her wine. Gary had his hands out in a pleading motion.

'Just listen to it all,' said Gary. He got up and paced.

'We will not use all our saving,' said Caz. She got up as well and stood in front of him. Hands on her hips.

'If the play is a success, which we know it will be. We will become the directors of the club. It's what we always wanted,' said Gary.

'It's what *you* always wanted,' said Caz. She looked sharply at Gary.

'If we are cautious, we could just spend a small part of our savings,' said Gary.

Gary was so desperate to be director he argued and argued until he wore his wife down. She only agreed to a small part of their savings being used. Gary was not listening by that point.

Hidden Garden Tearoom, Plympton-on-Sea, UK

Hilda was serving tables in the garden when her arm was grabbed. 'Hey!' she shouted. A few other guests looked around. When they saw she was alright, they went back to their conversations.

'Sorry,' said Len Russell. It was he who had grabbed her arm. 'I wanted a chat.'

'I'm not like that,' said Hilda, bristling. 'I don't go out with married men.' Hilda started to walk off.

'Oh no, I don't fancy you at all,' said Len.

Hilda stopped, turned back around to Len, and looked shocked. She said, 'well that's nice. Am I not beautiful enough?'

'Well, I mean,' said Len. 'You are, of course, a very attractive woman. Any man would be lucky to go out with you. But as you say. I'm married.'

'Quite right too, totally inappropriate. As my pops always said, fiddles are important,' said Hilda.

'Fiddles?' said Len. He was looking around with furtive glances.

'Yes dear, or was it violins? Something about being faithful anyway,' said Hilda. She walked back towards him and stood face to face.

'Fidelity perhaps?' said Len.

'That's what I said. Do listen,' said Hilda. She shook her head.

'Oh, yes quite. Anyway, I wanted to speak with you, Mrs Shilton, on a very important matter about your tearoom,' said Len.

'I could see something wasn't right between you and your wife,' but I'm not sure that I'm the one to solve it.'

'No, it's not that, I have another...' started Len.

At that moment Councillor Mildred walked into the garden and over to Hilda and Len, and said, 'hello Leonard, are you having a little chat with Mrs Shilton?'

'I thought it important to apprise her of a few things,' said Len. He looked nervously at his wife.

'Really? About your wrongdoing, was it?' said Mildred. She waved a piece of paper in the air.

'Len's wrongdoing? I think you're getting confused dear.' said Hilda. She looked at the wafting paper. 'What have you got there?'

'I think he wanted to own up to something he's done,' said Mildred. Her eyes pierced Lens'.

He shuffled from foot to foot. Then looked at his feet, back at Mildred, then at Hilda. Then said, 'I, I, perhaps I was mistaken. There isn't anything I needed to say.'

'That's what I thought. Come on, Lenard, let's go home,' said Mildred. She grabbed his arm a little harder than was strictly necessary, and they walked off.

Hilda stood watching them leave. She wondered what on earth all that had been about? But she soon forgot about it. There were far more important things to do. She never dwelt on the negative. Some might wonder why she was even keeping the tearoom open. Just four months to go before the lease would be forcibly bought from her and she would lose everything. But that was in the future. In Hilda's eyes, there was always hope. Live in the present and enjoy that. You may not see tomorrow.

Sheriff's Office, Marlan, Ohio, USA

In the sheriff's office in Marlan, Ohio. They had questioned Orville for hours about the murder of the young woman in Marlan State Forest. They had caught him 'red handed,' and Sheriff Gerwin saw it as a straightforward case. Forensics and other evidence were likely damming. Gerwin had expressed his opinion that there was hardly a need for a trial in a case like this. Just as well lynch mobs were no longer active in Marlan. Gerwin would not be a helpful defender of due process in this case.

Sitting in front of Sheriff Gerwin and his deputy Coleman, Orville had pieced together what had happened. Wilbur must have drugged him and set him up. Orville realised silence was his best recourse and so he refused to say anything until his lawyer arrived. That was taking a long time. The interview ended, and they returned Orville to his cell. Half an hour later, he was taken through to a room where his lawyer, Vance Jurgen, waited. Orville's first words were, 'I didn't do it, Vance.'

'I know, only an idiot would murder someone and stay by the body. You're no idiot. Besides, they got a 911 call. We can guess who made that,' said Vance.

'It must Wilbur. The last I remember, he had me tied up somewhere. Kept asking me about Ruby... Oh no! I told him her address. You need to get a message...,' said Orville.

Vance cut in, saying, 'It's alright, she's safe.' Vance informed Orville of his call to England and Ruby's subsequent move to safety. She was now back at the White House, staying as a guest.

'Why did he set me up?' asked Orville. He slumped in his seat. The exhaustion of the last few days catching him up.

'My guess, he wants you to suffer,' said Vance.

'Yeah, he always hated ma and me. Blamed us for keeping him locked up. I guess he's done ma in. I'm next.'

Vance opened his briefcase and said, 'first off, we need to prove your innocence. That ain't gonna be easy. Wilbur has set you up, well, and proper. But I have some ideas.'

Chapter Eleven

May 1937

Central London, UK

Life is strange. There are many echoes and reflections. Dates and days that are significant in different ways. Times that reverberate down the years. Places that have importance acting like crossroads of time and purpose. 1937 is such a year. In autumn of that year Pearl's twin sister, Ruby, suffered a life-changing event. Wilbur Stanley, another twin, murdered her adoptive parents. For her life changed in Marlan, Ohio. She ran away to New York and many years later became head chef at The White House.

For Pearl and Ruby's unmarried mother, Victoria, life changed in 1920. After falling pregnant with a smooth-talking man, her life fell apart. From a life of comfort and riches, they banished her to England. London became a crossroads of time and purpose. There, they forced her to give up her children. It's a place Pearl grew up and met Hilda. But also, a place that Ruby set off with her new adoptive parents back to the birthplace of her mother, America. Crossroads and reflections. Life has a strange way of bringing things around and around.

In 1997, Hilda and Pearl would leave from London Heathrow to fly to America and re-discover Pearl's twin sister, Ruby. Bringing things around in a circle.

***

Times, dates, and places have a strange way of interweaving in our lives. On the 14th of May 1937, another significant day played out. It appeared so ordinary, just another cold and windy day in London. Two days after a momentous event, the coronation of King George VI. Seventeen-year-olds, Hilda, and Pearl had wrapped up warmly as they walked around a chilly central London. Hilda bounced along in her usual jaunty style. This was long before trainers could give her a helping hand. She turned to Pearl, and said, 'what a ripsnorter of a day this is.'

'What?' said Pearl. Half looking at Hilda.

'I was saying what a ripsnorter of a time we're having,' said Hilda. She watched far too many movies and used a lot of the expressions she heard in wildly inappropriate ways.

'What does it mean?' asked Pearl, stopping, and looking at Hilda.

Hilda looked at the ground, up at the sky, and then screwed up her eyes. Her eyes opened wide, then said, 'having a great time.'

'Well, why didn't you say that?' said Pearl. She started walking again.

Hilda skipped a little as she caught up and said, 'where's the fun in that? I like to use new words.'

'So long as I understand what you're saying,' said Pearl.

Hilda continued to skip and even hummed a cheery tune as she kept pace with Pearl, then said, 'this is aces, compared to the coronation day.'

Pearl glanced at Hilda, then wrapped her coat and scarf around herself tighter. Hilda just swished her head, and said, 'you know what I mean. More fun. I know it's not warmer.'

Two days earlier, they had been part of the crowd cheering a rather surprised King George VI on his coronation day. He had never expected his brother Edward to abdicate after falling in love with Wallis Simpson, the American divorcee. But then no one had seen that coming.

Hilda and Pearl lived near each other in Kilburn, a short distance from central London. They were neighbours. Kilburn is part of London, predominantly Irish at the time. But neither Hilda nor Pearl's families hailed from the Emerald Isle. It wasn't until 1997 that Pearl discovered all about her true origins.

In 1937, Pearl and Hilda still lived at home with their respective parents. A trip into central London was a rare treat. Partly because they were busy working and partly due to cost. They both worked at the same place, having joined the same place after they left school. Trips into the city were very unusual. What was the point of going into the city unless you did something there?

They had spent the coronation day with Hilda's parents. This had given them a taste for another, more fulfilling trip. The coronation was a disappointing day for the two young ladies. Not because of any lack of interest in the Royal family. They were both ardent royalists. Just because it was such a long and exhausting day, to see so little, because of where they had been standing.

Two days after the coronation, Hilda turned up at Pearl's house, just after breakfast. Mrs Parker, Pearl's adoptive mother, answered the door. Hilda said, 'oh, hello Mrs Parker. Is Pearl in?'

'She's just finishing her breakfast,' said Mrs Parker.

'I'll come in and wait,' said Hilda. She pushed past Mrs Parker and walked into the kitchen. There at the small table sat Pearl. Her father was in an armchair with a blanket on his knees. 'Howdy, Mr Parker,' said Hilda. She'd been watching too many westerns at the cinema. He looked up at her, open-mouthed. Hilda also nodded to her friend.

Pearl choked on her toast and, coughing, said, 'hello.'.

Mr Parker had lost a leg in an accident at work. His wife needed to stay and look after him on Coronation Day. He spent most of his time sat in the armchair of that room. Or so it seemed to Hilda. Once Pearl had hurriedly finished her breakfast. Under the serious gaze of her parents, Hilda and Pearl headed up to Pearl's bedroom. Hilda explained her plan to go back into the city. She had been frustrated by the glimpse of it they had seen at the coronation. Her suggestion was that Pearl grab any savings she had. Hilda already had hers in her purse. Then they could have a treat out.

Their treat was morning tea and cakes at Lyons Tea Shop on Tottenham Court Road. J Lyons Tea Shops were extremely popular in the 1930's, and they were lucky to get a table. As usual, the quality of the tea and cakes was excellent. They sat in the crowded tea shop and Hilda felt like royalty. She tried out a few waves. Copying the ones, she had glimpsed the royal family doing in the coach and on the balcony the other day. Pearl asked, 'what are you doing?'

'A royal wave,' said Hilda. She had just waved to a table full of WI members. Three of them had noticed and were discussing between themselves what was wrong with the young lady at the table near them. One of them decided she was simple and waved back. Hilda and the lady waved at each other for a while. Then the WI member got bored and turned back to her friends.

'Don't embarrass me,' said Pearl. She was far too late asking that.

Hilda continued her waving around the room. A young girl sitting with her mother and, obviously bored, spotted her. She waved back. Hilda noticed her response and waved specifically at the little girl. She stood up and came over to Hilda. Her mother was deep in conversation with a friend at her table and didn't notice. The little girl, aged about three, arrived at Hilda and Pearl's table. Shee looked at Hilda expectantly. She had waved at her. There must now be a reward, surely. Hilda realised this was her expectation and reached for a sugar lump.

'Here you go little girl,' said Hilda, handing it to her.

The young girls' mother had noticed her absence and, seeing a strange young lady handing her daughter, something ran over. She said in a high-pitched voice, 'stop!'

Everyone in the tea shop, including the young girl, watched her mother running. Unfortunately, a waitress pushing a cart of cream cakes was also distracted by the squeal. She let go of her trolley. J. Lyon's made sure that their trolleys were well oiled. There is nothing worse than a squeaky trolley. Except perhaps a smoothly freewheeling trolley full of cream cakes you run into. The lady running towards her child may well have preferred the trolley to have moved less easily into her path. The trolley full of delicious treats was certainly not the place she wanted to be sprawled across. But she did. Her white blouse covered in chocolate and cream. J. Lyon's staff showed great concern for the lady's white blouse. They said all the right things. But their eyes looked at the mess of cakes all over the floor, expressing a wider concern.

Afterwards, Hilda and Pearl promenaded arm in arm towards Oxford Circus. They had rushed out of J. Lyon's tearoom before any repercussions. The last thing they heard, as the door shut, was the lady say loudly, 'my new blouse!' It had seemed funny to them. But then they were young. So perhaps we can excuse it as youthful ignorance. Although that would be harder to apply later in life to Hilda's antics. Perhaps she just never grew up. Is there a Paula Pan?

Having reached Oxford Circus, which is a bit like a crossroads. Then they headed down Regent Street. Just as well they were not playing Monopoly. Or they might have had a big payment to make. Their plan was to visit Buckingham Palace again. This time without the crowds. So, they planned to approach it from The Mall. What a lot of visitors to London don't realise is just how close things are to each other. Walking is an excellent way to get around in London if you are fit enough and know where to go. There are plenty of buses and, of course, the famous London Underground or tube. Also called London Transport by the workers on that system. After all, it's not all underground. Hilda and Pearl were saving their money for other treats and didn't use it for their travels. They were young and fit. The famous black London cabs were not even a possibility for them, on their budget.

At Buckingham Palace they stood and watched the changing of the guard. Hilda stood next to one soldier who was guarding the gate. He was wearing a red uniform and a Busby hat. She pulled a silly face. But he didn't smile. It tempted her to tickle him, but Pearl stopped her. They stood at the gate and stared through to the palace. But they couldn't see the Royal Family. Perhaps they were out or resting from all the parading two days earlier.

Afterwards, they headed up Constitution Hill towards Hyde Park. They continued up the outer path of the park until they came to Speaker's Corner. A popular place for people to stand and speak publicly. Unfortunately for a young man, he had chosen that morning to speak there for the first time. Hilda stopped to listen; the crowd listening was small. Pearl, Hilda, an old man with a stick who may have just been stopping to catch his breath. Two women were on a nearby bench, but they seemed to be chatting, rather than listening. There was also a large flock of pigeons; can we count them when they are pecking and feeding? They didn't seem all that interested in the young man. The only person who was concentrating on the man was Hilda. Pearl was looking around and hopping from foot to foot.

The man started speaking, 'these are dangerous times, and we must be cautious.' He was not loud or sure of himself.

'Here, here, I agree,' said Hilda. She clapped. 'You might want to speak louder, though. I don't think those two can hear you over their chatter.' Hilda pointed accusingly at the two women on the bench. They were oblivious to her comments.

The man was surprised. They had warned him of hecklers. But not expected agreement and encouragement. He half smiled.

'Carry on, we're enjoying it,' said Hilda. She looked at Pearl for agreement. But found that she was looking around for a bench to sit on.

The speaker checked his notes and coughed. He looked at the back and front of his papers.

'Have you lost your place?' said Hilda, walking up to him. She took his sheets of paper and looked at them. 'What scruffy handwriting. Did your teacher never tell you to write neater?'

'Ah, well, umm, yes,' said the man. He tried to take his papers back.

'What's this word?' said Hilda. 'Reflame? I've never heard that word before. Pearl, have you heard of reflame?' Pearl had spotted a seat and was heading for it.

'It's not reflame, it's reform,' said the man. He was still trying to grab his speech back.

'Oh, I see. Well, I'll let you get on. You have an audience to entertain,' said Hilda. She waved towards the couple of people. But the old man with the stick had recovered and was now walking off. The two ladies on the bench had finished their catch up and were leaving. Hilda handed the man his speech back. Unfortunately, he had not gripped it before the wind took it and blew it away. 'Never mind, I'm sure you'll remember it. Abyssinia.' Hilda watched far too many American films. Abyssinia was a way a lot of her favourite stars abbreviated 'I'll be seeing you.'

Hilda went over to fetch Pearl, who had only just sat down. The poor man watched his notes fly into the park. If Hilda had looked behind her as they headed off, she would have seen him leave. He walked sluggishly, head down back to his lodgings. No doubt he learnt a valuable lesson that day in public speaking. Not only to avoid Hilda. The young ladies headed to Oxford Street and did some window shopping in the stores. Hilda had a thought. She turned to Pearl and said, 'isn't the BBC around here?'

'I think so,' said Pearl. They asked directions and ended up at Portland place. As they drew near to the impressive BBC Broadcasting House building, they both stopped and looked up. Hilda whistled, and said, 'this was a corking idea; I've always wanted to see the BBC building.'

'Me too. I wonder if anyone famous will be around,' said Pearl.

Since leaving school three years earlier, they had worked as waitresses and shop assistants. Neither was feeling fulfilled.

'This is aces. That's where I want to work. I wonder how you find a job there?' said Hilda.

'Don't be silly,' said Pearl. She almost added 'Hilly,' but resisted. 'They won't want to employ you or me.'

'As my pops always says, you don't know until you eat a pie,' said Hilda.

'Are you sure he didn't say "you don't know until you try?"' said Pearl, screwing up her face.

'Oh yes, that's the one,' said Hilda. With that she walked boldly towards the entrance. Pearl, not being as brave, just waited and watched.

Hilda marched up to the imposing entrance doorway and entered. On the other side George, the doorman, blocked her entrance. He was a large, squarely built man in a uniform. He was ex-military and obviously thought he was still armed and at war. With the way things were going in the world, he may soon be again.

'Halt, where do you think you're going, young lady?' said George. His arms held in a position that suggested an imaginary gun. Just as well, it wasn't real, or many uninvited visitors to the BBC would have ended up in hospital.

'I have an appointment,' said Hilda. She tried to sound convincing.

For a moment, George was silenced, but regaining his authority, he said,

'with who.'

'I think you mean, with whom,' said Hilda, hoping she'd remembered her grammar correctly. Not that English had been a strong subject for her. No subject had been strong for her.

'Don't you talk gobbledygook to me, young lady,' said the doorman. He stood his full five feet eight inches. Most of his imposing appearance came from his muscular build and hard looking features.

'I am here to see the big boss,' said Hilda. She attempted not to show her nerves.

'What big boss?' said the doorman. He loomed over Hilda.

'The,' said Hilda. She wracked her brains for the right title she read the Radio Times cover to cover every week. 'The... Director General, Sir William Haley.' Hilda felt proud of her memory.

George was taken aback. He said, 'he's expecting you?'

'Of course... I'm his.... granddaughter,' said Hilda, bluffing.

'Ah... well... umm... you'd better go over to the reception desk and tell them you're here. Sorry to have bothered you, Miss Haley. I didn't know,' said the doorman. He stepped back.

'That's alright my good sir, I will say nothing to grandpops,' said Hilda. With that Hilda strode over to the reception desk. On arriving, she leaned across and said quietly, 'I'm here about any employment that might be available.'

Miss Barnard had worked on the BBC reception desk for years. Now in her early forties and unmarried, this was her life. The day-to-day tedium of meeting so called celebrities who had massive egos and fat pay checks was not novel anymore. Any enjoyment it once held was long gone. Every day was the same. On seeing the wide-eyed, red-haired girl with a twinkle in her green eyes, a wide smile and such a bubbly nature, Miss Barnard smiled. Any change to the routine could be fun. She looked across at George, almost filling the doorway. Anyone who could get past George without a steam roller was worth getting to know.

'What can you do?' said Miss Barnard. She leaned across the desk.

'I'm a waitress at the moment, but I can sing and dance,' said Hilda. She did a few dance steps.

Miss Barnards' looked crestfallen. Her smile disappeared, and she sat back. Then said, 'well, we don't need singers and dancers, we have those by the bucket load. We are also full up with waitresses.' She looked at her desk. There was a pile of papers and on top a note marked urgent. 'I don't suppose you can cook?'

'Absolutely, I am a corking cook,' she said. In a slight exaggeration, Hilda had been taught to cook by her mother. 'I have cooked for groups of... hundreds.' This boast had no foundation of truth, unless heating a large pan of porridge for fifteen people at guide camp counted.

'Perfect, our last cook left under a cloud, and we have been desperately searching ever since. Let me call someone,' said Miss Barnard. She made a call and then told Hilda. 'Go up the stairs and along, room seven on the right. Mr Petifer will see you.'

The stairs felt like they should be in a movie set, wide and sweeping. Hilda tap danced up them. No one took any notice. But then this was the BBC, full of entertainers. At the top of the stairs the corridor was long and had a marble floor. She counted off the rooms and found number seven.

Sitting in front of Mr Petifer, Hilda was looking around, wide eyed. His office was panelled in light oak, and he had a green leather covered desk. He was leaning back in his leather chair, studying Hilda. She jumped when he spoke. 'Which culinary school did you attend?'

Several of her teachers had noted that Hilda had a very creative imagination. One had been slightly more direct and accused her of lying. Which Hilda thought very unfair. She stretched the truth at times. But after all, wasn't that the idea? Wasn't truth meant to be stretched, didn't it need exercise? It always seemed to Hilda that her mother and father did exactly that. Truth was a very flexible thing in her upbringing. In later life, the reason for her parents' less than truthful attitudes would be clearer. But in her younger years, they were her role model.

'The Henrietta Grimbald school of catering,' said Hilda. She felt pleased with herself to have turned her mother's maiden name into a catering school.

'I'm sorry, I've not heard of that one. Where is it?' said Mr Petifer.

'That's quite all right, no need to feel bad about your ignorance,' said Hilda.

Mr Petifer sat forward and lent on his desk, red faced, and said, 'I meant where is it?'

Hilda smiled innocently. She said, 'well, why didn't you say. It is in Kilburn, of course.'

Mt Petifer frowned, and asked, 'Kilburn?'

'Yes,' said Hilda. She had a beatific look on her face.

Mr Petifer pursed his lips, screwed up his eyes and then looked at the ceiling. He got up and walked over to his filing cabinet. Fetching out a file marked 'canteen urgent.' He flipped through it. On the top were scribbled notes from department heads pleading with him to fill the vacancy fast. He glanced at the job application 'In tray'; it was empty. He sat back down and placed the file in front of him. He may well of had another reason to want to fill this vacancy pronto. The cloud under which the last cook had left involved Mr Petifer. A certain out of office hours dalliance that turned sour. One of them had to leave and it certainly wouldn't be him. He opened the file to a blank form at the back, and asked, 'when can you start?'

'Today, is that soon enough?' asked Hilda.

'I think tomorrow would be fine. Bring in your national insurance card. See you at 8am sharp,' said Mr Petifer.

***

As Hilda walked past reception, she thanked Miss Barnard and told her she had got the job. Miss Barnard smiled and said she looked forward to tasting her food tomorrow. Hilda stopped, looked at her, grimaced and then headed towards the exit. As she crossed the large foyer, her father, Bert, was just entering the door and walking towards her. They both stopped and stared at each other. 'Golly, Gee, hiya pops,' said Hilda. She was gobsmacked. She really needed to watch less American films.

Bert stared at her for a moment. Then asked, 'what are you doing here?'

'I have a job in the canteen,' said Hilda.

'Right O,' said Bert, then quickly disappeared up the stairs with just a nod to the doorman and receptionist.

Hilda realised she hadn't asked why he was there. When she passed George on the way out, he said, 'so, you know the secret lot, eh?' Nodding towards her father's disappearing back.

'What do you mean?' asked Hilda. She looked at the stairs, now empty, and shrugged. 'Well, see you tomorrow in the canteen,' said Hilda. She waved and left a puzzled-looking George standing by the door. She skipped outside to an anxiously waiting Pearl, who asked why she had been so long. Pearl was incredulous that Hilda had got a job at the BBC. She was almost speechless that it was as head chef in the canteen. She stated the obvious, saying, 'but you even burn the toast.' Hilda just wafted that comment away with a wave of her hand. She was too happy to be bothered by reality.

All the way home, Hilda kept bursting into song and doing small impromptu dances. When she was happy, singing and dancing just burst out from within. There were a few points when Pearl pretended, she wasn't with her. Particularly when they were passing a crowded bus stop. The people queueing tried to stand a little further away as they passed.

At home that night Hilda was the busiest she had ever been. She had returned home and demanded her mother show her how to cook for a 'great multitude.' Her mother just stared at her until she explained about her new job. Once Hilda's mother had stopped laughing, Hilda convinced her to help prepare for some semblance of mass cooking the next day. When Hilda's father returned home, he retreated from the steam and noise filled kitchen to his quiet garden. He had a small shed he liked to sit in and smoke his pipe. Hilda seldom saw him do any gardening. One time Hilda had joined him in his shed. All it contained was a seat, shelves of books, a box of tobacco with his pipe, and a silver flask he kept swigging. No gardening tools were obvious. Unless you counted an old rusty spade in the corner.

Later that evening, Hilda went out to see her father in the garden. He was sitting outside his shed, smoking his pipe, and reading. She asked him why he was at the BBC. But he told her it was top secret. Hilda never fully understood about her father's work for MI5, or the secret service as it was called then. She knew it was something secret and important. In the late 1930's they had an office at Broadcasting House, where they vetted BBC employees for security.

That night, Hilda collapsed exhausted into bed at 10pm and dreamt of giant carrots chasing her around enormous saucepans. She was being rocked around in a pan of bubbling water. When she opened her eyes, she realised her mother was rocking her awake. She said, 'it's 7am, time you were getting ready Hilda.'

BBC Broadcasting House, London, UK

At the BBC kitchen, Mr Petifer, the man who had interviewed Hilda, was showing her around. He said, 'these are your staff, Penny, Madge and Yve.'

They all looked much older than Hilda and were staring at her in disbelief that this was the new head chef. Mr Petifer told them she had trained at a well-known academy in London. He never bothered checking if it existed.

'I'll leave you to get on with lunch. Everyone will be glad to not have to go out for lunch anymore or bring in sandwiches,' said Mr Petifer.

Hilda wasn't so sure that would still be true after they had eaten. She looked at her staff, and said, 'right, let's get started. Do you all know what you're doing?'

'Once you tell us what we're making,' said Madge, smirking.

'I think we will make sausage and mash,' said Hilda, nodding her head. She had seen a movie character playing a ship's captain. In that he nodded his head as a way of saying, 'right carry out my orders.' But her staff were not as obedient. They just stood and stared at her.

'Is that it?' asked Penny. We normally have three mains and two puddings.

Hilda frowned and said, 'ah, right, well you get peeling the spuds and swede Penny. Yve, you peel some carrots and chop some onions and Madge, chop up some stewing steak. We will make a hot pot as well. Any ideas for a third dish, or the puddings? I like suggestions.'

'Well...' said Penny, hesitantly. 'They always like egg and chips, then you can't go wrong with spotted dick and custard and jelly and sponge.' As Penny spoke, Madge looked disappointed that Penny had been so helpful.

'Great, well, it sounds like you have done all this before, so I'll let you do what you know best. I will, of course, be checking on your work as you progress,' said Hilda. She thought what a simple job this would be. Much easier than being a waitress.

Two hours later, Hilda was less convinced of just how easy the job was. Onions were burning, pans were boiling over, and she was being asked her opinion on so many things that she knew nothing about. Her three assistants were great at preparing and chopping vegetables. They were fine watching and stirring pans, so long as someone told them when things were ready, how much seasoning to add and what else to put in. They were assistants rather than cooks. That should have been obvious from the fact none of them applied for the job of head chef.

'Right, there's an hour till lunch,' said Hilda. 'We need to get things shipshape and Bristol.'

'Isn't there a bit missing?' said Yve.

'Is there,' said Hilda. She investigated the nearest pan and tasted it. 'No, it seems fine to me.'

'I mean Bristol,' said Yve. She was staring at Hilda.

'We can't be worrying about Bristol now,' said Hilda. 'We have a meal to prepare. Bristol can look after itself.'

'She means fashion,' said Madge.

'You'll need to think about your clothes in your own time,' said Hilda. She gathered her troops to make a push and get things finished for lunch.

This was where Hilda's mother's influence and years of cooking for her family kicked into action. Hilda may have never cooked for so many before, but she could cook. Albeit that Pearl was right, she burned toast occasionally. Hilda remembered what her mother had said last night, 'don't panic, just do things a step at a time, add ingredients little by little and taste.' Getting rid of the burnt onions and turning the gas down on the pans, she felt in control.

Lunchtime came and eager BBC staff filed into the canteen. They had heard that there was a new cook, an expert, head hunted from some fancy restaurant, apparently. Orderly queues formed, as is the British way. Mouths were watering, and the smell was generally good, although there was a background smell of burnt onions, not altogether bad. It seemed to add an extra piquancy. Caramelised onions give a great smell to a kitchen.

In the kitchen panic was rising. Madge had glanced out at the growing queue and taken delight in causing additional anxiety. Hilda was supervising the dishing out of the various concoctions into large serving dishes. Unfortunately, she had not realised or been told they needed preheating. By the time everything was ready to serve, the meals were not hot.

Once everyone had been served and they were sitting eating their meals, Hilda looked around at the tables while people ate and chatted. Now and then, she noticed a face screwed up on taking a mouthful. She didn't know this was because the food was cold rather than lacking in taste. Fortunately, the diners were British and when she asked how everything was, they all answered how lovely and fine and wonderful it all was. Apart from being cold, they had little to complain about. Yes, the gravy was a little lumpy, as was the custard. The meat was chewy, but that was the quality of the meat. On the whole Hilda had come through by the skin of her teeth. Perhaps she had not proved herself a cordon bleu cook, but certainly everyone assumed she was a professional cook having a bad day. They allowed for first night nerves. It was the BBC, so many of the customers were actors, directors, and producers. The idea of a bad first night was quite acceptable.

***

Hilda was never a brilliant head chef. The food at the BBC canteen was always acceptable, rather than wonderful. It was better than the food at the new canteen. When the BBC moved to the television centre, Wood Lane. The canteen there became renown as a place you did not want to eat. So perhaps Hilda should have been proud of her achievements.

Because Hilda worked at the BBC, Pearl kept asking her for tickets to the radio shows they broadcast from there. Now that she had a friend at the BBC, it only seemed fair that she should be able to visit and meet all the stars. Hilda kept telling her it wasn't as glamorous as it sounded. But she loved it, really. Most days, she met one of her idols. She was working at one of the great centres of entertainment in England. The only thing that would have made it better would have been to dance and sing for an audience. Although that did not stop her from dancing and singing around the kitchens. Much to the surprise of her staff. She particularly enjoyed using the pans as drums. Finding it a nuisance when they were taken away for cooking.

Sometimes Hilda could sneak into the studios and watch her favourite programmes being recorded. But once or twice she would call out or applaud at the wrong moment and then get thrown out. She learnt to keep quiet, to a degree. Her favourite thing was to copy dances. But after being expelled for being too noisy, she bought some soft shoes. Once she had her new shoes, her dancing exploits continued unabated. She was often seen mimicking moves at one side of a studio. Those who did not know her assumed she was an understudy, warming up.

***

Hilda knew she must try to get tickets to a BBC show for Pearl and one day an opportunity came up, quite by chance. The Big Band show was looking for extra audience members for the upcoming Saturday night. An entire group of people from a local club had to pull out last minute, and they really wanted a full audience. So, they asked the staff to come and bring friends and family. Hilda grabbed two tickets and pretended to Pearl that she had tried hard to get them. Even though it was a radio show, the audience wore full evening dress. Hilda and Pearl were no exception. They both wore their best party frocks.

***

The night of the Big Band show finally arrived. Pearl had been excitedly chatting about it for days. The audience all filed in. Pearl sat next to a lovely man called Arthur, who was about her age. He had gentle manners and a deep, soothing voice. Hilda was stuck next to an elderly lady who spent the evening coughing and sneezing. Whenever the floor manager looked for the culprit, Hilda quickly pointed to the guilty party.

Pearl spent every break whispering to Arthur. But he seemed keener to lean across her and try to talk to Hilda. She found him rather boring; he was a civil servant, something in the tax office. She wasn't keen to know more. At the end of the evening, Pearl asked if she could meet Arthur another time. At first, he was reticent, but after Hilda said that she wanted to go as well, he quickly agreed. They arranged to meet at a local tea dance. As Arthur left, he smiled and waved more at Hilda than Pearl. Which seemed rather odd. But Arthur had a plan.

It was during her time at the BBC that Hilda solved her first murder. But that's a story for another time. There just isn't enough time to go into all that now.

Chapter Twelve

August 1998

Prison Transport, Marlan, Ohio, USA

Sat in the airless prison transport, Orville Stanley felt a sense of hopelessness. He was on route back to the county jail. At his arraignment hearing, his lawyer, Vance, had failed to convince the judge of his innocence. Too much physical evidence stacked up against him. The only defence they could offer had been that his brother wished to cause him trouble. But no evidence tied Wilbur to the crime scene. He'd been very careful to make sure of that. The fact Orville lacked any motive for killing the woman gave the only glimmer of light. But the state prosecutor took the line that Orville must be a psychopath.

A date for his trial had been set, and bail refused. Months of waiting trial at the county jail lay ahead for Orville. It hadn't been built for long-term use, nor the number of prisoners it currently held. But the county justice system lacked funding for improvement. Once Orville had a court date, he had no illusions of being found innocent. Everything pointed to him spending many years in prison. Or possibly the death sentence. That was a real possibility in Ohio. He could see no way out. His brother, Wilbur, had set him up for murder a second time.

Plympton-On-Sea, UK

Back in the UK, the mood was altogether lighter at the Plympton Playhouse Club meeting. We sometimes describe smiles as beaming. Presumably because they shine brightly, like a light source. Gary and Caz sat at a table, greeting the arriving club members. Their smiles were so broad and beamed so brightly that it's a wonder the entering members didn't need sunglasses. Or have to squint. In no other way did Gary and Caz resemble a light. Their despicable actions in ruining Hilda's play might well qualify them for a ranking in the realms of darkness.

'Welcome, welcome,' said Gary. He was so effusive that Lilly scowled at him.

'Are you all ready?' asked Lilly. 'We can't afford any more mistakes.'

'Yes, yes, here you go,' said Gary. He passed her a script and pushed her aside simultaneously. Caz had nothing to do but sit beside her husband and copy his smile.

Once everyone had sat and received scripts. Gary told them the play's name, 'They should have asked me.' He then asked them to have a quick scan through the script. Papers were shuffled and glasses adjusted. A few coughs and a couple of giggles. It was a comedy, after all. Perhaps more than a few giggles might have been a better sign.

'Have you got the gist?' asked Gary after about fifteen minutes. Most people nodded. Some were still concentrating on the script and didn't hear him.

'It's alright, I suppose,' said Lilly. She was still glancing through the script. 'All depends on production and casting.'

'I've been working on casting,' said Caz. There was a collective start, as she spoke up for the first time. 'We both felt that some younger blood was needed.' Most members around the room nodded. 'We've approached the local college. They have a drama class.'

The members shuffled in their seats, mumbling. Lilly asked, 'how old are they?'

'This is a senior college. The student's range in age from seventeen to about nineteen, I think,' said Caz. 'Oh, there may be a few older adults returning to catch up on...'

'They don't need to know that,' said Gary. 'No adults are coming along.'

'Yes, quite, I'm sorry.' Caz studied her script.

The members nodded and quietened down. There were a few relaxed smiles. They had all gone through a difficult time a few years earlier. The previous director had opened the group to younger children. It had seemed a great idea. It widened the scope of what plays they could put on. However, they had no members capable of directing or managing children. No one was able to keep any semblance of order. After one particularly dreadful week, the parents stayed around to supervise. The real reason was to prevent a repeat of the previous week's meltdown. No one wanted a repeat of that week. The kids had been running around, shouting and laughing. Drinks got spilt, members bumped into. Somehow a painting of the Plympton Playhouses' founder got ripped, and a vase ended up smashed on the floor. The director had ranted and raved, shouted, and threatened, all to no avail. No one was keen to repeat that experience. The Plympton Players never learnt how to 'manage' a group of children into a group of young actors. They gave up trying and closed their doors to anyone younger than 18 years of age. They added a proviso that if they gained a director with the requisite skills, they would discuss it again. Gary and Caz lacked those skills. They had been the worst with the children. At the time Gary had shouted at one of the young lads and caused the parents to complain to Lilly. She and the other members were relieved that it was older children who were coming.

'I suppose that's old enough to behave in an adult fashion,' said Lilly, demonstrating the lack of children and teenagers in her life. 'It should prevent a repeat of the issues last time.' She stared at Gary. He was looking at his script. He had several teenagers in his wider family. Caz had convinced him these young people from the college were needed. If they were anything like Tom and Tim, his brother's two, heaven help them all. That's what he'd said to Caz. 'Don't worry,' she'd assured him. He glanced at her and frowned.

'We *both* think it'll be fine,' said Caz. Gary coughed loudly, then looked back at his script. 'They'll be here to audition shortly. We wanted to tell you all first.' Then, under his breath, he seemed to pray.

Almost on cue, they heard a ruckus in the outer hallway. Banging and laughing, shouting, and talking. A group of six teenagers entered en masse.

'Whoa! We're ere,' said Trudy. She liked to state the obvious. Her clothing was almost as bold as her entrance. Hilda would have liked her. What a pity she couldn't be there.

'Come in and sit down,' said Gary. He waved towards some seats. 'Be quiet about it.'

The teenagers entered and sat down. They were not quiet about it. 'Hiya!' 'Shuv up a bit,' 'This free?' 'Cool!' and various other comments filled the air as they found seats. Along with much giggling and arguing.

Once all went silent, or at less noisy, Gary said, 'I want to do a read through tonight. See how far we get.'

Scripts were handed to the young people and after much rustling and Gary assigning temporary parts to people, they began.

Everyone looked at act one, scene one. Lilly pointed out that the first act only needed two actors. She said, 'why don't we jump on to scene three? That way, the young people can be involved.'

'I am methodical,' said Gary imperiously. 'I like to do things logically and in order.' Caz was nodding sagely. As his wife, she no doubt had much experience with his methods.

The two people playing the only two parts in that scene sat forward, scripts in hand. They flipped back and forward in their scripts, then nodded that they were ready. Everyone else looked bored. Gary saw the response and said, 'you all need to concentrate. To do your part well, you must *feel* the whole play.' Trudy spluttered a repressed laugh. Gary stared at her. She looked accusingly at the young lad next to her. He looked around the room, wide eyed and open-mouthed. Then the entire group of youngsters laughed for about five minutes. Gary eventually got them to be simmer down and the run-through of the play could begin.

Gary started by reading out the setting so that everyone would understand what was happening. He said, 'Barry,' he nodded towards the actor playing the part, 'and Loraine,' he nodded at that actor. 'Are at home in their front room, in an average house.' One of the club members asked why it had to be an average house. Gary gave her a withering look. She shrugged and looked at her script. Then Gary said, 'Barry,' another nod. 'Is sitting in front of the TV half watching a football match. While Loraine.' again a nod, 'is reading a magazine.' The actor playing Loraine said, 'does it matter that I don't have a magazine for the read through?'

'Use your imagination, you're an actor,' said Gary. He muttered something under his breath.

'An amateur one,' said the actor playing Loraine.

Then a debate ensued about other props, such as the TV. Gary interrupted loudly and said, 'this is a read through. Use your imagination. Now, let us get on with the first act.' The general noise and hubbub subsided.

The actors looked at their scripts. The actors playing Barry and Loraine looked at each other.

'What are you doing?' said Gary.

They spoke almost as one, 'the stage directions.' The actor playing Barry explained, 'it says we look at each other.' The actor playing Loraine nodded and pointed at her script.

'Ignore those for now. Just read the lines,' said Gary. He was shaking his head.

The club members all grumbled, but the read through continued. The actor playing Barry said, 'they should have asked me.'

Then some discussion about the stage directions followed. As the actor playing Loraine was meant to look up from her magazine. In the end she said, 'eh, what now?'

'They should have asked me,' said the actor playing Barry.

'Oh yes, the font of all knowledge,' said the actor playing Loraine.

'I'm not saying I know everything…,' said Barry.

'Really!' said Loraine.

'I am just saying, what with my medical background an all,' said Barry.

'Medical background! You're a hospital porter, for goodness' sake! Ideas of grandeur,' said Loraine.

'Yes, well, I see a lot, especially when people aren't looking,' said Barry.

'Is he a pervert?' said Trudy with a leering grin.

'No, he's not a pervert,' said Gary. He spoke louder than needed.

'He sounds like a pervert,' said Trudy. She looked at her mates; they all agreed. A few of the club members were nodding.

'Well, he's not,' said Gary. He looked around the room. 'Can we please get on?'

'It says he spies on people,' said Trudy, holding up her script, pointing.

'No, it doesn't,' said Gary. He was turning red. 'It says I see a lot, especially when people aren't looking.'

A five-minute argument followed, whether that meant he spied on people. In the end, Gary told them that whatever it meant, they must carry on. A few people grumbled, but eventually agreed. Gary pointed to the actor playing Loraine to continue. Everyone said they had forgotten where they were. So, he reminded them, that Barry had just spoken the line, 'Yes well, I see a lot, especially when people aren't looking.' Which almost started the whole argument off again.

The actor playing Loraine carried on, and said, 'I'll bet.'

'They should have asked me, that's all I'm saying. Nothing more,' said Barry.

'You're just full of yourself today, aren't you? I shouldn't have given you those King Edward spuds,' said Loraine.

'It's just with all this stuff,' said Barry.

'Stuff?' said Loraine.

One of the club members put their hand up and coughed. The two actors playing Barry and Loraine stopped. Gary looked up from his script to see why the play had ground to a halt yet again.

The cause of the interruption said, 'umm, excuse me, I don't like that bit.'

'What bit?' said Gary.

'Stuff,' said the lady, a long-time member of the club. A few other members nodded.

'Well, you're not here to critique the play. Just to be quiet and listen,' said Gary. He was sounding extremely cross.

'There's no need to be rude,' said Lilly. She defended the club member. 'I have to agree that it was getting boring.'

'It's hardly got going yet. This is the second interruption,' said Gary. His face matched the vermillion velvet curtains.

'Give it time,' said Caz. 'It's funny later.' The club member flicked through the script to the end. She was frowning. 'When?' they asked.

'You need to see it acted out,' said Caz. She looked at her husband. He was turning puce.

'We haven't got time for interruptions. Just shut up and listen,' said Gary. His lips curled.

'This aint much fun,' said Trudy. She got up. Her mates followed her example.

'Wait!' said Caz. It will be soon.

'Ow soon?' said Trudy. She stood staring at Caz.

Caz looked pleadingly at her husband. Then said, 'maybe we could skip to their scene?'

'I have already said that we will do this in order,' said Gary. He spoke through gritted teeth. 'Anyone who doesn't like that can just lump it.' He stood and lent forward. His knuckles were white, pressed on the desk in front of him. He glared at the young people. They glared back.

***

Later as Gary and Caz sat on their own in the hall. Caz stared at her husband accusingly. He was shaking. The caretaker walked in and asked, 'have you finished? Time I was locking up.'

Gary and Caz got up and left. As they were walking out the caretaker said to them, 'oi, you've left all these scripts on the floor. I'll just bin em, shall I?' Gary shouted a rather unpleasant reply.

Plympton-on-Sea, UK

Ever since they had bumped into each other at the harbour, Hilda and Karl met up regularly. They alternated between meeting at his house and hers. One Thursday evening, Karl was at Hilda and Pearl's flat. He had joined them for a meal and now they were all sitting drinking sherry and listening to music. Karl said, 'have you heard, Gary and Caz had a disaster?'

'Weren't they the couple backstage for Hilda's play?' said Pearl, getting up to fetch some crisps.

'That's right, they were going to direct a play after Hilda's failed. I reckon it was them who messed up Hilda's though,' said Karl.

'Water under the bridge,' said Hilda. She looked happy and relaxed.

'Sounds like they got what they deserved,' said Pearl. She brought a bowl of crisps in and placing them on the coffee table in the middle of the room.

'I would agree,' said Karl, nodding. 'But Lilly was telling me it leaves the Plympton Theatre in dire straits. She asked the trustees for one last chance.' He took a handful of crisps from the bowl.

'Oh dear,' said Hilda. She eyed up the crisps and then got up and headed to the kitchen. 'It's such a delightful little theatre.' She called across from the kitchen.

'Lilly was asking if I had any thoughts, and I do. But I wanted to talk to you first,' said Karl. He looked at the two ladies.

'Really? Whatever for?' said Hilda. She was still in the kitchen, having taken out a pack of chocolate biscuits from the cupboard and put them on a plate.

'Do you remember all those years ago? I always said that I fancied writing a musical. But I was too busy with my commissions. After Lillian died, I wrote one. It's all about you Hilda,' said Karl.

'All about little old me. How special,' said Hilda. She skipped through with the plate of biscuits. They bounced up and down on the plate.

'Well, not just you, all of us, really. I called it The Fabulous Four. Remember that name?' said Karl. Hilda smiled at the memory. Karl took a proffered biscuit from the plate. Hilda also handed them to Pearl and then placed the plate on a side table next to her seat.

'Aren't the Beatles called that now?' said Pearl. She took some crisps in her other hand and munched on them.

'We called ourselves that and I called my musical that, long before the Beatles,' said Karl, smiling. He sat back in the chair, sherry glass in hand.

'How wonderful,' said Hilda. She took a biscuit and nibbled it.

'I want you to be in it. I will direct it,' said Karl. He had a sip of his sherry. 'If I wrote a musical just about you it would end up being all about murder and mysteries.'

'That's true,' said Pearl. 'Ever since you were a child you've love blood and gore.'

'That's not fair,' said Hilda. 'People just seem to die in mysterious circumstances around me.'

Karl laughed, 'it's just as well the police don't see that as suspicious and blame you.'

Hilda stared at Karl. 'Anyway, you were saying about your musical?'

'Yes, it's all about the four of us, back in the thirties and forties. Lots of music and singing.'

Hilda leapt up and span across the room singing, 'another opening, another show...' she kept spinning and singing as she continued around the room. Karl and Pearl watched her and laughed.

'I take that as a yes?' said Karl.

'What do you think?' said Pearl, looking at her friend spinning and dancing around the room.

William and Louise Shilton's House, Meedham, UK

That same evening in Meedham; William was asleep in front of the TV. Louise had given up trying to keep him awake.

Their usual nightly routine was to take turns sleeping through their evening's viewing. Louise had slept through most of an earlier murder mystery. Every time William noticed, he gave her a nudge. She would miss a key plot point and wake, asking what was happening. By the time he explained, they missed the next key bit. So, he had tried to keep her awake. They had long ago agreed that sleeping early evening spoilt their sleep at night. Now the murder mystery had finished, and William was missing most of a DIY programme that he had chosen. Louise's method of waking him was to whistle loudly. It worked most of the time. William had tried the same technique but was never as good at whistling.

The DIY programme finished. Louise got up and turned off the TV, then said, 'Wake up, it's time to go to bed.' William jerked awake and looked around the room.

'I want to watch that programme on DIY,' said William.

'You mean the one that just finished?' asked Louise. She was walking towards the door. The phone rang, and she jumped. 'Who would ring at this time of night?'

William reached across from his seat and picked up the phone. 'Hello... Mother!?... whatever's the matter?'

'Is she alright?' asked Louise, walking over and trying to listen in.

'What show?' asked William. 'But wasn't that cancelled?'

'Why's she phoning about a show?' Louise was straining to hear by putting her ear near the phone handset.

'A musical... slow down... all about you? Oh, I see, and your friends,' said William. He was looking at Louise and shaking his head. 'You know the time?... I'm sure you are excited.... But it's still very late.... Well, that is exciting news.'

Louise whispered to William, saying, 'Sunday Lunch.'

William shook his head. Louise was nodding. He was shaking his head. But said, 'Before you go, are you free for lunch on Sunday?... Oh... you are... excellent... well goodnight then. See you Sunday.'

Gary and Caz's Hilkins house, Meedham, UK

A cat ran out. Cats know when to make themselves scarce. Gary and Caz's neighbours could have taken detailed notes on the argument within. At the kitchen sideboard, Caz may have been making lunch. At least Gary assumed that was why she stormed out of the lounge. He popped his head around the kitchen door, took one look at his wife and was about to leave, but Caz noticed him. She glanced at the stack of plates in front of her. Ones bought as wedding presents by Gary's mum. She picked one up and felt its weight. Then carefully replaced it. Gary entered slowly, head down. 'It wasn't my fault.'

'Not your fault! Just whose fault was it, the dogs?' asked Caz. Their boxer, Duke, looked up from the safe place he'd found in the corner. As he wiggled backwards, further under the sideboard, only his nose poked out. If they played hide and seek later, Duke would win.

'I was trying to say it's no good crying over spilt milk,' said Gary. He stared at Caz as she lifted a pan, held it aloft, then carefully placed it on the stove, shaking and breathing hard. Gary continued, 'we can get our own back on that, that... woman.'

Caz span round holding a spatula. 'What about our savings? We paid out for the scripts, the advertising, the costume rental. Now we have nothing, no play, and no money.' She waved the cooking implement like a conductor's baton.

'Revenge is sweet,' said Gary. 'It may not get our money back. But we might feel better.' His wife picked up a knife, hefted it in her hand. Then turned to the sideboard and chopped the onions in what seemed a rather vicious way.

The advertising around town which announced the new musical about Hilda Shilton and friends rankled. Gary and Caz planned and schemed. Maybe if they got away to Caz's mother, an idea would come. At least they would be away from Plympton.

Chapter Thirteen

June 1937

Church Hall, Islington, London, UK

Back in 1937, two weeks after Hilda and Pearl had first met Arthur and Karl, they were outside a Church Hall in Islington. Arthur's planning had come to fruition. He'd arranged a foursome at a local dance. Pearl had been hesitant and said to Hilda, 'I don't enjoy lying to my parents. It was bad enough the other week.'

'They wouldn't have let you come,' said Hilda. 'They're old stick in the muds. Still living in Victorian England.'

'It's only to keep me safe. I think we should leave,' said Pearl.

'And miss out on a dance, don't be daft,' said Hilda. As she was speaking, they saw Arthur arrive. He had brought a friend, Karl Dansk. The four of them sat chatting for quite some time before Arthur got up the courage to ask Hilda to dance. He chose the right thing to ask. Hilda loved dancing with anyone at any time. Pearl was miffed, watching Arthur dance with Hilda. In her mind she saw herself dancing with him. But really, she was happier chatting. The idea of dancing worked better in her imagination. As Pearl sat talking to Karl, he told her he was a musician and composer. But he had a fiancé, Lillian. She was just ill that evening; hence, his being alone. Pearl found him an interesting man to talk to. His knowledge of music kept Pearl enthralled.

While Pearl and Karl chatted, Hilda and Arthur tripped around the dance floor like professional dancers. They were the perfect dance partners for each other. It was this dance that changed Hilda's view of Arthur from a boring civil servant to an object of affection. Arthur didn't need the dance to change his view of Hilda.

The evening wore on and Arthur was ready to sit down, but Hilda was just getting into her stride. She seemed to have an excess of energy. The band gave the dancers a break and play a tune for them to just sit and listen to. Everyone sat down, everyone except Hilda. She stood in the middle of the floor and sang the words of the song they played: 'Love Is the Sweetest Thing.' She sang while swaying around the floor.

Hilda sang loudly and well, and as she sang, she often seemed to look at Arthur. He stood open-mouthed in amazement; this was the girl of his dreams. He had to marry her. I don't think any other potential suitors in the room would have argued. He could have her and that was fine by them. It wasn't that they thought she was a poor singer or dancer. She was reasonably pretty, too. Most people in the room would probably rather that their girl didn't get up and sing to them in public. People are so shy and retiring. Something to do with British reserve.

At the end of the evening Karl said that he was keen for them all to meet his fiancé, Lillian. So, he arranged for a trip out on a picnic near Dover the next week. Arthur wanted any excuse to see Hilda again. She was finding an increasing desire to see more of him. Pearl was happy to go along. If she could come up with an excuse for her parents.

Ramsgate, Kent, UK

The following Saturday, Karl borrowed his father's Rolls Royce. The Dansk family originated in Sweden, having made their money in wood and paper. Karl's father had emigrated to England and set up a publishing company. He rivalled the Swedish part of his family in wealth. Karl was born in England into a situation of comfort and wealth. But his father had ensured that he grew up understanding the value of people and money. This upbringing had saved him for being like so many of his contemporaries; selfish and uncaring. Indeed, he had met Lillian when working at an inner-city homelessness charity. Many commentators over the years suggested that Karl's music sprang out of an understanding of real people and actual situations. He was never afraid to get involved in people's lives. Even if that caused him personal pain.

Having borrowed the Rolls Royce, Karl drove Hilda, Arthur, and Lillian down to Ramsgate in Kent. Pearl was ill, with the same illness Lillian had the previous week. Passed to her when she had her long chat with Karl. She was not happy to miss out. When Hilda met up with her before she left, Pearl said, 'don't find any bodies on the picnic.

'I don't set out to find them,' said Hilda. They were talking about the murder Hilda had stumbled upon a few weeks earlier.

Hilda promised she would do her best and tell Pearl all about the fun outing on her return. At least Pearl didn't need to lie to her parents. They would have been no keener for her to go off in a car with a strange man than to a dance. Having Hilda as a chaperone was not acceptable in their eyes.

In the 1930's you could still drive a motorcar onto the cliff path near Dover. Which is exactly what Karl did. He took his father's big and heavy Rolls down very close to the edge. Perhaps he enjoyed the squeals and shouts from the ladies. Arthur was much more restrained uttering the occasional 'steady on old man.' The heavy car drew extremely close to the edge, then stopped in time, well just. Brakes in those days were a lot less reliable.

Hilda's squeals were of delight rather than fear. She loved the sense that the car could sail off the edge and into the English Channel and was wishing she had brought her costume. Lillian was just screaming from sheer terror. It's a wonder that she continued to love and trust Karl after that trip. It's strange the way love works. Her love for him grew.

Once the car had been parked safely. Facing sideways, at Lillian's insistence. That may have been a good safety precaution as handbrakes were also less reliable in those days. They all disembarked. Getting out of such a stately vehicle felt like leaving an ocean-going vessel. They fetched a small table and four chairs from the boot and setup. This was a luxurious picnic. No sitting on rugs on the grass. Then the Fortnum and Mason's food hamper took its place on the table, ready for lunch. A fanfare should have sounded, or a butler been on hand. The occasion looked so grand. The champagne, cheeses, crackers, pâtés, foie grass, cooked meats, breads, fruits, and fish were unpacked. Then placed onto fine China and with silver cutlery and handed out.

'Are there extra people coming?' said Hilda, staring at the massive feast.

'Just us,' said Karl. He popped a cork.

Hilda and Arthur gazed in wonder; they had never eaten so grandly. It wasn't Karl's normal meal either. He wanted to treat his guests. After the repast, everyone sat back, unable to move for about an hour. Hilda didn't usually sit still. She was the first to regain her energy and leapt up, saying, 'anyone for a hike?'

'I beg your pardon?' said Lillian. She looked up from her seat. Her eyes were only half open.

'I'll join you,' said Arthur. He looked bright eyed at the idea.

'Count me out,' said Karl. His eyes remained closed.

Hilda and Arthur walked off down the path. There was a lightness in their step, despite the heavy meal. They spotted a pathway to the beach below and followed it. The track was narrow and steep. In the 1930's Hilda believed in stout, sensible footwear and kept her footing every bit as well as Arthur. He looked disappointed that she didn't need to hold on to him all the way down.

On arrival at the bottom, they found themselves all alone on a small pebble beach. Walking on the pebbles was hard work, but they struggled on and made it to the water's edge. Small waves lapped the shore, moving the stones and making a relaxing swooshing sound. In the 1930's Hilda still wore dresses. She had on a lightweight summer frock that reached just above her ankles. She also had on some thick white stockings. Asking Arthur to look away, she removed her shoes and stockings. Then she hooked up her skirt and wrapped it around her legs, at about knee height. Meanwhile, Arthur removed his shoes and socks and rolled up his trousers. He couldn't help but glance at the exciting view of Hilda's ankles and calves. Together, they paddled in the cold water. Neither of them seemed aware of the stones or the icy cold water. It was as if the entire world existed only for them. Just for that moment in time.

Hand in hand, they stood in companionable silence. Hilda felt a strange electric tingle holding Arthur's hand. A seagull whirled and swooped in the distance. He turned towards her. She looked up into his eyes. He opened his mouth to speak.

'Hello, you two,' said Karl. He crunched on the stones down the beach. He was arm in arm with Lillian.

Arthur turned around and said, 'I thought you didn't fancy a walk, old man.'

'Almost the moment you left, Lillian here said. Let's go and catch up with them,' said Karl. He and Lillian had reached the water's edge.

'That's not quite true, Karl. It was you, twisting my arm,' said Lillian. She was looking at the cold water and shivered.

'Didn't take many turns,' said Karl, smiling.

Arthur and Hilda walked out of the water and joined their friends on the beach. By the look of their hobbled walking, the sharp stones had become more noticeable. Sitting on the beach, the four of them talked of everything and nothing, as young people do when they really want to talk of love.

***

Some might think that Arthur was very rash and quick acting. They might not believe in the idea of love at first sight. Such notions being fanciful to them. But Arthur had experienced love at first sight. Hilda had discovered love at first dance. In the 1930's, love and marriage went together like... I don't need to finish that rhyme. Talking of horses and carriages. As Hilda thought back to that day at the beach, she pictured princes and princesses, horses, and carriages. But then she had a very fertile imagination.

Arthur was more practical. He wanted to marry Hilda, minus any horses, and he eventually got an opportunity to ask her, a week later. He had asked to meet her again when Karl dropped her off at the end of the trip to Ramsgate.

***

Arthur and Hilda's fourth meeting was less lavish than the trip with Karl. One set at a level Arthur could afford. They went for a walk by the Thames and then bought some fish and chips to share sitting on the Embankment. As they sat close together, staring at the murky water. A fogginess descending around them. They found themselves in a small white cloudy space, just the two of them. It had a cosy feel to it. They had set off on a sunny Saturday afternoon. The weather had changed and now, as they sat on the bench by the Thames, an ethereal light tried to break through the fog.

Arthur was sitting sideways, gazing lovingly into Hilda's eyes. He said, 'I... you probably wouldn't even consider this. But... I really love you.'

'Why wouldn't I consider that?' said Hilda.

'That's not the bit I meant,' said Arthur. He wriggled on the bench. 'There's more.'

'Oh, have I jumped the gun?' asked Hilda.

'You never do anything wrong. You're perfect,' said Arthur.

'I don't think my mum and pops would agree with that,' said Hilda, pursing her lips. 'At school, pops used to say, "you need to pull your finger out, Hildy." I think he wanted me to work harder. Although why that involved my fingers, I don't know? Maybe for writing, do you think?'

'Umm, yes, maybe,' said Arthur. He gazed into Hilda's eyes, 'But you're perfect to me. I really love you.'

'That's really spiffing. I love you too,' said Hilda.

'Gosh, thank you... Well, the thing is...,' said Arthur. He gulped, 'You see, that being as I love you and all, and, and with you loving me, which is awfully wonderful, I was thinking whether....'

A bus tooted its horn on the road near them, and they both jumped. Hilda said, 'gee whiz! That was loud.'

Arthur breathed deeply then said, 'yes well, as I was saying, umm, I wondered if you would do me the honour...'

Hilda interrupted him, and asked, 'you want to marry little old me?'

'Oh, well yes, if that is alright and everything,' said Arthur.

'Golly, yes, it most certainly is alright,' said Hilda. She kicked her legs in the air and clapped her hands. Then she gave Arthur a big kiss. After a minute, she stopped and looked at him in shock. 'I've just thought. You'll need to ask pops.'

Arthur recovered from the kiss. He came out of his beautiful dream and said, 'Is he frightfully scary?'

'Not to me he isn't, but I think he can be to other people. But I'm sure you'll be fine,' said Hilda.

A Public House, Kilburn, London, UK

Arthur met Hilda's father, Bert, at a public house near his home. Bert's usual job was interrogating foreign spies. This made him a hard man for a potential son-in-law to approach. Choosing a pub as a venue was a poor choice. Arthur arrived early and made sure he found the ideal table in the saloon bar. Bert walked in and looked around. The look on his face was one of disgust. He found Arthur and sat down.

'What would you like to drink?' asked Arthur.

'You drink here a lot?' asked Bert, looking around.

Arthur stood ready to fetch the drinks, and said, 'no, no, I, I, hardly ever drink, really, this is just because of you.'

'You think I'm a drinker?' Bert stared at Arthur, open-mouthed.

'I, I, I'm not saying that, not at all,' stammered Arthur.

'Oh, I see. You think I frequent public houses?'

'We, we, we could, could go for, for a walk instead...,' Arthur left his question hanging.

'Oh, I see. You think I'm teetotal?'

'No, not at...,' said Arthur.

Bert interrupted. 'I'll have a scotch, single malt, whatever decent one this place has. Make it a double.' He was used to throwing those he was interrogating off balance.

'Ah, alright, fine,' said Arthur. He headed to the bar. Glancing up at the price of single malts in shock.

As they sat with their drinks, Bert started with the reason for such haste. He asked if Arthur had got Hilda pregnant. Arthur had just taken a sip of beer and choked on hearing that question. After reassuring Hilda's father that was not the case, he was then cross questioned about his prospects, current financial state, and future. Arthur hardly touched the rest of his drink. While Bert requested two refills. They jointly agreed, or rather, Bert decided. That it would take two years to save up and be ready to marry Hilda.

***

When the two years were up, the war broke out and two years became eight. It was a long engagement. But Arthur loved Hilda so much that he didn't mind. He told her he would wait forever. She was much more impatient and found the delay a big nuisance.

1939-1945

During World War II, Arthur, and Hilda both had postings in England. Hilda was in the WAAF (Women's Auxiliary Air Force) along with Pearl. During their time there, they learnt to drive large vehicles. Arthur was based at The War Office, working in procurement. Hilda never knew that her father had found a job for Arthur with the secret service. He certainly worked in procurement, but not for things he could talk to Hilda about. Fortunately, Hilda never asked. Karl was in an ENSA (Entertainment National Service Unit) and toured England and France, bringing comfort and relief through his music. It's a pity that Hilda couldn't have joined. Although perhaps her exuberance may have tested the patience of those running the shows. Lillian worked in a factory manufacturing medical supplies. Many of Karl's most well-known pieces were written during the war. The sights he saw, the anguish, pain, stress, sadness, and suffering, seemed to tap into a creative streak he never fully regained. The four of them, and many times Pearl, would meet up as often as they could. With four of them working in London, they just had to wait until Karl was nearby and see if they could co-ordinate their leave for get-togethers. Occasionally they could, and when that happened, it was brilliant.

One time they had planned to meet up, but last-minute Arthur was called in to work urgently. Which Hilda thought odd of someone who worked as a buyer. 'Surely, they could have waited until the morning?' she said. Arthur explained it was more complicated than that. He couldn't tell her the truth. His job involved setting up all the practical needs for agents to go undercover in France. The currency and equipment that they needed. Following the loss of contact with an entire group, they had to urgently send in a new person to set-up a new one. Arthur was called in to equip her with all she needed.

The next day as Hilda walked past the Church Hall, where they would have danced the night before, she stopped still. The sign that advertised the dance was under a firefighter's foot. A pile of smoking rubble stood in the place where the hall had once been. A team of people were clearing rubble. That night, Hilda kissed Arthur extra softly. He looked at her, puzzled.

February 1946

London, UK

After the war in early 1946, Hilda and Arthur were married. Karl was the best man and Lillian and Pearl, maids of honour. The next four years felt to them all, like one long party. Rationing was still in place, but they were back together. They called themselves, 'The Fabulous Four.' By this point Pearl had moved off to a new job outside London and they all lost contact with her. She got married and had a whole new life. Hilda,

Arthur, Karl, and Lillian discovered a shared love of jazz. It influenced Karl's music, and they went to clubs and venues that others saw as edgy and out there. Karl found his talents in demand internationally, even within the US movie industry. The crowds they mixed in became wealthier and more famous. Hilda and Arthur became more distant from them. By the time William was born in 1950, Karl and Lillian were spending more time in Hollywood than England. It was also in 1950 Hilda and Arthur moved to Croydon. Between 1946 and 1952, Hilda had somehow managed to stumble across two murders and help the police solve them. That was additional to the one in the late 1930's. No wonder Karl said her life was full of murders.

In 1952, Hilda and Arthur moved to the suburbs, a small town called Stoke Hind. Arthur died a few months after their move of a heart attack. William was only two. Hilda raised William on her own. Karl and Lillian were so busy that they came over less and called less often. Karl and Lillian moved permanently to California, USA. Life changed and moved on as it always does. The fabulous four were forgotten. Hilda's life became a lot quieter, for a few years.

Chapter Fourteen

September 1998

Ohio State Penitentiary, USA

Orville Stanley walked stiffly down the narrow corridor because of the complex series of straps and handcuffs attached to his hands and feet. An overhead light flickered. They had not fixed it since the last time he took this walk. Arriving at a door, he had to wait while a guard unlocked it. They led him inside and attached his shackles to the table in the centre of the room.

Vance Jurgen, Orville's lawyer, arrived the moment he had sat down. The guard entered a windowed room next door. Orville slumped over the table, breathing heavily. He appeared to be studying the handcuffs. His mind was in another place many years earlier and some miles away. He jerked slightly when Vance asked, 'how are you?'

'Seriously?' said Orville.

'Stupid question, I guess,' said Vance.

Orville lifted his head slowly and stared at Vance, then shook his head. He could see no hope in those eyes. 'I won't even ask. It's obvious.'

'I'm sorry, you need to prepare yourself for...' started Vance.

'I'm prepared for the worst. Reckon I have been since he tried to drown me.'

'Trial dates set, October 20th. Judge Kimber,' said Vance.

Orville glanced up, fear in his eyes.

'I know, Killer Kimber. Always pushes for the death penalty. I'm not a God-fearing man, but reckon we need to pray for a miracle,' said Vance.

Orville gave out a mirthless laugh. 'That's all I've been doing.'

William and Louise Shilton's House, Meedham, UK

William had a night in on his own. Louise was out with her work colleagues watching the latest movie release, 'You've Got Mail.' William had no interest in a soppy romance. Even if it was dressed up as having something to do with technology. That was another thing he had no interest in. Lying on the sofa, half watching TV, William drifted to sleep. A familiar voice woke him. 'Enjoying Mastermind?' Josh laughed. He had let himself in with his key.

'What? Who? Oh, it's you. Why are you here?'

'Nice to see you too, dad.'

'I didn't mean it like that.' William sat up and rubbed his eyes.

'Yeah, I know. I've come round to chat about gran. What are we going to do about this lease problem?' Josh sat opposite his dad.

'What can we do?' said William. He shuffled around in his seat.

'She'll be homeless if the lease holder takes possession of her tearoom and flat. Can she live with you?' asked Josh.

William leapt from his seat, and said, 'she may be homeless, but she won't be penniless. I'll find her a nice retirement home.' He headed to the window and stared out.

'You have loads of space here,' said Josh. He was waving his arm expansively. 'I'd have her stay with me, but my flat's just one bedroom.'

William looked around at his son and said, 'I had enough time with my mother in my childhood.' Then he started pacing around the room. He ran his hand through his thinning hair.

'I don't get it; gran's such a laugh.'

'You two are peas in a pod.' William glanced at his son. 'You're outgoing, like her. I like peace and not being noticed.' He stopped in front of Josh and looked down at him.

'Sure dad. Gran told me about your love of acting at school. You're no shrinking violet.'

William looked at his feet. There was a smile playing on the corner of his lips. 'That was a long time ago.'

Plympton-on-Sea, UK

The members of The Plympton Players had a sense of déjà vu as they gathered for a third time to hear about a play that would save the theatre. 'Oh well, third time lucky,' said one of the older members to another. The other member shook their head.

'I'd be glad to actually get a part in this one,' said an older, frail member. Given that the new production was a lively musical, they may have been overly optimistic.

Karl, Hilda, Pearl, and Lilly were sitting at the front table. Pearl had reason to feel déjà vu herself as she handed out scripts and kept notes. Lilly welcomed everyone, explained that Karl was directing the new play, and handed over to him.

Karl stood up and said, 'hello everyone, for those who don't know me, I used to be a well-known musician and composer, Karl Dansk.' There were a few giggles, especially from the older members. Some had already asked for his autograph. 'I have written a musical about a time that my wife and I used to spend with Hilda and her husband, Arthur.' People looked at each other, puzzled. 'It's not as boring as it sounds. Just to give you a taster, it includes the time Hilda nearly hijacked a train.' There were gasps around the room and everyone stared at Hilda. She was smiling, clapping her hands, and kicking her legs. Lilly said, 'I beg your pardon? Mrs Shilton is a criminal?'

'No, no, no, you'll need to read the script. It's all hilarious,' said Karl. He looked at Lilly and smiled.

A local PC, who was a club member, said, 'breaking the law is no laughing matter.' Any idea of laughing policemen could be squashed after viewing his demeanour. Just as well that he was off duty.

'I agree,' said another voice. There were a few nods.

Hilda looked like she could leap up and dance around the room at any moment. Karl brought order and said, 'it wasn't a criminal act. Well, it didn't become a criminal matter. You need to read it or watch the play.'

Hilda added her two-penneth worth, and said, 'oh yes dear, we got as far as the driver's cab and then the station master agreed to drive the train. We only threatened him and the other station staff. It was all light-hearted fun.' The policeman looked like he was searching for his handcuffs. He just had an itchy nose and was looking for a tissue.

Pearl spoke up before Hilda continued with any more detail and caused a riot, by saying, 'I think you should tell us more about the play, Karl.'

'Right, thank you Pearl, it's called the Fabulous Four and...' started Karl.

'Isn't that a pop group?' said a voice from the back. A lot of voices agreed.

'Similar, but no,' said Karl. He wiped his forehead. 'That's the Beatles, Fab Four.'

'Not very different,' said one voice. There was a lot of agreement. Karl asked if they could continue. Then another voice said, 'have we got talented enough singers?' There was a lot of mumbling, chatting and discussion about the club's lack of singers.

'I have written it to be easy to sing, and a few singers from a local society have agreed to help us,' said Karl.

'Not the Somershire Singers, is it?' said an old man sitting at the front. He had a dour expression and a deep voice. If he had worn a long black robe and carried a scythe, he could have passed for The Angel of Death.

'Yes, it is Rose's group,' said Karl. He sat back in his chair and sighed. He looked around the room. A discussion started on whether the Somershire Singers, led by Rose Dune, were trustworthy, reliable, and desirable. Some of the Plympton Players had belonged to that group under its previous choir leader. A person they all admired and respected. They left when Rose took over. 'She likes all these modern, un-tuneful songs.' Was one opinion. The fact that the group had grown in membership, popularity, and awards was ignored. Eventually, they all agreed to give the group a try, just this once.

Just as that issue was sorted, two others were raised. One person said, 'what about musicians for the band, and how about dancers?' One of the older ladies who had hobbled in with a stick told them all that she was a fantastic dancer. Those who knew her patted her hand and said, 'yes of course you are.'

Karl could finally continue. He said, 'don't worry, I have it all in hand.' He did not want another lengthy discussion and so he didn't tell them who he had chosen as musicians. After answering all the remaining questions. He allocated the initial parts, and they could finally start their first read through.

November 1978

Karl had mentioned to the Plympton Players about a certain incident back in 1978. A rather curious incident. Whilst Karl and Hilda hadn't met for fifty years. What Hilda didn't know was that Karl's wife, Lillian, had seen her in London in 1978. Why she chose not to make herself known is something we shall never know.

A Country Lane, Stoke Hinds, UK

Perhaps we need to start a few days earlier. Hilda was trying to get in shape. A run seemed the best idea. So, she enlisted the help of her neighbour, Betty. She had a simple job, to cycle beside Hilda as a pace keeper. A job that Betty took to with great gusto and all seriousness. After all, it was a tremendous responsibility to be asked to carry out such a task. She cycled along shouting over her shoulder, 'keep going, come on Hilda.'

'I am going as fast as I can,' gasped Hilda. Huffing and puffing but doing very little actual running. Betty was getting further ahead. Rather than pace setting, she was leaving Hilda behind. Perhaps she hadn't quite got the idea of her job after all.

'Well, you need to be faster,' shouted Betty from the comfort and ease of her cycle. She had to keep stopping, turning around, and cycling back to Hilda.

'I only have little legs,' said Hilda. Pointing at her legs. She obviously had to stop to do that.

'The training book didn't mention leg length,' said Betty. She didn't sound very sympathetic. But Hilda had chosen her as a pacesetter, not as a comforter. So perhaps she was fulfilling her role after all.

Hilda stopped running or rather walking briskly yet again and looked seriously at Betty. 'Well, it jolly well should.'

'Don't get cross at me, Hilda,' said Betty. They were on a deserted country lane. Hilda had stopped for another breather, not that she needed it. Betty pulled her cycle up by Hilda and stared at her friend seriously. 'I'm just doing as you asked.'

This was the first time in her life Hilda had dressed in a purple tracksuit bottoms and white trainers. She so loved them that in later years, she wore that outfit all the time. She started panting heavily, which was a surprise, given how little actual running she had done. It was probably for effect. Given that her friend was now in earshot. Hilda stood up straight and said, 'right, let's try again.'

'Just don't blame me if you can't keep up,' said Betty. She set off far too fast.

The experiment in running had come about after Hilda realised, she was getting a little plump around the middle. She decided exercise was the obvious way to lose weight. After sharing the idea with Betty, her first suggestion had been eating less. But Hilda was having none of such ridiculous and extreme suggestions. Her grandma had a saying, 'fresh air and exercise were all you needed.' She'd lived to the grand old age of 64, so she must be right. Mind you, that only gave Hilda 6 more years to live. But she was sure things had improved since her grandma's days. People seemed to live longer now; maybe Hilda didn't even need exercise. Thinking such happy thoughts, a few yards down the road Hilda said, 'right oh, that's enough for today.'

'But you've only run for about a quarter of a mile,' said Betty. She looked over her shoulder and fell off her bike.

'As much as that! In which case, I feel well pleased with my progress today. Back to my house for tea and crumpets,' said Hilda. She set off back toward her home. Faster than she had run so far. The tea and hot buttered crumpets were calling her.

'But Hilda…' started Betty, but she found she was talking to a rapidly receding back. She climbed back on the bike and pedalled. It was hard to catch up with Hilda on the return trip. Perhaps a treat of crumpets at the end was the way to get Hilda moving on the outward trip.

***

Later, Hilda and Betty sat in the small front room of Hilda's cosy cottage in the village of Stoke Hinds. They were in a pool of candlelight due to yet another power cut. To the news, it was 'The winter of discontent.' But sitting in front of Hilda's open fire, on which she could heat a pan or kettle, with a plentiful supply of cut wood. Power cuts were no issue at all. The house was warm, the crumpets were tasty. As for the lack of TV, with a voice like Hilda's that was no problem either.

'Time for a song, I think,' said Hilda. She tried out a few notes.

'Ah, well,' said Betty. She spoke over Hilda's warm up. 'I can't stay too long. Ernie is expecting me soon.'

'Just three or four then,' said Hilda, bursting into full song.

Betty half-heartedly joined in. She eventually escaped at 10pm. The power was back on, and Ernie was watching a film. He looked less concerned at her late arrival than she had expected. Perhaps he hadn't expected her earlier, after all.

When Arthur, Hilda's husband, died in 1952, Hilda needed to work to top up the widow's pension she received. It was the only way to pay the bills, put food on the table and clothe William. Even after William had grown up and left home in the 1970's, she still needed to work for her own needs. So, she commuted daily to London, as local jobs had not paid enough. Recently all the train strikes, made getting to and from work increasingly difficult. Although Hilda had no problem with the occasional power cut, train strikes were another thing entirely. She needed to get to and from her workplace.

Doran and Sarn's Solicitors, London, UK

Then came a peculiar Friday in November 1978. Hilda had worked hard all morning at Doran and Sarn's solicitors, where she worked as a general clerical assistant. It came to lunchtime and Miss Minchin, a very important client, arrived with some urgent paperwork that needed sorting. Mr Dandy the Clerk and Miss Watson the Secretary were both out at the same time. A coincidence, obviously. Hilda missed the fact it was becoming an increasingly regular lunchtime coincidence. Besides, what business is that of ours to comment on? We do not wish to gossip. The fact Mr Dandy was married was his affair. Miss Watson was free and able to do whatever she chose. That was entirely her affair. Perhaps an unfortunate choice of word.

Miss Watson rarely gave Hilda anything to do beyond filing and making coffee. Jobs that she carried out to a reasonable level of accuracy. You can't get tea and coffee wrong. Well, there was that one time, but it's best not to dwell on Hilda's failings. She put files into the cabinets extremely well. Most filing at Doran and Sarn's never needed to be referred to again. Perhaps just as well. It found its way into the filing cabinets; did it really matter if it ended up filed under the first name or the surname? Not unless you wanted to retrieve it.

One thing was certain, Hilda found working there rather tedious and often daydreamed. Sometimes Hilda wondered if working was just as boring as school had been. Work had one enormous advantage over school; They paid you for work. At Doran and Sarn's, they paid her even when she made mistakes. Perhaps they would have changed that had they had known of all her mistakes. Plus, the great thing for Hilda was that neither Mr Doran nor Mr Sarn ever took a cane to Hilda's nether regions. A regular experience during her schooldays.

On this rather strange Friday, the important client, Miss Minchin, was so pressed for time she insisted Hilda help her out. She could not wait around for Mr Dandy or Miss Watson. Hilda was always keen to help anyone in need. She was eager to show all the skills she had picked up by watching Mr Dandy and Miss Watson. She didn't really see the partners at work. They were always in their private offices; as they were that day, with a 'do not disturb' notice on the door. Hilda wondered if they just slept in there all day. As Miss Minchin was so pressed for time, Hilda decided this was her moment to shine and show that she could rise beyond making tea or filing. They all underestimated her, something which had happened often over her life. But Hilda would show them how wrong they were. They thought all she did was daydream. Hilda pictured the praise and adulation that would come from everyone when they realised just how clever she really was. 'Oh Hilda, we underestimated you.' 'Hilda, take this pay rise.' 'Hilda, would you consider becoming a partner?' 'Hilda, would you like your own office?' she imagined the furniture she would have and the pictures on the wall. Obviously, she would have a pot plant. Maybe an aspidistra, 'the biggest aspidistra in the world.' She hummed the song. Then she came back to reality by Miss Minchin saying, 'Mrs Shilton, why are you humming? Can you help or not?'

'Right, yes. Now, I'm not exactly a legal expert, Miss Minchin,' said Hilda, in a slight understatement. 'But I have worked here for ten years. You can't help picking up a few things. I will do my best and as my pops always used to say, "your best is all we can expect Hilda," and he was a brilliant man.' She picked up a pen and a legal pad to write on. At least everything would be written on the right paperwork. That's an important start.

At that moment, just as Hilda was distracted by Miss Minchin, Lillian Dansk, Karl's wife, and Hilda's old friend, walked in. Hilda didn't look up. She just said, 'if you could please take a seat. I'll be with you in a moment.'

Lillian looked shocked to see her old friend after so many years. No doubt she felt guilty for not having been in contact before. She took a seat and watched. Waiting to be noticed. Hilda was far too busy listening to a complex request from Miss Minchin. Who said, 'I would like to make a bequest for some chattels to be willed to my heirs. I also wanted the partners to mediate in a litigation proceeding for me and investigate an issue of a relative who died intestate.'

Hilda checked the few scribbled notes she had written: 'request to chat about hair. Needs medium to contact dead relative who died of intestinal problems.' Then she told Miss Minchin: 'I think I have all that. I will pass it on as soon as Miss Watson or Mr Dandy returns.'

Lillian was shaking her head in awe. She must have been impressed at her friend's grasp of legal matters. Realising how occupied her old friend must be, she got up and said, 'I'll call back another time. I can see you're busy.'

'Righto,' said Hilda. She didn't notice her long-lost friend. Lillian left with one last glance at Hilda. She passed Miss Watson on the stairs, who looked flushed and dishevelled after her lunchtime meeting with Mr Dandy. As Miss Watson entered the office, she saw Miss Minchin and asked how she could help.

'It's alright, your assistant has taken notes on everything,' said Miss Minchin, pointing at Hilda.

'If I could just double check the fine details,' said Miss Watson. She knew Hilda was just about suited to tea making and filing. Her experiences of Hilda doing anything more had not been encouraging. Fortunately, after taking a correct note of

Miss Minchin's requirements, she never compared her notes to Hilda's. Although the downside of that is, it left Hilda in blissful ignorance of her error. Hilda went home that day feeling she had finally started on her legal career. She felt she was on her way to becoming a legal legend.

Just as Miss Minchin was leaving, Mr Dandy walked in. He also looked a bit flushed and in disarray. He exchanged a furtive glance with Miss Watson, then headed to his desk. Every so often, they glanced at each other, smiled, and looked down again. Hilda thought this odd behaviour and quite unprofessional. 'Still,' she thought, 'not everyone can have my legal professionalism.'

Mr Doran came out of his office later that afternoon, to announce that they would close early. He had heard on the radio that the rail strike was bad that day and wanted to ensure everyone got home safely. Hilda wondered why he was listening to the radio in his office during business hours. Miss Watson passed on the message from Miss Minchin before she left. They chatted about no hair, no mediums were contacted, nor intestinal problems discussed. Hilda was not in earshot when the message was conveyed, so she left with full confidence in her understanding of legal matters. But no knowledge of the visit from her friend Lillian.

Hilda got ready to leave, putting on a knee length blue wool coat over her jacket and skirt, then donning a matching blue bonnet. The red gloves and scarf stood out a bit. The weather outside was very bitter, and she hastened towards the tube station with her head down. Many people must have had the same idea to leave early, as the station was crowded, even at 3:45 pm. As Hilda and the rest of the commuters walked down the escalator, she mused, not for the first time, why they were all so impatient. Surely, the moving stairway moved fast enough on its own without them walking. In reality, no one wanted to just miss a tube train by a few seconds. As she neared the bottom of the escalator, there came that mixture of swooshing sound, gust of wind, and smell that happens as a train approaches. The tension in the crowd increased. Which platform was it approaching? Was it theirs? Everyone sped up. The wind and noise increased as Hilda entered her platform. It was her train. The platform was already crowded. But she pushed forward alongside everyone else. The train arrived, and the doors opened. No one got off, but the entire platform attempted to get onto the train; and succeeded. It was a squash, but no one seemed to mind. They just pushed harder. Hilda knew how a sardine felt, but without the tomato sauce. There was no need to hold on to the handles. Everyone held each other up.

For a country as reserved as England, a tube train trip is an intensely intimate way to travel. On a tube at rush hour, everyone is so close to each other, they are almost one entity. Travelling by tube at rush hour, you get to know your fellow passengers inside out. You could no doubt give their measurements to a tailor or dressmaker. At the arriving station, which was thankfully the next one, everyone burst out. Exiting the train was like a jack-in-the-box springing open. People shot from the train towards the train station platforms.

Hilda knew the route blindfolded; she had done it for years. She also knew the timetable. Glancing at a clock, she could see a train was due to leave in two minutes. She was glad to be wearing flat shoes and so ran. Up the escalator, pushing past other startled passengers across the station towards her platform. It must have been all that running practice with Betty coming to the fore. On arriving at the platform, crowds were gathered, but no train was in sight. She asked a fellow passenger if he knew what was happening. He told her the train was delayed while waiting for a driver because of the strike. Everyone waited, the crowd increased, time passed, and time passed.

***

Standing a few yards from Hilda were Karl and Lillian. When Lillian left Hilda's workplace, she had been meeting her husband. They were waiting for the same train but would get off at an earlier stop. They might as well have been a hundred miles away. The crowd was so dense, neither could see the other. Each stood in their own space, an island apart within the sea of people. Lillian was talking to Karl, she said, 'Hilda looked so changed, so professional.'

'You're sure it was Hilda?' asked Karl.

'She's unmistakable,' said Lillian.

'That's true,' said Karl.

'You should have seen her taking notes about a complex legal case,' said Lillian. A man with a suitcase tried to squeeze past them. He just succeeded.

'Maybe she took some legal training?' said Karl.

'Perhaps, but she never seemed that logical to me,' said Lillian. They moved to one side as another few people passed and they realised they were in a busy place.

Forty minutes later, a train pulled up at the platform and the gates opened. Greyhound races don't have a faster start than the people at those gates. Passengers burst through, flashing their tickets at the staff manning the gates, and ran to the train to secure a seat. Hilda was quick as a hare and headed for her carriage near the front. Karl and Lillian were far behind. They didn't often travel by train. But their car was out of action, so they had decided on the train. Karl had a meeting with some record producers in London and Lillian had planned on updating some trust papers. Doran and Sarn's solicitors had been recommended to her. Her usual solicitors were on the other side of London. Just as well, the papers were not urgent, as they were still unsigned. Karl and Lillian sat in the carriage next to Hilda's. They were fortunate that they found a seat.

***

For those who have not experienced a 1970's UK train, a description is needed. The doors opened via a turning brass handle, and then only from outside. On arrival at a station, you must pull down the sliding window and hang out of it to open the door. Most passengers opened the doors while the train was still slowing down. On a busy commuter train, people have disembarked before the train stops. On a train that is leaving people often run after the train, opening the door as they run beside it, then leap on at speed. Slamming the door behind them. One wonders why electronic doors were brought in. All the fun has gone out of rail travel. Oh yes, it's much safer now.

The layout of the inside the carriages varied slightly. Each carriage was open with no corridors by the late 1970's. But within each open carriage, they divided the seats into sections. These were groups of four seats, two facing each other across a footwell or a table. They echoed this on either side of a central walkway along the entire length of the carriage. Occasionally, a separation panel was placed part way down a carriage. There were also sometimes rows of two seats behind each other, facing in one direction. Again, either side of the walkway. First-class carriages had larger gaps between the seats.

This was a British train, so everyone sat in silence reading or looking out of the window. Brits are also creatures of habit, sitting in nearly the same seat every day with the same people that they totally ignore. Which makes you wonder why they sat together. Perhaps it was the comfort of familiarity. The growing knowledge that your fellow passengers will do nothing shocking, like speak to each other. Hence Hilda heading for her carriage of people she regularly sat with and ignored.

***

Hilda sat down that day and noted that all her usual travelling companions were present on either side of the table. The other three had also got off work early that day. Although with the train having left so late, perhaps it was near its usual time. It is a wonder they had all claimed their usual seats. Perhaps they had glared at anyone who dared sit in them or move towards them. A British stare is a fearful thing.

Sitting across the table from Hilda, there was the tall slim, greying man in his 60's reading the Times. A man of medium build and dark curly hair in his 30's reading the Daily Express. Sat next to Hilda was a serious-looking young man in his teens with shoulder length dark hair. He was reading a book with a plain brown plastic cover. As usual, Hilda wondered what was he reading? She tried smiling; it had the normal effect, none. The young man held his book at an angle so that she could not read it. No matter how hard she tried.

The train left ten minutes later. At each station en route, more delays occurred. The longest being a twenty-minute delay at Garsham, but eventually the train got going again. However, on arrival at Great Missleham, an announcement came over the intercom that the train would proceed no further. All passengers should disembark and find their own method of onward travel. Fortunately for Karl and Lillian, this was their stop, and they were already disembarking. This was not the case for Hilda and her fellow passengers. It would leave them stranded fifteen miles from Stoke Hind. No direct bus ran to Stoke Hind, and a lot of stranded passengers needed travel.

The Times reader put his paper down and said, 'what's going on? This is unacceptable.'

The Daily Express reader slammed his paper on the table and said, 'I'm not having this. We have waited and waited, now they just stop altogether. Enough is enough.'

The young lad just looked red faced and flustered. He put his book in his shoulder bag.

Hilda stood up and said, 'This isn't right, they can't do this. Come on, let's go and see what's happening.'

It was a complete shock. Totally unacceptable and un-British. Someone should have written a letter to The Times. Everyone was talking to each other, oh yes, and the train had stopped. The passengers were pouring off the train. Hilda and her group joined them. There was a belligerent mood. You could feel the tension. Outside the train, a few passengers were gathering around an unfortunate railway employee. They were even talking to him. It was hard to believe you were in England. People were putting aside their discomfort and speaking very loudly indeed.

Karl and Lillian were struggling to cross the platform. Crowds of people talking to each other got in their way. To gain the exit, they had to pass Hilda's carriage. They did this as she and all her fellow passengers burst out of the carriage door. Karl and Lillian could proceed no further. In front of them, a band of angry passengers had surrounded the railway employee. They looked around and in between the crowd of people to see what was happening.

One of the angry passengers was saying to the railway employee, 'It's only another two stops, why can't you carry on?' To say the other passengers were not looking happy is an understatement. The poor railway employee looked in danger of being struck by an umbrella. He may even have had some very strong words said to him. He could obviously sense the rising anger as he was trying to escape the crowd and gain the safety of his office. This was a decidedly un-British crowd. Absolutely not cricket, not cricket at all.

Hilda and her band of followers pushed to the front of the crowd. Hilda said to the agitated worker, 'Now you there, who do we speak to in order to get this train moving?'

'You can't speak to anyone. It's stopping here,' said the railway worker. He was still trying to back away towards the shelter of his office.

'Don't you go running away,' said Hilda. 'Can you drive a train?'

'Well, technically yes, but it's not that... I can't actually be cause...,' started the worker. He was still trying to hide.

'I can operate a train,' said a voice in the crowd. It was a middle-aged man in a business suit. He didn't look like a train driver. No overalls or little peaked cap with Train Driver written on it, or anything. The crowd focused on him.

The railway employee stopped trying to escape and said, 'You can't do that sir, it's against the rules.'

Hilda had to shout to be heard and said, 'Well, if you refuse to drive it, I think the passengers will have to take control. Now we have someone who can drive the train for us. Who's with me?'

The crowd had grown around Hilda and a general roar of assent went up. It needs to be understood that in the 1970's train driver cabs had no electronic door locks or special keys to start. Anyone could open the door to the cab, get in, and push a few levers to operate it, if they knew which ones. It would be illegal, of course, but possible. The passengers were not thinking about minor issues like the law. They wanted to get home. That was much more important. They'd started talking to each other, for heaven's sake. What was a minor thing, like a railway bylaw after that shocking start?

Karl and Lillian glimpsed Hilda through the cheering crowd. They looked at each other in amazement. They were learning new things about Hilda. Things that later ended up in Karl's musical. Things the policeman in Plympton Players was unhappy about.

'Where's that man who can drive the train?' said Hilda. He came forward and Hilda held his hand up, saying, 'Our champion. To the cab! Come on, everyone.'

Then she half remembered a stirring speech she had learnt at school. This was her moment to inspire the troops. She hopped up on a box. Unfortunately, it had never contained soap. She said to the crowd: 'What happens here today, good women will teach their daughters. From this day to the end of the world. We few, we happy few, we band of sisters and brothers. Today wave your brollies with me.' Hilda waved her brolly madly. One or two in the crowd copied. 'You who wave your brollies with me shall be my brothers and sisters…' she hesitated and looked at the pigeons in the rafters of the station roof. Then, as if struck by a powerful emotion, she said, 'People in bed will be sorry they missed out on this great day.'

Everyone was silent and stared at Hilda, puzzled. Hilda leapt off the box and grabbed the potential train driver and pushed him forward. It's a pity she lacked a chariot and sword to impersonate Boadicea. Chest thrust out; brolly held aloft like a sword. Oh, if only she could have ridden on a chariot. Even a railway trolley would have sufficed. The crowd gathered around her, anyway. Cometh the hour cometh the woman. Hilda led her army forward, that great horde of passengers. No longer puzzled by her speech. They blindly followed her. We all follow a strong leader. Even the silly ones.

There was excited chatter, laughing, cheering, and general merriment in the crowd now. The earlier tension had gone. People's power was winning through. If anyone had forgotten that Britain was great, they needed to be present at that moment. Churchill would probably have had them arrested. But he may also have been jolly impressed with the British fighting spirit shown. 'Never, never, never, give up.' 'We will fight them on the platforms.'

Karl and Lillian joined the rear of the crowd as it surged forward. Hilda and the new driver led the way, and the railway employee ran behind, pleading and trying to be heard in his walkie-talkie. 'The passengers are high-jacking the train. Help urgently required.'

It was an amazing sight to see, like something from a Hollywood movie where the hero takes control of a city once occupied by the enemy and vanquishes the foe. As the actor and martial arts instructor, Bruce Lee has been quoted as saying: "The successful warrior is the average man with laser-like focus."

They had pushed the passengers far enough, and they were turning on the system. These average men and women, with their laser like focus on getting home. It had turned them into warriors. The worm had turned. Victory was in their grasp.

As Hilda and the would-be driver arrived at the train cab, so did the station master. He was panting and red faced, having run full pelt to beat the crowd. Having heard the urgent radio call and on entering the platform, he'd been spurred into action by the sight of passengers storming the train. After being momentarily thrown by Hilda's speech, who wasn't? The station master now stood in front of the driver's door, and said, 'OK, you win. I'll drive the train the rest of the way.'

The biggest cheer you can imagine went up from the warrior passengers. Some pigeons who were happily sitting on the station roof heard the sudden roar, and in their panic and showered good luck on the passengers below. Even Karl and Lillian cheered, and they were already at their destination. The station master was as good as his word and drove the train the remaining way to Stoke Hind. The passenger revolt had won without the need to break any laws.

In all the remaining years that Hilda travelled on that train, the passengers never spoke to each other again. Although the next morning when Hilda did her usual smile at everyone, the young man with the long hair smirked back. Then he carried on reading his book, 'The Fog' by James Herbert. As he flipped open the book Hilda saw his name, Mike Nevin, written on the inside cover. 'Odd surname,' she thought. 'I won't forget that.' She promptly did. But then it's a very forgettable name.

Hilda settled back in the train carriage and smiled to herself. Two successes yesterday, she thought. First, I've helped a client at work. Second, I led a revolt against the railways. The passengers won a marvellous victory, all because of me. One day they might make a statue of me and put it at a station in London, my right arm pointing towards Stoke Hind. No, maybe that's too much. She closed her eyes and daydreamed about books being written all about her life. All she needed was an author ready to write them.

Once Karl and Lillian got home from the train trip, they thought to contact Hilda. It had been too long. They had lived out in California, USA, for several years and now they were back in the UK. But things got in the way. It never happened, and so a missed opportunity came and went. A year later, they went back to California for a few years. Karl's work was at its height.

***

When Karl shared this story with Hilda. Her response was, 'no use buying spilt milk.'

'I think you mean crying,' said Karl.

'Oh, I do as little of that as possible, dear,' said Hilda.

'I can see that,' said Karl, laughing.

'As I always say, life is too short to have bears with fudges. You and Lillian were always wonderful friends. You couldn't help having busy lives,' said Hilda.

'Bears with fudges. Thank you, I think,' said Karl, smiling.

We know the response of the Plympton Players. It remains to be seen how the story will add to Karl's musical. After all, his musical is meant to save the theatre. Be quite good if someone could save Hilda's tearoom as well.

Chapter Fifteen

September 1998

Hidden Garden Tearoom, Plympton-on-Sea, UK

On the morning after the Plympton Players had done their practice run of Karl's musical, Hilda and Pearl were having breakfast. 'It wasn't all bad,' said Hilda.

'True,' said Pearl, 'There were bits where no one spoke or sang.'

'Don't be a sourpuss, dear.' Hilda munched her cornflakes.

'Well, there's not a lot to be happy about. We only have six weeks to practise and put the show on,' said Pearl.

'It'll be alright on the night,' said Hilda. She got up and danced around the room. 'You see, I have the moves all practiced for my main dance.'

Pearl watched Hilda, open-mouthed. Not a pretty sight, as she had just taken a mouthful of porridge. She shook her head and chewed her mouthful. Perhaps it was surprise at Hilda's dance moves or that she had a dance at all. Whatever the reason, things were not looking great for Karl's musical.

Josh's Photographic Studio, Meedham, UK

Later that same morning, Josh was reading his post. His assistant asked if he was free to do a portrait which had been booked for his other assistant. They'd just called in sick. Getting up, he walked over to meet the client. Beth Jenkins stood up to greet him. Some would describe the experience the two of them had as 'love at first sight.' Others call it 'being hit by a thunderbolt.' Whatever the phrase, they both stood still and stared into each other's eyes. Josh barely breathed. Time stood still for them both. Josh's assistant setup the backdrop for the portrait, then came across to tell him it was ready. The assistant opened her mouth to speak, then looked at the obviously love-struck couple and smiled. She walked off to the back of the studio, shaking her head.

Josh shook himself into action and took a couple of steps forward and said, 'I, I, umm, I'm, the, urr, umm.'

'Yes,' said Beth. She obviously spoke gobbledygook.

Josh opened his mouth to speak again and closed it. Then he finally said, 'you wanted a...'

'Yes,' said Beth. She took a tentative step towards Josh. She must have been a mind reader too; at least of Josh.

'Right,' said Josh. He pointed out the direction to walk. Their eyes locked together, each seeking something deep within the other. As Beth drew closer to Josh, his arm outstretched for directions; it brushed hers. They both gasped as if they'd received an electric shock. No, something far more pleasurable, judging by their expressions.

'Sorry... accident,' said Josh.

'Yes,' said the loquacious Beth. Staring at Josh through very large brown eyes. Eyes that in the upcoming years, Josh would often gaze into.

Josh guided her more carefully and less physically to the photographic area. Their eyes never leaving each other. This caused a few issues as they crossed the studio. There were a few bumped knees on route. But neither seemed to notice. Isn't love glorious? Having instructed Beth where to sit, Josh then spent longer to arrange the lighting than ever before. Beth's auburn hair shone. Rosy cheeks glowed rosier that day than ever before. Full red shiny lips quivered. Perhaps some of the radiance in her looks came from the presence of Josh. He was obviously affecting her. In arranging her for the portrait he did, with her permission, need to waft her shining auburn hair aside, straighten her perfect shoulders and gently lift her shapely chin. Each touch bringing the same joyous electricity as earlier. It's difficult to know why he adjusted her position. She was obviously already perfect in his mind already. With tremendous effort Josh looked away from Beth's eyes and at his camera. But only long enough to set up the photos. Every opportunity he looked at her again. This was either love, or they had both gone completely crazy. Some would argue that the two states are very similar.

It will be no surprise that after the portrait shoot, they could not part. Josh, finally regained partial articulation and asked Beth for a drink. They headed to a local bar and started getting to know each other beyond the colour of each other's eyes.

Plympton Council Offices, Plympton-on-Sea, UK

Councillor Mildred Russell was looking very important as she sat behind her large desk at the Plympton Council Offices. She read through proposals and gave her approval or denial. Mildred elaborately ticked or crossed the applications. The onyx Parker fountain pen she used bore the inscription 'To M with love from L.' Her husband had bought it as a Christmas gift. Its delicate gold-plated nib flowed so beautifully on any forms she had to sign or approve. She had also recently used it in a far less beautiful way. Signing the forms that were to drive Hilda from her home and business.

The phone on her desk rang. The operator said, 'It's a Mr Ling. He says he's phoning on behalf of The Conglomerate.'

'I'll take it,' said Mildred sharply. She whispered into the phone. 'Why are you calling me here?'

'We have informants everywhere,' said Mr Ling. 'This simple old woman at the tearoom has friends at the highest level of government.'

'What are you talking about?' asked Mildred. She broke the nib of her pen on the form beneath it. The ink was flowing across the page. She looked at the mess and scowled.

'I hope you have everything tied up tight?' said Mr Ling sharply.

'Yes,' said Mildred, grabbing a piece of blotting paper. 'No one can stop us. It doesn't matter what friends she has.' She hung up, then dabbed absentmindedly at the ink-covered form. She pressed the button for an outside line and dialled a number.

Plympton Playhouse, Plympton-on-Sea, UK

At the Plympton Playhouse, everyone gathered ready for rehearsals. All except Karl Dansk. He would normally have been there waiting. Karl had enlisted one of the regular club members to help him. She had injured her leg, but still aspired to be involved. Acting as his prompt and doing admin. Karl's assistant hobbled over to Hilda and asked, 'have you seen Karl?'

'No dear,' said Hilda. She turned back to a group she had been chatting to. They were shaking their heads in agreement. No one had seen him.

The lady who had approached Hilda said, 'he isn't answering his phone, and he is usually here half an hour early at least.' She looked worried.

'Pearl and I will knock on his door; he may just have nodded off. We're none of us getting any younger. Are we?' said Hilda to Pearl. Who then frowned at Hilda.

Harbourside Cottage, Plympton-On-Sea, UK

Hilda and Pearl headed off to Karl's cottage at a cracking pace. Pearl had to ask Hilda to slow down. Perhaps Hilda's observation about age had been correct. At the cottage, Hilda knocked hard on the thick oak door. She didn't press the bell. It was an ongoing issue for Karl. Why did no one ever ring the bell? Perhaps it was in the wrong place, and no one noticed it. There was no answer to Hilda's bashing at the door, and all the lights were off. Hilda told Pearl to wait by the door in case Karl answered it belatedly and she headed around the back to check the kitchen door. This was the life she enjoyed, investigating, exploring, searching. Whoops, she tripped on a stone down the dimly lit side passage. The cottage was all on one level and detached from any other. The side path was narrow, but the rear garden was extensive and mainly grass. It was 7.45 pm, and the nights had drawn in.

Hilda arrived at the rear garden; it was in shadow. Some of this could be put down to the tall trees and hedging that surrounded it. On gaining the rear of the house, Hilda noticed the kitchen window was ajar. A glow emanated from all the electrical appliances inside. So many seemed to have digital clocks and displays. Hilda thought they looked like the Blackpool Illuminations. Although that spectacular seaside town may take issue with the comparison. At the back were both a large French Door and a glass-panelled kitchen door. Hilda first went over to the French Doors. Locked, as expected. She peered inside. The dining area was empty. Karl's dining and kitchen area were all one large space. She then tried the glass-panelled back door, also locked. She knocked - no answer. Karl was not in the kitchen. Now came her breaking and entering skills. Honed in previous investigations. Obviously, she must do this, after all, Karl wasn't answering the door. Perhaps he was injured. This was an exceptional circumstance. In an exceptional circumstance breaking into a friend's house was a necessity. He might need rescuing.

The open kitchen window was low, and Hilda was very fit and nimble. So, she clambered through it and onto the kitchen worktop on the other side. She hadn't noticed that it contained plates. These made a rather impressive crashing sound as they hit the tiled floor. Hilda hoped they weren't Karl's special set. The ones he kept for best. She was very careful as she continued her covert entrance. But still sent the cutlery that had been next to this fine crockery, onto the floor, to join the broken plates.

The whole racket made by the breaking and crashing of Karl's crockery and cutlery was certainly enough to have drawn his attention, had he been in. No one came to investigate. She could therefore assume that either he was out or in some dire need. This spurred Hilda on to investigate more urgently. She hoped fervently that Karl's body would not be her next one to discover. As she swung her feet around, ready to hop onto the floor, her trainers caught a rack containing glasses. Fortunately, it only wobbled a bit. Which was just as well. They looked a very fine set of glasses. She steadied the rack and jumped onto the floor. A loud screech from an unidentified source caused her to spin around and knock the rack with the glasses for a second time. It wobbled impressively, but all the glasses stayed on it. Hilda realised the screech was merely the neighbour's cat. It had followed her into the kitchen. She continued into the house, shouting, 'Karl, are you here?' There was no answer.

Hilda saw movement by the kitchen window, so she walked back to it fast. Was it her imagination? She had left the window wide open, and she could see into the garden. The lawn looked eerie in the half-dark. A black blur whizzed in front of her and a howl filled the air. She swatted the apparition, missed, and hit the rack. Sending it and the glasses it contained flying across the kitchen floor. The sound they made was much more impressive than the plates or cutlery. The black cat, which had paused momentarily on the kitchen sideboard, was terrified. It leapt back out of the window and across the lawn. Hilda had always found that cats cause such havoc. She looked at the floor. What a mess the cat had caused. Seeing that she had frightened off the ghostly apparition, or rather the cat. Hilda walked on through the kitchen. A sensor high in the corner flickered. She entered the hallway, still calling out. This was like playing hide and seek. She almost felt like shouting 'boo!'

It was the most excitement she had enjoyed in ages. She must repeat this game soon. Karl might disagree once he saw the damage.

***

Outside, Pearl was wondering what Hilda was doing and considering going around the back to find out. When a hand gripped her shoulder and she screamed. A security guard said, 'Can you explain who you are, and why you're here?'

Pearl span around, still shaking. Once she saw the uniform and that there were two security personnel before her. A man and a woman. She calmed down a bit. Then said 'I, I, well, Pearl.'

'Well, Pearl, are you related to Karl Dansk?' said the male security officer. He towered over her.

It was at this point that Hilda opened the front door and said, 'No one's home, it's all clear. You can come in now. Though a cat's broken a few things in the kitchen.'

The two security officers stared at Hilda and the woman said, 'And you are?'

'And I am what, dear?' asked Hilda. She blinked hard. There was a strong streetlight behind the lady.

'Your name?' said the woman. She was reaching for some pepper spray. They could carry nothing else.

'My name? What about it?' asked Hilda. She glanced between Pearl, the man, and the woman. 'Do you want to come in for a sit-down Pearl? You're not looking at all well.'

'What right have you to enter Mr Dansk's house, madame?' asked the man. He drew himself up to his full six feet five inches.

'Mr Dansk? Oh, you mean Karl, well, his kitchen window was open. So, I climbed in,' said Hilda.

'Breaking and entering,' said the man. He grabbed his radio. Then Pearl said, 'Hang on, Hilda doesn't mean it that way.'

'Don't I?' said Hilda. She looked puzzled. 'Mind you, there was a ghost...'

'Hilda!' said Pearl.

'What?' said Hilda innocently.

Pearl turned back around to the security officers, she held her hand's palm out, and said, 'We are Karl's friends. He is meant to be directing a musical tonight. We came here to find him.'

It took a bit more convincing and some showing of ID before the security officers believed them. Karl had a silent alarm and employed a company to monitor it. They locked his house. Securing the kitchen window and allowing Pearl and Hilda to clear up the broken glass and plates. Then, after a few stern words to Hilda, they left.

Hilda stood outside Karl's house and looked at Pearl, and said, 'now what? Where can he be?' The sun had totally gone, and they were standing in the pool of light cast by a streetlight.

'First thing, tell the group. Maybe we could run the practice tonight?' said Pearl.

'Oh, I don't think so. There are some new bits to be sorted,' said Hilda.

A man walked by with his dog. He stared at the two women standing by the streetlamp. Hilda and Pearl headed back to the club with the news. Most people had already given up and left. A few stalwarts remained. The practice that night was called off. Karl still hadn't returned the next day or for the next three days. Everyone was getting worried. Especially Lilly. This was the last hope for the club. She had pleaded with the trustees for this last chance. Now everything was falling apart.

Chapter Sixteen

September 1998

Hidden Gardens Tearoom, Plympton-on-Sea, UK

Hilda and Pearl returned home and had a fitful night's sleep. Hilda dreamt of dancing in a park. There was a brass band, but all the musicians were animals. The trumpeters were foxes, an elephant played saxophone, and a bear trombone. A tiger on tuba, of course. None of this seemed unusual in a dream. Hilda was dancing with her husband Arthur; he was a teddy bear. Well, you'd expect that. Pearl was there dancing with a long-lost friend. As Hilda danced by the bandstand, she noticed Karl was conducting the brass band. He turned to her and nodded. Hilda spotted Lillian dancing, gliding beautifully around. It mesmerised Hilda. Then Lillian turned into a bird and flew away.

Hilda found herself in the Hampton Court maze. All the hedges were pink. She was in the centre alone and could hear Lillian calling to Karl in bird song. She flew down and landed near him. He was calling for her. Lillian transformed back into herself.

Hilda was in the air looking down as Lillian and Karl tried to navigate the maze; trying desperately to find each other. But they kept getting lost and going the opposite way. Next, Hilda found herself in the maze again, and she felt lost. She had a sense she needed to find someone - but didn't know who. Intense sadness hit her, and she shouted, 'Arthur, Arthur!' The sense of loss increased, and tears filled her eyes. She ran through the maze, trying to find Arthur. But he was gone. She shouted even louder, 'Arthur, Arthur, Arthur.' A hand was shaking her, and she woke staring up through tear-filled eyes at Pearl.

'Are you alright?' asked Pearl.

Hilda's tears formed rivulets down her cheek. It took her a while to realise that she had been dreaming. But as she woke more fully, she said, 'I know where to look for Karl.'

Pearl patted Hilda's hand and said, 'it was just a dream.' But Hilda sat up in bed and wiped her eyes. 'I mean it, I really know where Karl is.'

'But dreams...,' started Pearl.

Hilda cut her off, saying, 'this dream was about an actual place we used to visit.'

As Hilda was adamant, they bought tickets on the next train to London. Taking overnight bags just in case it took them a while to find Karl. That was Pearl being sensible. Hilda just wanted to rush out of the door. What they hadn't planned on were train cancellations. This was a time of many cancellations. They sat in the station most of the day. When they eventually got on a train, it only went part way, and they had another long wait. All due to major signalling errors on the line. As they waited on the platform, Hilda remembered back to 1978. 'Where was an amateur train driver when you needed one,' she thought. A man in a smart suit walked by. She shook her head, 'no, those days are gone.'

The Foremost Inn Hotel, London, UK

On finally reaching London, Hampton Court would only have been open for another hour. It would take longer than that to get there. So, they travelled part way and found a hotel. Pearl negotiated a last-minute deal for a twin room, bed, and breakfast.

Pearl did not find sharing a twin room with Hilda a restful experience. The snoring was the least of her problems. Hilda went to sleep late, woke early, and she snored noisily. Add to that the fact that her idea of unwinding before sleep was to chat. Pearl was exhausted by the morning.

They were both hungry and ready for a full English breakfast. The hotel served an 'all you could eat' breakfast. You served yourself. Hilda licked her lips as they made their way to the counter. After filing their plates, Hilda put food in her bag. That soon filled up. Hilda passed things to Pearl. She then got another muffin in her own bag. Pearl had walked away. Hilda caught called her back and said, 'Shove that in your bag.' Passing her another croissant. It was the fifth.

'I don't think we're meant to do this,' said Pearl. She glanced around, red-faced.

'Nonsense, it says all you can eat breakfast,' said Hilda.

Both of their bags were now nearly at full capacity. But Hilda was trying to squash a few things down and asking Pearl to do the same. One of the hotels serving staff had watched them for a while. At first, she ignored the two old ladies. But this was becoming extreme. She walked over to Hilda and was about to speak, when Hilda saw her and said, 'Ah, I'm glad you're here, you've run out of yoghurts.'

'I've come over to ask you to stop,' said the staff member.

'Stop? Stop?' said Hilda. 'I beg your pardon, young lady; I think I've misheard you.' She picked up another pat of butter and tried to fit it in her bag.

Pearl tried to slink away, but Hilda grabbed her arm and said, 'My friend, Pearl and I are doing nothing that needs to stop. Are we Pearl?' Pearl stared at the staff member, open-mouthed. 'You see, my friend agrees.'

'You're filling your bags with food. I've been watching from over there,' said the staff member. 'One or two bits is common, but you are packing them to capacity.'

'Absolutely, we have, and I would like to carry on. If you fetch those yoghurts. Then I can ask that kind young man at the hot counter to load my plate with sausages, hash brown, eggs, beans, and bacon,' said Hilda. 'Have you got any spare bags out the back I can use?'

'I don't think you understand,' said the assistant. She looked around for a manager.

'It's you who doesn't understand. I want to fill lots of bags with all I can eat. As your advertising says,' said Hilda. She pointed at a poster on the wall.

'We have an all you can eat, breakfast. Not an all you can possibly carry,' said the staff member. She looked pleased with herself. She even smiled.

'Don't you get clever with me. My mother always said, "it takes a wise man to know what he…" That's not it. "Many a fool takes…." no, that's wrong. "It takes a wise fool to…" no, no, that's not right, I know. "It takes a wise man to know what he doesn't know." Was that it? Anyway, you know what I mean?' said Hilda, nodding firmly.

The assistant looked at Hilda and said, 'I'm not trying to be clever. Our rules are that you can eat as much as you like.

But you can't just fill your bag to overflowing.' She saw a manager at a distance and waved. He was looking in the wrong direction.

'Ah, but this is how much I can eat today and maybe tomorrow. Is there a problem with your arm?' asked Hilda.

'But you're not eating it,' said the assistant, looking frustrated. You're emptying the contents of the sideboard into your bags. She gave up on waving at the manager.

'It's how much I can eat over the next day or two, dear; it will do me lunch and tea, maybe tomorrow's breakfast,' said Hilda.

'But, but, that's just not, no, that's not it,' said the staff member. Turning puce.

'I am only a poor pensioner; my friend Pearl is even poorer,' said Hilda. She pointed towards Pearl, who had walked fifteen feet away. 'You're penniless, aren't you, dear?'

'No, I'm not and don't drag me into this,' said Pearl as she moved further away.

'Well anyway,' said Hilda. She did a stage whisper. 'She gets a bit confused.' Pearl looked cross. 'I'm certainly a poor pensioner.' Hilda looked at the staff member over her glasses, and said, 'and I can only afford one meal a day. Are you really going to begrudge me food?' Hilda put on her best pathetic look.

Several other customers at nearby tables had overheard. They were looking from the staff member to Hilda. They did not seem pleased. It was hard to tell if they were cross with the disturbance or the big hotel chain starving a poor pensioner. The staff member decided it might be the latter. She gave up and said, 'just this once. But please don't make a habit of it.'

'Right O. Now if you could just fetch those yoghurts, one of each flavour, and that carrier bag if you have it. I'll order my second full English,' said Hilda. She headed to the hot counter, leaving a bewildered staff member staring after her. 'Oh, and can I have four more of those mini cereal packets?' Hilda shouted over her shoulder.

The rest of the customers went back to their meals. Some shaking their heads, others planning to increase their own daytime top ups. Pearl had already returned to their table to await Hilda. After a few minutes, Hilda joined her with a plate piled high. It contained five sausages, four rashers of bacon, three hash browns, three eggs, four tomatoes and beans. On a side plate were five slices of toast. She looked at the space in front of Pearl and asked, 'Where's your full English dear?' Pearl just shook her head, muttering, 'Bless your belly.'

A little later, after their small repast. Hilda and Pearl set off to Hampton Court. The place where Hilda felt sure they would find Karl.

***

Hilda and Pearl arrived at Hampton Court and paid for the entry. Hilda kept complaining of a stomach ache. But Pearl had little sympathy after all she had eaten. As they strolled through the extensive grounds, it brought back memories for Hilda. Plus, it took her mind off how full she felt.

***

Walking through the grounds transported Hilda back to the late 1940's, just after the war. When the four friends used to picnic there. This was after Pearl had moved away. Hilda remembered one hot Saturday afternoon in the summer of 1949 when all four of them had been sitting under an oak tree. They were glad of the shade. Hardly a puff of wind cooled them. Bits of twigs and insects kept dropping onto their food from the tree above. Lillian was upset about it. In Hilda's eyes, she was always delicate and fussy. Karl had joked about the insects adding to the delights of their meal. Lillian stormed off. Arthur told Karl to go after her and eventually he did. But he couldn't find her, so Hilda and Arthur joined the search. Hilda suggested they try the maze. She was right. Lillian had taken refuge in the maze but got lost. When they eventually found her, she was sitting in the centre, having tried to find her way out a few times. She was sobbing. But so pleased to see them all. That hot and memorable day Lillian had told them all, 'We should never lose touch with each other. This is special, what we have.' Then she had an idea and called them 'The Fabulous Four.' They had all shouted, 'The fabulous four!' Over and over.

Karl had got so carried away with the moment that he got down on one knee, in the centre of the maze, and proposed to Lillian. Arthur congratulated him, saying, 'Well old man, you'll be joining us, old married men.' They all felt so close in that place. It was a special feeling, a significant place. They knew it would last forever. The optimism and energy of youth. Nothing had turned out as they planned. Arthur died three years later. Karl and Lillian drifted apart from Hilda. After that, Hilda had entered years of boring work to make ends meet.

***

Now Hilda was back at Hampton Court, and the memories were coming back. Hilda was not one for soppy sentimentality. But she felt a sharp pain in her gut as she walked towards the maze with Pearl. Arriving at the entrance, Hilda felt a fluttering inside. As if she had drunk a fizzy drink. They entered the maze. The high green hedging encompassing them, shutting out the early morning sun. They shivered as they entered. The shadowed interior of the maze felt cold. Hilda had to stop. Pearl said, 'are you alright? You look so white. Is it the cold?' Hilda shook her head. She was just feeling the power of memory, the emotions of loss, and the sense of place. It transported her back over the years, to experiences she had long forgotten. These were things Hilda never dwelt on or processed. They hit all at once and with tremendous force, bringing her to a stop. All strength drained from her, and she felt that she could have collapsed onto the floor. Instead, she bent forward and held her knees. After a few minutes, Hilda said, 'onwards!' She marched on, full of vigour, her old self. Maybe not fully her old self.

Hilda had hoped that her memory of the maze from years earlier would come back, and they would walk straight to the centre. That didn't happen. They must have gone up every blind alley. Even ending up back outside at one point. But eventually they found the centre. Karl was not sitting there awaiting their arrival. Just a young couple, enjoying the seclusion as Hilda and the others had once done. The young couple looked up at the unwelcome intrusion. They drew apart, got up and left arm in arm. Hilda and Pearl sat and rested.

Hilda claimed she heard it first. But Pearl was the first to say, 'is that crying?'

They followed the noise and found a dark lump on the grass behind a bench. Drawing closer, they discovered a heavy coat covering a person on the ground. Hilda whispered. 'Karl?'

The crying stopped, and the coat moved.

Leithly Hall, Somershire, UK

A Prime Minister is also a local Member of Parliament for a constituency. Prime Minister Nicholas Martin was the MP of Somershire and in attendance at a party fundraising event. It was being held at the home of one of his greatest supporters, Jayne, The Duchess of Somershire. The same duchess, whose diamonds Hilda had rescued the year before. Nicholas, or Nick as his friends knew him, was standing on the terrace, drinking wine. Something he did rather a lot of. He was alone. Earlier, he had been inside and surrounded by sycophants. Now he was escaping for a breath of fresh air and a peaceful drink. His security detail stood at a distance.

The Duchess walked out of the house and across to Nick. She said, 'Enjoying yourself?'

'Absolutely,' slurred Nick, in a very un-prime minister-like fashion. He walked towards a bench. Was that a stagger? His sixth glass of wine arrived, and he took a bigger slug of it than from his previous glass.

Jayne looked at him, shook her head, then asked, 'What are you doing about the tearoom issue?'

'The tearoom issue, the tearoom issue, the tearoom issue,' chanted Nick, in a sing-song voice. 'What tearoom issue?' Nick seemed to wake up. He shook his head and stepped heavily to one side. Then sat on the bench with a thump.

'The lady who recovered my diamonds,' said Jayne. 'Her tearoom. Don't tell me your blasted secretary didn't pass on my message.' She looked down at Nick seriously.

'Oh that,' said Nick, rather offhandedly, wafting his glass free hand and spilling some of its contents. 'Yes, I got the message. I am the Prime Minister, you know. I don't have time for things like that. So, I passed it on.' He had finished his drink and was showing a nearby server that he wanted another.

'Who too?' asked Jayne. Her eyes locked on Nicks'.

'Kerridge,' said Nick. His drink arrived promptly, and he grabbed it on the second try.

'Kerridge!' shouted Jayne. 'You give him things that you want to forget about.'

'You mean it's important?' asked Nick. He appeared to be trying to focus on Jayne but failing.

'Put it this way, you're here to raise funds for your re-election campaign. I think you might get a few pounds from some people here. Correct me if I'm mistaken. I am your principal contributor?' said Jayne, already aware of the answer. She took a sip of her drink and looked at her garden. Then she looked back at Nick. 'On a completely different topic. This poor old lady rescued my diamond, and I would hate her to lose her home. So, if you could help her...'

'Right, got you, priority number one.' The PM stood up, steadied himself, and then called one of his assistants over. 'Get me the Attorney General on the phone.' He hiccupped and then giggled.

'Do you mean the car phone, sir?' asked the assistant. He didn't seem surprised by the condition his boss was in.

'You can use my office phone,' said Jayne, smiling. The PM laughed and walked a wobbly line towards the house.

Hampton Court, London, UK

While Hilda's legal problems were being talked about by the highest in the land. She and Pearl were sitting on a bench in the centre of The Hampton Court maze. A rather unkempt Karl was sitting on the next bench. They had asked him to sit downwind and at a distance on account of the smell. He had been sleeping rough for a couple of days.

'I remembered about this place,' said Hilda. She stared at Karl.

Karl tried to focus on her through red-rimmed watery eyes. 'Lillian was my life.'

'I know dear,' said Hilda. She felt a pang a pain as she spoke. 'She was unique. The two of you changed my life.'

'I'm so sorry we weren't there when you needed us most,' said Karl. He got up and walked over to Hilda, stooped, and hugged her. They both cried. Pearl looked awkward as she sat next to Hilda. She got up and walked around the centre section of the maze.

Karl and Hilda stayed hugging for a while. Then they sat in silence. In her mind, it transported Hilda back to that same place fifty years earlier. The optimism of youth. The four of them, planning an unknown future. All the trips they would take. How they would both have lots of children. Live next door to each other. Their kids grow up together and maybe even marry. A fairy tale and, like all fairy tales, the wicked witches of time, illness, death, and reality tore it down.

Hilda didn't dwell on failure, pain, and distress. Her happy endings were not fairy tales, but hard work and pushing forward with a joyous nature. She felt the pain of lost opportunities. She felt loss and grief. Just as she had done so many times before. But just as she always did. Hilda did not wallow in that sadness. Or stay in darkness. She didn't allow the weight of sorrow to crush and destroy her. Hope bubbled up within her, and she stood. Taking Karl's hand, she said, 'Lillian and Arthur would want us to keep on living. I have a motto. That I will live until I die. Join me in that. I don't give up.'

Karl looked up at her. The glint of life and joy shone through her tears. He gripped Hilda's hand and stood, at first shakily but then firmly. Then he said, 'you're right, I can almost hear your Arthur say, pull yourself together old man' He took a deep breath. 'I *will* live until I die. I haven't been living these last eight years.' He smiled. 'I'm so glad I bumped into you again, Hilda.'

It drizzled. Hilda looked at the sky, then at Karl and said, 'Lillian would say if you can't smile in the rain, when can you smile?'

Karl gulped, and choked back a tear. Then straightened up and said, 'Hilda, Pearl, we have a musical to put on.'

Arm in arm, the three of them walked out of the maze. Well, they tried to. It took them several attempts, but eventually, they made it to the exit. It's only in fiction that things go really smoothly.

Early October 1998

Meedham and Plympton Canal Basin, Meedham, UK

On the same morning that Hilda and Pearl were finding Karl, Josh Shilton and his girlfriend Beth were walking down the canal in Meedham. They saw only beauty. With cameras around their necks and smiles on their faces, they viewed a scene invisible to others. There is an expression about only having eyes for each other. It must have applied to them.

The canal they were walking down was the same one that can be seen from the boardroom of TSU Plc. At least it would be visible if they pulled the blinds up. Old tyres and shopping trolleys littered the canal itself. Potholes made the towpath a trial to traverse. Although they were hard to spot, because much of the path was overrun with weeds and unkempt bushes. The once busy and vibrant industry on the canal banks was now tumbled down wrecks. Yet as Josh and Beth walked hand in hand, they appeared to be in paradise. Beholding each other, more than the scenery. Now and then they would stop and take photos of a now defunct lock or a few reeds. It seemed almost incidental to their reason for being there. They were oblivious to the puddles of muddy water that passed for a canal. Looking at their faces, it was apparent that they saw a different scene. A vision of paradise. If only their perception could have been captured on paper for those planning the canal's revival. It would have motivated the work. Josh and Beth took their beautiful scenery with them and saw what they wanted to see. If all around them had been a desert, they would have seen a field of billowing flowers.

Josh turned to Beth and said, 'I'm so glad I met you.' She blushed and looked at a muddy puddle. Then, gazing into his eyes, she said, 'You're the best thing that ever happened to me.' For a moment, it looked like Josh was going to say something else. Then he gulped, and they walked on in their mutual bliss.

***

William and Louise Shilton's House, Meedham, UK

Is there such a thing as double déjà vu? A feeling that you've felt that you've done something before, twice. A kind of double experience of the memory. Remembering a memory of a memory. Well, if there is then Louise was about to go through it on the Friday after Josh and Beth had wandered down the canal. She arrived home and had a knock on her car window. Except it wasn't William, and she didn't scream. Her son Josh stood, smiling at her car window. William may well have complained that she didn't scream. After all, Josh was doing the same as him a few weeks earlier. But perhaps it was that famous mother's intuition for their children, that prevented the fright. The connection they enjoy that is so unique. Or just the fact that she spotted his car in the drive and saw him get out and walk towards her. Whatever the reason, no screaming occurred to bring their neighbour Ted running.

Opening her car door, Louise said. 'Lovely to see you.' Then she gave Josh a hug.

Their neighbour Ted watched them and smiled. He had no compulsion to phone the police. William might well consider that unfair. But life is not fair, and that is a fact William may have to accept. Once inside, mother and son sat at the kitchen table with a cup of coffee, Josh looked thoughtful.

'It's lovely to see you, but I have a feeling you're here for a reason,' said Louise. She sipped her coffee and waited.

Josh was silent for a while and then said, 'How do you know if someone is right?'

'A girl?' asked Louise. She stared intensely at her son.

'A woman.'

'I think it just feels right. What's she like?' Louise smiled at her son.

Josh let out a long breath and then looked at his mum. 'Wonderful, like no one I've ever met before.' He sighed. Then got up and paced around the kitchen.

'Pretty?' asked Louise.

Josh stopped pacing and stared at his mum. 'Does that matter?... I'm surprised you asked. But yes, very, and funny too. I just can't help smiling when I'm with her. I don't want to be apart. We'd be together now, but she's working.' He continued pacing.

'What does she do?' asked Louise. She followed her son with her eyes.

Josh spoke as he walked. 'She's a carer, at Tall Trees nursing home. She loves caring for people. Her mum had to go in there after a serious stroke. She so enjoyed visiting and helping that she changed her plans.'

'Plans?'

Josh stopped again and looked at his mum. 'She was on a teacher training course. Then her mum got ill. Decided to get a job at the home her mum was in. So found it fulfilling and stayed.'

'Sounds a wonderful girl... sorry woman,' said Louise, smiling.

Josh sat back down. He sipped his coffee, then said, 'You'll get to meet her. But not yet.'

'Whenever you're ready.'

After Josh had left, Louise sat in the kitchen for a while staring into her now empty cup. William came home a little later than usual for a Friday. He was flustered and said, 'Sorry, I know it's date night, but being a director, they are putting more work on me at the moment.'

Louise just nodded and told him dinner would be delayed. William reminded her they ate out on a Friday. She seemed distracted, got up, and went upstairs to shower and change. William had changed long before she was ready. At the restaurant, when they were eating their dessert, Louise said, 'Our little boy is growing up.'

'You've just noticed,' said William, snorting.

'Not physically,' said Louise, playfully punching William on the shoulder.

'Ouch,' said William.

'I hardly touched you,' said Louise.

Louise said to William, 'I meant, he has a serious girlfriend. Sounds like he's in love.'

William stared at Louise and said, 'Really? He didn't say anything to me.'

Louise smiled and looked at her glass of wine. She held it up, ready to chink glasses, and said, 'to our son, growing into a man.'

'Our son.' William chinked glasses with Louise.

William and Louise were still at the restaurant chatting about the prospect of their family growing. They were even planning grandchildren. Leaping a lot of steps and making many assumptions.

Plympton Playhouse, Plympton-on-Sea, UK

Karl, Hilda, and Pearl had made it back to Plympton from London. The Plympton Players were relieved to see Karl back, especially Lilly. They were ready for the final full dress run-through of Karl's musical. Members of the Plympton Players were up on the stage in full costume. This was a full-dress rehearsal. Karl was in the auditorium near the front. There were a couple of club members dotted around in the auditorium, ones who had either not wanted or not been chosen for parts. They were all interested to see how it went. Some might say that they were hoping to see another disaster. But the only two that would really apply to were Gary and Caz. They had gone off to visit her parents, having chosen not to be around.

Karl had the club member with the injured leg sitting next to him. She would act as prompt and take notes. After much debate on the merits and disadvantages of live over recorded music, they opted for a live band. Karl had called on old contacts in the industry to come and play. After much chasing around and persuasion, they had agreed, seeing it as a charitable act, to save the theatre. The eclectic group of musicians had never played together as one group and lacked practice. But Karl was optimistic that their professionalism would overcome all problems.

***

Gathering the group of musicians had been more complicated than Karl expected, and he was glad he started it a few weeks earlier. When Karl had phoned his old friend guitarist, Purple Knight, he was in the UK on a tour. Karl caught him backstage after an argument with his stage manager. The timing was perfect. The stage manager was getting very stressed by Purple Knights' staging requirements and was not a patient man. The manager was at the end of his tether that evening. Purple Knight walked out from a practice and complained about everything. The lighting was too dim, the pyrotechnics unimpressive, the centre section of the stage, was not high enough, speakers were not big enough. Even the colour they had painted the set was not purple enough. So, it went on. In the end, the stage manager said, 'And you're not good enough.' Before storming off.

Purple Knights' agent and manager were trying to find a replacement ready for the next night. No one wanted to work with him. He was known as a temperamental and unreasonable rock star. Almost a requirement, you would think. At that point, Karl had called, singing his praises, and telling him how wonderful he was. It was the ego boost he needed. He agreed to help Karl straight away. Fortunately, the dates of the show coincided with gaps in his tour schedule.

***

When Karl tried to track down bassist Jura, that proved tricky. No one had seen him for six months. Karl tried some other bassists he knew. They were busy. One of them knew where Jura could be found. He had bought a small Scottish Island and was living there, almost as a hermit. Karl called in a favour from a friend in Scotland, who owned a private helicopter. After a train ride to Scotland, they set off to the island onboard the helicopter. A quick hop across from the airport to the island. When they arrived, there wasn't much sign of habitation, apart from a wind turbine and a basic hut. But as they came into land, a man ran out from the hut and waved at them. He was shouting, but once they landed, and Karl had the door open, they could hear him.

'Clear off! Private island,' he shouted.

Karl could just make out Jura's distinctive demeanour. Despite his beard, long hair, and rough clothing. Karl got out of the helicopter and walked towards Jura, saying, 'it's me, Jura, Karl.'

Jura stared at him and then walked closer, and said, 'Karl?'

After an emotional welcome, they sat and chatted in the small and basic shelter. Jura was adamant he would never leave the island. He would die there. He had given up on modern life with all its trappings.

'I hate to do this, old friend,' said Karl. He took a deep breath. 'But I'm calling it in. Garth Lodge, Sept 5th, 1963.'

'No, you promised you'd never call that in,' said Jura. He was wild-eyed and looked around. The helicopter pilot had gone for a walk. No one was in earshot.

'I need your help desperately, just as you needed mine that night. You said, Any Time, Any Place,' said Karl. He sat forward on a wooden bench. Jura perched on a very basic cot type bed.

'You said you did it as a mate,' said Jura, standing up. His head almost touched the curved corrugated steel roof.

'I did, but now I need your help... as a mate,' said Karl. He stood next to Jura and put his arm on his shoulder.

As the helicopter lifted off, it had three passengers. The island was empty. A few rabbits came out and stared at the disappearing noisy aircraft. After the aircraft had gone, they bounced around the open grass, occasionally stopping for a nibble.

***

The legendary drummer, Lionheart, was in a terrible mood when Karl phoned. The tax man had sent him an enormous bill. Just before the call, he had been complaining to his cleaner. She had responded sympathetically. But hearing about a tax bill for more than she might earn in a lifetime must have been hard. Lionheart had employed her on less than minimum wage because she didn't have the right immigration papers.

'Lionheart? It's Karl.'

'Karl who?' said Lionheart. As he held the phone to his ear, he noticed a patch of his deep shagpile carpet the cleaner had missed. He pointed to it. She shrugged and unwound the cable on the vacuum cleaner again.

'Don't be daft,' said Karl. He was sitting in front of his fire, in his cottage. 'Karl Dansk, of course.'

'Yeah well, not in a great mood today. Dunno why I live in this godforsaken country. They tax the life out of me,' said Lionheart. The cleaner started up the vacuum. It was noisy. He said to her, 'Hang on a minute. I can't hear myself think.'

'But you told me...,' started the cleaner. Then she just gave up, switched off the vacuum and went off to the kitchen to clear up.

'You got someone there?' asked Karl.

'Just the cleaner,' said Lionheart. He watched her head to the kitchen.

'If you have a big tax bill, my timing is excellent,' said Karl, staring into his fire. 'I think you can claim charitable gigs against tax.'

'Tell me more,' said Lionheart. He looked down at his recent tax demand.

'Chat to your accountant,' said Karl, smiling.

The thought of saving money had convinced Lionheart to be charitable. The three major artists joined a few lesser-known ones that Karl knew. He had formed a decent ad hoc group. They even practised before the event. It wasn't perfect, but Karl was sure it would be alright on the night.

***

The Overture

The band tried out the overture, and Karl was right it worked well. Their professionalism was winning through. No one could see the guitarist Purple Knight stick his tongue out at his ex-band member, bassist Jura. He'd fallen out with him over copyright issues years ago. Jura himself was far too preoccupied with missing his island. The drummer, Lionheart, was free to pull all the faces he wanted; hidden behind his partition.

Pulling faces was always what he did best. All such antics would be invisible on the night. After the practice was over, Purple Knight was planning on telling Karl that he needed a better place to play. He was too squashed in for a star of his calibre. Despite everything, the run through of the musical got underway.

Act One – Scene One

It was a typical musical. The opening scene had most of the cast on stage for a rip-roaring, toe-tapping number. It had a rhythmic beat and a repetitive refrain. The number was designed to get the audience clapping along, in their heads, if not physically. The words 'Fantastic Four' repeated far more times than seemed helpful or strictly necessary. What was happening wasn't immediately obvious and appeared to bear no relation to the rest of the story. It was almost as if it was only there to open the show dramatically, rather than being part of the plot. Anyone who has seen a West End musical would recognise the style. As if they all begin the same. A slight variation of tune and some different words.

Dancers leapt over each other and around the stage. The club had invited members from a local dance and gymnastics group to enable such scenes. Hilda had aspired to be a person leaping. But common sense had prevailed; eventually. But only after a lot of arguments and even then, Hilda had tried very hard to sneak on stage. Actors slid across the stage at speed. They spun around each other and created human towers, some of which had people leaping over each other from hidden trampolines. Actors on wires flew across the stage. Lines of people marched, danced, leapt, pranced, and span their way around the stage at dizzying speed. The overall spectacle was a sight to behold. It was meant to be. This was the grand opening number. Designed to grab the attention of the audience. Wow, them and make them say, 'That was amazing.' As Hilda thought back to her accidental but very enjoyable time on the Broadway stage. She couldn't understand why Karl had not allowed her to dance in this opening number. But that dance piece was less acrobatic than this one.

Karl had brought in a West End choreographer to organise the dancing and she had let her imagination run riot. Karl had given her more freedom than she had ever experienced, and she used it to the full. She complained that the stage may not be big enough. She need not have worried; the Plympton Stage was almost as large as a professional stage. The major limitations were the lack of space for the many scenery flats and a small backstage area. But ingenuity and skill overcame everything. The choreographer would not let such a marvellous opportunity pass her by. She found a way around every limitation. It was just as well that the musical didn't require a full-sized helicopter-like 'Miss Saigon,' which may have tested the ingenuity of even the best brain there.

Karl and his helper nodded their head in satisfaction at the end of scene one. They gave the actors a rousing round of applause. The other club members dotted around joined in and even shouted out some hurrahs.

Karl and the other people watching sat in awe as the actors, dancers, and singers performed. They laughed, they clapped, and they even cried. During the break, which was placed where an interval would be in the actual live show, Karl went backstage. He wanted to congratulate everyone and encourage them. But Hilda grabbed him and took him to one side. She had an issue with how little she was in it. 'As the musical is all about me,' she said. 'Not just you, remember?' said Karl.

'Yes, I know dear, but you are directing. Young Dereck is playing you. I must say he is rather better looking than you,' said Hilda.

'Oh, do you think so?' asked Karl.

'Well, yes, he is a very handsome young man,' said Hilda. They both watched the talked about young man as he passed them. He did look rather well built and chisel-jawed.

'I suppose so,' said Karl.

'Anyway, my point is that as I am the only one of the original Fabulous Four in the musical. There really ought to be more of me in it,' said Hilda.

'But Hilda,' said Karl. He glanced at the floor. 'How do I put this? I set most of the musical in the past. When you were well... younger.'

Hilda drew herself up to her full height, and looked up at Karl and said, 'are you suggesting I am too old to play myself?'

Karl pulled a few very odd faces and said, 'I suppose I am.' He then walked off to chat to some other actors. Hilda watched him go. She looked as if he had slapped her.

Act Three – Scene Four

The final scene of the last act was ending. Even though he had written it, Karl had an expression of joy and a few tears. As the last words were spoken, he leapt to his feet and shouted, 'Bravo!' then clapped passionately. The other people watching were also standing, shouting, and clapping. After Karl had recovered his composure, he went backstage again, this time making sure he avoided Hilda. He addressed the company of actors, saying, 'that was brilliant. Do it like that Monday night and we will have a runaway success.' Let's hope he is correct.

Chapter Seventeen

Mid-October 1998

Hidden Garden Tearoom, Plympton-on-Sea, UK

After the show's rehearsal, Karl joined Pearl and Hilda at their flat. They were sitting down to a takeaway meal of fish and chips. Merlin was showing great interest in the fish, so Pearl got up and gave him his tea early. Hilda had forgiven Karl for his rudeness about her age earlier; she was not one to hold grudges. Hilda also reasoned that it was too late to increase the parts she played in the musical. Fish and chips were a treat she always enjoyed, and she decided it would make a wonderful celebration meal. They all ate in silence. Pearl looked at Hilda a few times during the meal. Possibly to make sure she was still alive. Silence and Hilda were not normal companions. But Hilda seemed to be thinking, then she put her empty plate to one side and said, 'This feels like the night before a great battle.' She sat forward on the edge of her seat and thrust her chest forward. 'We are like those knights of old.'

Karl looked at Hilda, his eyes shining. He finished a mouthful of fish and said, 'Sound trumpets! let our bloody colours wave! And either victory or else a grave.'

'I beg your pardon!' said Hilda. She stared at Karl. 'Go and wash your mouth out with soap, young man.'

'It's a quote from Shakespeare, Henry VI,' said Karl. His face looked like a cooked lobster.

'I don't care if your mate Henry Shakespeare said it or not, we don't allow swearing in this house, do we, Pearl?' said Hilda, nodding towards Pearl.

'He wasn't swearing,' said Pearl. 'He was quoting from the bard.'

'I know,' said Hilda. She stared seriously at Karl, 'and he should keep that kind of language for the bar.'

'The Bard, not the bar,' said Pearl. She had finished her meal and was getting up to clear the plates away.

Karl sat on the edge of his seat and said, 'Yes Hilda, William Shakespeare, our nation's famous writer and poet.'

'You really ought to make these things clear, you know,' said Hilda, handing her empty plate to Pearl. 'Rather than talking about your mate, Henry.'

'Anyway,' said Karl. 'I was agreeing with you. It feels like the night before a great battle. All our troops are sleeping.'

Hilda looked at her watch and said, 'it's only half past seven dear.'

'Metaphorically speaking,' said Karl, shaking his head.

Hilda looked puzzled; Pearl clattered about at the kitchen end of the room. This disturbed Merlin, who had fallen asleep after his tea. He stretched and strolled through to join Pearl in the kitchen.

Hilda got up and went to switch on the kettle and get out the cups to make a hot drink. Karl walked to the kitchen area and stood watching them and said, 'Give me the cups; And let the kettle to the trumpet speak, The trumpet to the cannoneer without, The cannons to heavens, the heavens to earth.'

Hilda looked across at him and said, 'You really say some very odd things. Are you quite alright?'

'Shakespeare again,' said Karl. He looked out of the window with a dreamy expression.

'Not your friend Henry again, is it?' said Hilda. Pearl was shaking her head.

'Hamlet,' said Karl, wafting a hand.

Once the drinks had been made. The three of them returned to their seats and sat again in silence. Hilda daydreamed about the coming day. She was dressed as a knight in shining armour. As she rode up to the stage on her magnificent stead, her page was waiting. He held the horse while she gracefully dismounted. Climbing easily onto the stage, Hilda found the cast of the musical awaiting her arrival. They were lined up in two rows, on either side of her. She took her place in the centre. Her silver armour dazzled in the spotlight. The music started and Hilda easily sprang and pranced around the stage. It was as if the armour weighed nothing. She leapt over towers of people, slid under their legs, and flew in the air on a wire. This was it, the role she was meant to have, that she had argued for. Even in heavy armour, she could easily do it. Why had they said no? As Hilda pictured herself flying across the stage in gleaming armour, she heard voices of adulation saying, 'Hilda, Hilda, Hilda.' They wanted more of her. Obviously, she was right. She should appear more in the musical. The voices grew louder. 'Hilda, Hilda, Hilda!' Then it seemed to become one voice, 'Hilda, Hilda,' said Pearl.

Hilda jumped a little on her chair and said, 'Oh, yes, what was that?'

'You were asleep, it was just as well your cup was empty,' said Pearl. She was standing next to Hilda, looking down at her.

'I never sleep early in the evening,' said Hilda. She stared at her empty cup, which she was holding at an extreme angle.

'Yes, well, while you were fully awake and snoring, I have been repeatedly telling you that Karl is leaving,' said Pearl. Karl was near the door.

'I heard you,' said Hilda, getting up. 'I was just thinking, that's all.' She headed towards Karl.

'It's been so good to be here with you both. See you tomorrow,' said Karl.

'We will win the battle,' said Hilda.

'It'll be a great show,' said Pearl.

Karl thanked them again, gave each a hug, and left.

Plympton Playhouse, Plympton-on-Sea, UK

There's an old saying, 'It'll be alright on the night.' Normally, people say it because a dress rehearsal has gone wrong. The assumption is that adrenaline will give actors the extra oomph they need to give a brilliant performance. As The Plympton Players and all the extra people Karl had enlisted gathered for opening night, they worried that the last rehearsal had been so good. How could they better it? This was not what usually happened.

Karl called everyone together backstage for a chat. He stood up in front and said, 'Don't worry, it will work out.'

Hilda stared at him and shook her head. She walked to the front and said in his ear, 'That's not a pep talk. Let me say something.'

'Thank you, but...,' said Karl. But he might as well have tried to stop an avalanche. No one who knew Hilda would let her loose on public speaking. Karl had seen her try a few times, and he wasn't keen to hear it again. Hearing only the thanks, Hilda turned around and shouted, 'Attention, quieten down.' Having got everyone looking at her, she started her pep talk. 'You all know me and the play that I put on. Well, that didn't work out. But don't let that failure put you off Karl's musical. After all, Karl is not me.'

Pearl saw Hilda talking and walked up to join Karl. They both tried to encourage her to stop. But Hilda continued: 'He doesn't even look like me. But we're good friends. This musical, as you know, is about that friendship... actually it's about the friendship between the four of us. My husband and I, Karl, and his wife.'

Pearl tried telling Hilda to end. Hilda ignored her and said, 'When you put on a show, it's always an anxious time. You think of everything that could go wrong. Well, just look at what happened to mine. That went badly wrong. Anything that could go wrong, did go wrong.' The actors and crew were looking anxious and looked towards the doors. Hilda was undeterred. 'We must carry on, don't give up, the British spirit is...' She spotted that one actor was of Asian origin and remembered she had just arrived, fleeing persecution. 'Sorry Meera, the human spirit, is that appropriate?' Hilda nodded towards Meera and felt pleased with herself. 'Or do I say, international spirit?' Meera looked puzzled. Hilda nodded. 'Alright, the human spirit is to push forward even when things are tough. We don't care if things go wrong, do we?' There was silence. 'Do we?' she shouted louder. A few voices responded, 'no.' So she shouted even louder, 'do we?' More voices joined in, and there were a few claps and cheers.

Pearl turned to Karl and asked, 'Are they clapping and cheering about things going wrong?'

'I have no idea what's happening,' said Karl. He looked at his watch.

The rest of Hilda's pep talk was similarly confused. At the end, people clapped, mainly in joy that it was finally over. They also felt a sense of relief. The musical couldn't be as bad as listening to that pep talk. Which gave a rising sense of hope. Hilda took full credit.

They hustled everyone to their places, and the musical could begin. They played the overture to perfection. Purple Knight behaved himself, no rude gestures. Jura and Lionheart were on form. As the curtain rose, the audience was on the edge of its collective seats. The press was poised, pens in hands. All the cast was on stage in darkness. The opening number was due to begin the moment. It began with a single beat on the bass drum. The beat should then be repeated and build in volume and pace, and all the other instruments would join in, and the lights increase in brightness. But as the cast stood in darkness, no sound came, apart from the first beat and a few coughs and chair squeaks.

Time is extended when you are waiting. Especially when things are awkward. Although Einstein's theory of relativity only talks of space and time. There should be a theory of time in relation to boredom/pain/embarrassment on the one hand. In these instances, time slows. Time in relation to fun/excitement/pleasure on the other hand. In these instances, time speeds up. This well-known, but unscientific theory of time and relativity that was happening at that point. As the cast stood in darkness and silence, time crawled by. If a clock had been on the stage, each second would have taken twenty seconds to pass. The tension was building. The critics' pens hovered over their blank pads. Karl's head sank into his hands.

Then, at last, Lionheart seemed to wake from a trance and hit the follow-on beats. The follow-on beats grew in volume and pace. The whole band joined in; lights rose in brightness as the dancing began. That opening delay was the only error in the entire show. Afterwards, the critics assumed it was a dramatic pause and praised its effectiveness. Karl told Hilda and Pearl; that he was glad it wasn't any longer. His heart could not have taken it.

The show received the most glowing praise any show had ever received at The Plympton Playhouse. There are West End shows that would have envied such reviews. They sold out every night and even had to put on an extra night. This was after a lot of negotiation with Purple Knight, Jura, and Lionheart.

***

After the show's end, a West End producer bought the musical. It ran for many years. Karl gave the substantial proceeds as an endowment to the Plympton Playhouse. Money enough to keep the theatre and the building open. The theatre's future was secure. Potential actors of all ages wanted to join the club.

***

Purple Night's return to his tour was not all as planned. He decided he enjoyed doing charitable work. So, he donated all his earnings and money to a children's charity and then found himself bankrupt. He was then inundated with offers for work. Every tour manager and agent wanted to work with him. His next tour made him richer than he had ever been. He gave half the proceeds to the same charity. They named him as its honorary director. A few years later, he was knighted.

***

When Jura finally returned to his island. He found it too cold and windy. He sold up and went to live in California. There he met and married a movie star. Their marriage lasted six months, and she sued him for half of his net worth. He went to live in a commune in the wilderness, where he found happiness and love. There are possibly apocryphal stories that he fathered three children. What is certain is that the commune became a place of pilgrimage for many Jura fans. One of its members changed it into something more akin to a theme park. Anyone wishing to visit now must book ahead and stay at one of the expensive, yet basic Yurts.

***

Lionheart returned home to find that his cleaner had... cleaned him out - financially. He was foolish enough to leave all his banking passwords and keys to everything around the house.

She escaped to a place without an extradition treaty with the UK. When she cleared out his safe, she took all the jewellery and cash, most of which was undeclared to the taxman. When emptying his bank accounts, she even found the money he'd hidden in offshore accounts away from the UK tax office. He wasn't as broke as he told Karl. At least he wasn't before his cleaner had stolen from him. When the police investigated, they found she was a notorious thief who impersonated cleaners for rich clients. She relied on them, not checking her references. By telling them she was an illegal immigrant and that they could pay her low wages. She had repeated this same scam three times, including him. But Lionheart was her biggest haul. Not that he told the police the total amount stolen. She even stole some art he bought on the black market, no questions asked.

Gary and Caz's House, Meedham, UK

Gary and Caz returned from their three week stay at Caz's parents. Gary had only agreed to go to her parents, to placate Caz, after he lost their savings on the failed attempt to become the new Plympton Players director. She wanted a break away from Plympton and without savings, they couldn't afford a proper holiday.

They had tried to come up with a way to hijack Karl's musical; but failed. Then they were banned from the club once it was realised, they had deliberately messed up the lighting and sets on Hilda's play. They just hoped the musical would flop. It sounded like a crazy idea. Why would anyone go to see it? While they were away, they just tried to forget it.

A pile of letters made it hard to open their front door as Gary pushed at it. He stood the wheeled cases to one side, picked up the post, and then continued inside. Caz walked in behind him, carrying a few loose bags. They both looked weary and, having left the cases and bags in the hall, headed for the front room.

The trip to Caz's parents had not left them refreshed. Gary and his father-in-law clashed. They were both opinionated and strong-willed. Maybe there is something in the notion that you marry a man like your father. The two men spent the holiday arguing. Nothing specific, just everything that they came across. They disagreed over politics. They had different ideas on how to fix a shelf. Caz's father was putting one up when they arrived. Garry had helpful and unwanted suggestions on how to do it. They argued over how to light a barbeque. They even disagreed about driving. After one particularly arduous trip, where Gary was back seat driving; they travelled in two cars on any further trips out. Caz's mum tried to counter the difficulties. She was a kind and caring person who had a knack for smoothing tensions and calming people. Her skills offset several situations that could have been very difficult.

Having left their bags in the hall, they sat on the sofa. Gary said to Caz, 'Aren't you gonna put the kettle on?'

'No,' said Caz. She closed her eyes. Gary huffed, got up, and headed to the kitchen. There was a knock at the front door.

'Why does no one ever ring the doorbell?' Gary said to Caz as he went to answer it. Denis, their neighbour, was standing on the doorstep. He had a pint of milk in his hand and a big grin on his face. He said, 'The moment she saw your car back, the missus, wanted me to pop round with some milk. Reckoned you wouldn't have stopped on the way back from your in-laws.'

Gary looked at the milk and said, 'Thanks, I was just making a cuppa.' He took the milk and started to close the door.

'You won't have heard,' said Denis, grinning. Gary stopped closing the door. Denis' grin continued to grow. His missus had come round herself and was just walking up the driveway. 'Have you told them?' she asked.

'I just got ere. Be patient,' said Denis to his wife. A couple of other helpful neighbours were also walking up the drive. One had a second bottle of milk. Another had a loaf of bread. They were providing more help than was usual after Gary and Caz had been away. Another neighbour was just arriving at the bottom of the drive to tell them he had watched their house while they were away.

Caz heard a lot of voices at the front door and came through to the hallway to investigate. She stood alongside her husband and stared out at the sea of faces and proffered goods. It was hard to make out every individual question. But there was a recurring one that was oft repeated, 'have you heard?'

'Heard what?' asked Gary.

The answer was such a cacophony that it was impossible to discern. Gary said, 'Be quiet! Denis, you tell us.' Denis preened himself, looked around at the gathered group of neighbours, and then back at Gary and Caz. He cleared his throat and said, 'While you were away, Karl put on the musical about Hilda, himself, and their partners. He brought in international stars to do the music. Dancers and acrobats from the local college.'

'They don't need all that bit,' said his wife. 'It was a tremendous success, and they saved the theatre. Plus, they asked Mrs Shilton to be the permanent director.'

'She didn't even direct it neither,' said Denis helpfully.

'You said that already, you told um, Karl did,' said his wife.

'Yeah, but the point is, that Hilda was asked to be director when he didn't want to be,' said Denis.

***

Denis and his wife walked home. He was grumbling to his wife, 'You jumped in with the best bit. I was gonna say it was a success.'

'Never mind that. I thought it was rude that they slammed the door in our faces,' said his wife.

The other helpful neighbours were also walking away, grumbling, and chatting about the ungracious attitude of Gary and Caz.

Dennis stopped and looked behind him and asked, 'What's that noise?'

'You mean the screaming?' said his wife. 'That'll be Gary and Caz getting used to the news.' She cackled in an unneighbourly fashion.

Late October 1998

Hidden Gardens Tearoom, Plympton-on-Sea, UK

A week after Karl's musical finished, the inhabitants of Plympton were thinking the owners of The Hidden Gardens Tearoom must be very famous indeed. Although it was early morning, there was a lot of activity. Parked outside the tearoom was a convoy of important cars and police vehicles. The

Prime Minister of Great Britain had just gone inside with his security contingent. Various other security personnel were positioned outside. A crowd of curious onlookers gathered and were held behind a cordon.

Although the press had not been notified of this unannounced visit. They had heard of it through 'a source' and several press and TV vehicles were positioned nearby. Much speculation was underway as to why the PM was there.

Inside the flat, Pearl was also wondering why she had such an important visitor. She was just offering Prime Minister, Nicholas Martin, a seat. Simultaneously, she pulled her dressing gown tighter around her. Apologising for not being dressed and explaining she knew nothing of the visit, or she would have been ready. The PM waved it off as being of no consequence and said, 'after all, we didn't tell you we were coming.' Then he laughed falsely. He grimaced, presumably a hangover from all the drinking the night before. Pearl didn't look amused. She would probably rather have had some notice.

'Do you know when she'll be back?' asked the PM.

'It varies, but normally about eight,' said Pearl.

The PM looked at his watch and said, 'any time now then.'

Pearl glanced at the clock. 'Maybe. By the way, I think I'll just get dressed.'

'Fine, fine, I don't suppose you have any drink?' asked the PM.

'Oh, I am sorry, what a poor host I am. Shall I make you a tea or coffee?' Pearl started towards the kitchen area.

'No,' said Nick. He glanced at what appeared to be a drinks cabinet and licked his lips. 'I'll be fine.'

While Pearl was in her room getting dressed, Hilda arrived back. There was much commotion downstairs and eventually she burst in saying, 'well I never. You won't believe what's happening outside. Someone manhandled me at my own...' She spotted the PM and asked, 'whoever are you dear? You look a lot like that chap I don't like. The one I didn't vote for...'

Pearl walked in before Hilda could say anymore and said, 'Hilda, may I introduce our Prime Minister the Right Honourable Nicholas Martin?'

'You are him,' said Hilda. She looked disgusted. 'That awful man.'

'As I always say, you can't please all the people all the time,' said the PM. He walked over to greet Hilda. He was holding out a hand for her to shake. She stared at it suspiciously.

'It would be good to please a few of us,' said Hilda. She decided she would rather not give him a handshake. So, she gave him a low five. Something she learnt in America from Chad.

'Oh, that was...' said the PM, moving his hand oddly. 'Well, umm, that's why I'm here to please you. Your friend, the Duchess of Somershire, asked me to help you.'

'Ah, Jayne, that lovely lady. We liked her, didn't we Pearl?' said Hilda. Nods of assent came from Pearl. 'Not sure what you can do, though. You're a friend of hers?' Hilda huffed.

'I gather you have a problem with your lease?' said Nick. He put on his best concerned look. It always played well on TV interviews.

'Do I?' said Hilda, looking puzzled.

'Yes, you do,' said Pearl emphatically. 'You are going to lose the house and tearoom because of some technicality.'

'Oh, that,' said Hilda. She sat on the sofa. 'Something will turn up.'

'It has,' said the PM. He followed Hilda and sat opposite her. 'Me, I've turned up.'

'I meant something good,' said Hilda.

The PM matched the red seat he was sitting on, but said, 'my best people worked on it, and they have found a solution. You won't lose your flat and business. You just need to pay the rent charges.'

'There you go, trying to get my money. Typical of your government. I'm a poor pensioner, you know,' said Hilda.

'Nno, nno,' said Nick, trying to get his words out. 'This is money you owe the leaseholder, not me.'

'I see, blind me with legalise. Then steal my money. Did you know the press is outside? They asked why you were here. I shall just tell them. It's to steal my money,' said Hilda. She got up and headed for the door.

The Prime Minister looked confused. Which is not surprising. He had come to tell Hilda good news, and she was about to tell the press he was trying to steal from her.

'Wait!' The PM shouted. 'I'll personally pay the few hundred pounds owed to the leaseholder.'

'That's very kind of you, dear,' said Hilda. She turned around. 'I might consider voting for you next time.'

'That's sorted then,' said a rather confused PM. 'I've saved your flat and business.'

'There's no need to boast, very unbecoming of a Prime Minister. Well, we must be getting on, a tearoom to open and all. I'm sure you have very little to do and can sit around all day chatting. But we are busy. A woman's work is never done, you know,' said Hilda.

'I am quite busy too,' said the PM in a squeaky voice. Hilda hustled him out of the door. 'I fitted this in especially.' He added. Hilda was unconvinced.

Outside, the PM gave an impromptu press conference. His staff had prepared a statement. The essence of which was that he was acting in a personal capacity in helping the friend of a friend in a legal matter. By the time the press chatted to Hilda and dug into the background, the whole thing blew up into a scandal. The PM misusing public resources and power for personal reasons. Instead of being re-elected the following year, he never served in public office again. In common with many ex-Prime Ministers, he became an international speaker. Published several books. Was co-opted onto the boards of international corporations and became wealthy and famous. That is until they found him guilty of fraud and insider trading whilst in power. He served eighteen months in an open prison. During his time there, he gave up drinking. Thanks to his cellmate, who introduced him to Alcoholics Anonymous. He came out a changed man. More sober, less focused on himself. The rest of his working life he dedicated to working for an international disaster aid charity. Something helpful came out of his meeting with Hilda, after all.

California State Prison, Lancaster, California, USA

While things are looking up for Hilda, things are very different in the USA. Penelope Kendal, AKA Bonbon, or B, a one-time friend of The Duchess of Somershire. Is languishing in jail in California. The year before, Hilda, Pearl and Ruby had been instrumental in her criminal endeavours being uncovered. This made them rather unpopular with her. Only the fact that she was a half-sister to Ruby and Pearl prevented her from having them killed.

Penelope still ran a worldwide drug, theft, extortion, and trafficking network from prison. She called that network, 'The

Conglomerate.' The same conglomerate that Mildred worked for. She ran it by communicating through her lawyer, Mr Ling, to underlings like Mildred.

Just to add to the confusion, Lord Lenard Russell was B's illegitimate son. She had shipped him off to boarding school in England from a young age and never visited. He had only 'seen' his mother when he was a baby. She bought him a false heritage and set him up with a nanny to look after him as a child. Once he came of age, he 'inherited' a title and property; all bought for him by his mother, Penelope.

Mildred didn't know that The Conglomerate, for whom she acted as a UK agent, was headed by Len's mother. B found the link amusing and an extra way to 'help' her son. She didn't believe in charity. This way, his wife could work for the profit they gained as a couple. Everything would have been wonderful. Had it gone to plan. But Hilda has a way of upsetting every plan.

Plympton Council Offices, Plympton-on-sea, UK

The same day that the Prime Minister visited Hilda. Councillor Mildred Russell was chairing a long and boring meeting. It was open to the public. A few attended to observe or bring up issues. But these had to be pre-agreed. At the end, there was a brief opportunity for any pressing additional issues. The meeting was ending, and no one brought any other business. Mildred said, 'Right in that case...' A young man ran in houting, 'Am I too late?'

Mildred peered at him from the front and said, 'Just in time.'

The man caught his breath, and then continued. 'I own the hardware shop on the High Street. Twice in the last month, my deliveries have been blocked by VIP convoys. No warning, no planning, no by your leave. We get The First Lady from the US of bloomin A. Now today, our own Prime Minister turns up. I ask you, what's next? A Papal visit? The Queen? Who is it we have living here? Some celebrity? A Hollywood A-lister? I thought it was just a couple of old biddies running a tea shop.'

While he spoke. Mildred turned white. She sat open-mouthed. A question had to be repeated to her several times before she responded. Even then, her only response was to get up and leave. Everyone stared at her empty chair.

Stonehouse Manor, Upper Plympton, UK

Arriving home a few minutes later, Mildred turned on the TV, and radio, and powered up her PC. Her answerphone light was flashing, but she didn't press it. There was a fax in her machine. A handwritten message in capitals said, 'CALL ME NOW!!!'

It also had threats and expletives. But the essence was that the sender was not happy that the plan had failed. The Conglomerate was desperate to contact her. She made the call in trepidation. Mr Ling gave her information that caused her to fall back in her chair. The Conglomerate was headed by Len's mother, Penelope Kendal, AKA B. She was extremely unhappy with Hilda. A woman who had already caused her imprisonment. Now that Mildred had failed in the plan to bring pain back to Hilda, all B's anger was directed solely at Mildred. She had failed her.

Mildred dropped the phone and ran upstairs to pack some essentials. She needed to escape the wrath of B. She'd heard they were ruthless. Len returned from a walk and found Mildred running down the stairs with just her case. 'Where are you going?' asked Len.

'It's all gone wrong,' said Mildred, sweating. 'That stupid woman has ruined it all.'

'You mean Mrs Shilton kept her home?' asked Len, smiling.

'You don't understand. I was going to make us a fortune. The Conglomerate was going to pay us for it. We could have bought a better house. Lived in comfort. Now it's all ruined,' said Mildred. 'and your mother...'

'What do you mean, my mother?'

'She's behind the Conglomerate. It's all her.'

Len had stopped listening part way through. He was staring at his wife. He said, 'My mother, the Conglomerate, what are you talking about?'

'Yes, and she's not a woman to be trifled with. I need to get away.' Mildred walked towards the door, saying, 'I'm taking the car.' She picked up the car keys.

'Hold on,' shouted Len. He walked over and stopped her.

Mildred stood still, a look of thunder on her face and said, 'How dare you...'

'I don't know what you are talking about. I've never met my mother, but she has looked after me. You can leave, but say nothing bad about her,' said Len. He pointed at the door. He appeared taller, stronger than usual.

Mildred hesitated. 'You'll find out soon enough.' She shook her head, then walked to the phone and called a taxi.

Chapter Eighteen

Late October 1998

Marlan, Ohio, USA

Across in the USA, Wilbur Stanley's was feeling very pleased with himself as he drove along the highway. Singing was not in his nature. But he had the radio on. His speed increased until he was flying along at eighty miles an hour. He had nearly reached his home. Don't they say that a lot of problems with driving occur 100 yards from home? He wasn't that close, maybe ten miles away. Sometimes it's the chance events of life that change everything. Everything had turned out exactly as he planned. They had charged his brother Orville with the murder he had framed him for. He was sure that in time, he'd track Ruby down. Now he had her address. Patience was his virtue. His mom used to say that. They were her last words. Wilbur laughed loudly.

Traffic Officer Laurie was about to go off shift. It was tempting to ignore the speeding Buick, but duty took over. He would be glad he pulled the car over and followed all the right procedures, keeping his hand near his gun. Wilbur made a big mistake that morning. He had been using Orville's driving licence as ID. Without thinking, he handed it to Officer Laurie. The moment he did so, he reached for his knife. Officer Laurie had Wilbur out of the car and handcuffed quicker than steer could throw a new cowboy. The radio check came back quickly. They listed Orville Stanley as in the State Penitentiary. Either he had escaped, or this man had stolen his ID. Either way, an arrest followed.

At the local sheriff's office, there were some surprised faces. A couple of weeks earlier, they had sent Orville to the State Penitentiary to await trial. They questioned him about how he'd escaped. When he pleaded the fifth, they called up the prison and had a bigger surprise. Orville was in his cell and gave them the explanation they needed. They must have arrested his twin brother.

They ran some checks, DNA, fingerprints and had Orville brought back to the local office. After that followed a complex series of investigation and court hearings before they could sort it all out. Although their DNA was the same, they discovered it was Wilbur's fingerprints at the first two murders. They arrested Wilbur for those crimes.

The last murder turned out to be tricky. Wilbur had set Orville well. The local sheriff turned out to be better than expected. Given the fresh evidence, he re-examined all the facts they had. His officers found witnesses who had seen Orville being bundled into the trunk of a car. A check of Orville's blood taken at the time of his arrest showed high levels of a sleeping drug. They put out an appeal for more witnesses. A group of teens came forward. They had been passing by and seen Wilbur take Orville out of the trunk down near the crime scene. When asked why they hadn't come forward before, they explained about 'borrowing' one of their parents' cars. The offence had now been discovered by their parents and punished. So, they had no more reason to hide it. Finally, after a few months in jail, Orville was freed, and Wilbur arrested for all his crimes. Orville asked them to investigate the death of his mom. They had ruled it accidental. She appeared to have drowned in the local creek while out walking. Once Wilbur had been found guilty of all the other murders, he admitted to murdering his mom. He escaped the death sentence but received life imprisonment.

Hidden Gardens Tearoom, Plympton-on-Sea, UK

Pearl was standing in the sitting room of their shared flat at The Hidden Gardens Tearoom. Hilda was walking from room to room, sorting things out. Pearl shook her head and said, 'after all that. I thought you wanted to direct the group. Wasn't that what started all this?'

'You know me, dear; I enjoy doing things for a while. Besides, it was Karl who directed the musical,' said Hilda. She picked something up, looked at it, and put it down.

'He doesn't want to do it. They have realised your play was sabotaged. Lilly was very apologetic,' said Pearl. She was following Hilda around.

'She can apologise all she likes; I have other plans,' said Hilda. She found a box and started putting bits in it.

'Right, while we are on that subject. I have something I need to tell you. I wanted to wait till after the show,' said Pearl. She tried to catch Hilda's eye. But Hilda was moving around too much.

'You want to go to America? Your sister has retired, and you want to share a house together,' said Hilda. She stopped and looked at Pearl. 'Besides, now that they've caught Wilbur, you'll be safe together.'

Pearl stared open-mouthed at Hilda and asked, 'how on earth did you know I wanted to join my sister?'

'I am not as stupid as I look. Wait! I mean, I'm not stupid. All those phone calls and secret meetings. I knew once Ruby retired... well, it was obvious. I put two and two together and got five,' said Hilda. She went back to loading the box. 'You will be taking Merlin, I hope?'

'Of course, and it's four by the way,' said Pearl, shaking her head.

'Four?' said Hilda, counting on her fingers.

'Yes, two and two are four, not five,' said Pearl.

'I never was very good at complicated arithmetic,' said Hilda. She went through to her bedroom with the packed box and came out with another empty one.

'Anyway, what are you doing?' asked Pearl. She looked around at the cases and packed boxes.

'You might well ask. Once I knew about your plans, I made a few of my own,' said Hilda. She put a few more things in the empty box.

William and Louise Shilton's House, Meedham, UK

William and Louise had a spare bedroom. In fact, they had two spare bedrooms and a spare bathroom. Hilda had already decided that she would move in with them. This wonderful news she had broken to them straight after the musical. They were still debating it a few days later. As they sat at the kitchen table drinking coffee, Louise got up and walked to the window and said, 'she can't live here permanently.' The bin lorry was just collecting the rubbish. 'It wouldn't work. I love your mother… in small doses.'

'I agree completely. We just need to get the alternative bought quickly,' said William. He sipped his coffee.

'Alternative?' Louise raised an eyebrow.

'Didn't I say?' said William. He bit his lip. 'You know Josh's girlfriend, Beth?'

'Of course, I do, more that you,' said Louise. She walked back to the table and sat down.

'Yes, well, when I met Josh for coffee the other day, he'd been chatting with Beth. She knows of a retirement village in Faringsea. Someone has just moved out of it and into the nursing home where she works. Josh and Beth took mother to see it. She loved it,' said William.

'That's wonderful,' said Louise, letting out a sigh.

'One snag, the family of the lady who moved, are selling it on her behalf. They want to wait until after Christmas. Make sure she settles into the nursing home,' said William.

'So, she stays for Christmas. Then moves out in the new year. That's not too bad, I guess,' said Louise.

'It might be a few months into the new year. By the time it all goes through,' said William.

'So long as it isn't permanent. How is the sale going on her place?'

'There's good news there. It's already sold, and she will have plenty of money in the bank after she buys her new home. A group of investors offered her nearly twice what she paid. Not a bad increase in a year. They have the idea of running it as a tearoom once owned by the famous Hilda Shilton. Just because she was friends with the US President and the UK

Prime Minister,' said William, laughing. Louise stared at him in astonishment.

Messrs Kerridge, Lister, and Jingle Solicitors Offices, Plympton-on-Sea, UK

At the office of Messrs Kerridge, Lister, and Jingle Solicitors, the police arrive. After Tim showed them through to the senior partner, Mr Kerridge's office. He returned to his desk. There are whispered conversations among the other junior staff. But Tim ignored them. He takes out an old and well-worn school photo. The face of Councillor Mildred Russell half smiles from its well-handled and creased surface. Or as he had known her at school, Milly. As he gazes at the creased photo, he must see only beauty, for he stares at it lovingly.

Mr Kerridge asks Tim to join them. Tim walks in hesitantly. 'The Hidden Garden Tearooms, that was a file you were handling, wasn't it?' said Mr Kerridge.

'Yes, that's right,' said Tim. He glances at Mr Kerridge and the two officers.

'Can you fetch all the files?' said the officer, who was standing next to Mr Kerridge. Tim checks for confirmation that it was acceptable to his boss.

On receiving a nodded approval, Tim heads out of the room, out of the office, and back to his home at considerable speed. He's unaware that one police officer has watched him leave from the office window and followed him. At home, Tim hurriedly packs a bag, grabs his passport, and heads out of his front door. The two officers are there waiting. One officer steps in front of Tim. 'Going somewhere?'

Later, at the police station, Tim confesses to everything. He is not a strong person. Probably the reason Mildred could manipulate him so easily. When he gets offered immunity from prosecution in return for information that would help in catching Mildred, he folds. He explains everything about Mildred's involvement. Giving the police every detail, he knows. How Mildred had asked him to pass her the ground rent request letters and to prevent any communication about it reaching the partners in his firm. Mildred had assumed that she could trust Tim and shared a lot with him. She had involved him in her escape to South America. She needed some paperwork he could organise for her. So, he had her address details there. A useful bit of information for the police. Perhaps his love for her was more of an infatuation, after all.

The surprise information for the police was about the council. That would be an equal shock to them. Tim had provided legal paperwork and advice to Mildred in her transferring council funds to her personal accounts. Money that was allocated for new council offices. Mildred had redirected it to her personal account.

Hidden Garden Tearoom, Plympton-on-Sea, UK

Hilda wondered, 'Had it really only been a year since Pearl and her moved to Plympton?' She was planning a party to say farewell to Pearl and to The Hidden Garden Tearoom. She'd invited their staff, Kelly, and Lauren. So, they needed extra help with catering. Hilda wanted everyone to be free to enjoy the party.

Hilda invited Karl personally and told him not to tell Pearl. He told her she was more likely to let it slip into conversation than him, which was true. But Hilda kept the secret. She then had invites printed and sent out to William, Louise, Josh, and Beth. Hilda liked Beth a lot. She could see that Josh and Beth made a perfectly matched couple. They were all surprised and delighted to get printed invites as they saw Hilda in person, so often. It was also unlike her to be so organised. She also gave printed invites to the Rev Hanley and his wife, Hilda, felt that was only right. The good reverend felt that he'd finally made the impact he planned as he was unaware that most of the town ended up getting an invitation. The mayor and his wife were obviously included. After all, he'd asked Hilda to open a building. Then Hilda spent the week inviting every customer who visited the tearoom. By the end of the week, there may not have been a person in Plympton who didn't have an invitation. Given the size of the tearooms and the amount of food and drinks Hilda had bought, it was fortunate not everyone came. The tearoom and gardens were full enough.

How Pearl missed all the hubbub of planning for the party is a complete mystery. Perhaps she saw it and ignored the fact. When the Saturday of the party came, Hilda had sent Pearl off on an errand. They decked the tearoom out in bunting and fairy lights. The party would continue into the evening and the garden would be used. It was an unseasonably warm and dry day. Food and drinks were laid out on trestle tables inside. Then the normal tearoom tables were all set up with decorations and had plates and cutlery to enable people to fetch their own food. Each table had candles inside glass covers. On the walls were banners saying, 'Good Luck in your new life Pearl.' Specially printed and organised by Josh.

The guests arrived at the planned time of four in the afternoon. Hilda had wanted them all there before Pearl arrived back at five. Apart from one or two stragglers, her plan worked.

It was dark when Pearl got back and walked up to the door of their flat. Hilda popped her head out of the tearoom door and called to Pearl, 'Can you come and look at something a minute?'

Pearl looked puzzled but went over to Hilda and walked into the dark interior of the tearoom. 'Is it the lights? Are they broken?' asked Pearl.

'Surprise!' shouted everyone, as they switched the lights on, and a few people set off party poppers.

Whether Hilda should have known. After all, Pearl had been a friend since childhood. Or Louise guessed. She had known Pearl for a long time. Maybe the local GP, who was in attendance, could have just sounded a note of caution about sudden surprises for elderly people. But we are not looking to apportion blame. This was a party, and no one can be to blame for trying to bring a bit of fun. Who could really have guessed that after the rush to town on Hilda's pretend errand? The lack of an afternoon drink. Then a sudden surprise. A loud noise and burst of light from darkness. Pearl would faint into a heap on the floor. Rather than shouting for joy. Who could blame the person who dialled 999? Thinking Pearl had suffered a heart attack. Who would reproach Pearl for being a little miffed at all the fuss caused?

It was later, after the doctor checked Pearl over and she recovered from the embarrassment that the fun could really start. Hilda claimed it all added to the overall excitement of the evening. How many surprise parties have you attended where the guest of honour collapses on arrival?

After she recovered, Pearl marvelled at all Hilda had planned and organised. The food got her seal of approval, as did the décor. Rev Hanley came over to talk with her about her unfortunate entrance. Hilda was nearby. He said, 'I wanted to condole with you, about the way things began.' Rev Hanley looked serious.

'What is it with you and the dole?' asked Hilda, shaking her head. The vicar tried to explain. But he was onto a losing battle. Hilda noticed a small mousey looking woman beside him and asked, 'is that Mrs vicar?'

'It is indeed my good lady wife, Mrs Hanley,' said the vicar. He made a sweeping gesture towards his wife. Mrs Hanley tried to disappear into the floor. She was holding tightly onto her handbag with both hands.

'It's alright dear,' said Hilda. She looked at Mrs Hanley's bag. 'We won't steal it. Got lots of money in there, have you?'

'Oh no, John doesn't allow me... I don't... I mean...,' started Mrs Hanley. She glanced at the floor.

'Tight, is he?' cut in Hilda. She looked sharply at the vicar.

'I beg your pardon,' said Rev Hanley.

'Yes, you may,' said Hilda.

'He's really not all that...,' started Mrs Hanley.

Hilda spoke over her, 'I noticed that about him, on the Sunday I visited your church. He needs to go back to vicarring school. Learn how to be a bit more joyous. After all, he has Good News to share. Don't you agree, dear?' asked Hilda, smiling at Mrs Hanley.

'Well, I...,' said Mrs Hanley. She glanced between her red-faced husband and the joyous face of Hilda and then said, 'You know, I think I do. I very much do.' She stood up straighter and a change came upon her. She looked less like a mouse and more like a lion.

'Well, I never did. We need to be leaving,' said the vicar sharply.

'You go, I'm going to enjoy myself with these lovely people,' said Mrs Hanley. She walked over to Hilda and took her arm.

Rev Hanley watched her open-mouthed. Then he huffed and walked home. He had a sermon on obedience to write. He was supposed to be writing one on love, but that could wait. There was enough love around already and far too little obedience, especially to him.

'How wonderful to have you join me,' said Hilda. She grasped Mrs Hanley's arm, and they jauntily walked through the crowds' greeting guests.

The mayor and his wife had a large gathering around them. They were discussing Councillor Mildred Russell. Hilda pushed her way into the group. They left Mrs Hanley on the outside. But in her new emboldened state, she was soon in cheerful conversation. In the group's depth, Hilda said, 'did I hear something about Mildred? Is she alright? She was always so lovely to me.'

The mayor looked at Hilda in shock and said, 'Umm, you obviously don't know what's happened, Mrs Shilton.'

Pearl was nearby and overheard the conversation, too. She gained a place next to Hilda and asked what the mayor was talking about. He shuffled around, coughed, and then said, 'Councillor Russell was involved in rather a serious fraud. The police are involved. It was her who stopped the letters reaching you about your ground rent. She has escaped the country. Plus, she stole a large amount of council money.'

'I knew it. She always seemed very odd,' said Pearl. A few people near her agreed.

'What about poor Len?' asked Hilda. 'He's such a nice man.'

The mayor looked at Hilda and said, 'They aren't sure if he's involved. He's been arrested. They're investigating.'

'Poor man, I'm sure he's innocent,' said Hilda.

'But Hilda, how do you know?' asked Pearl.

'I just do,' said Hilda. With that, she walked off. She was going to re-join Mrs Hanley but found her so happy in a little gathering that she left her to enjoy herself.

Hilda headed off to find Josh and Beth. They were in the garden, staring into each other's eyes as they sat hand in hand at a small table. It was tucked away in a pleasant corner behind a rose hedge. The candlelight in the centre gave their faces a soft rosy glow. The fairy lights strung along the fences and around the bushes added a romantic air. Hilda walked up and said, 'I'm glad I found you.'

'Oo, gran,' said Josh.

Beth looked up dreamily and smiled. Then back at Josh. She sighed. Hilda shook her head and said, 'You two seem to be madly in love. I do hope Josh hurries up and asks you to marry him.'

They both jumped and let go of each other's hands. Josh said, 'What makes you say that?'

Hilda laughed and shook her head saying, 'It's quite obvious dear.' With that, she walked off.

Beth stared at the tabletop. Josh bit his lip. He started to say something but stopped. Beth glanced up and held her head to one side. Her hair fell over one eye in a very fetching manner. Josh took a deep breath and said, 'Beth, I was wondering...'

Just then, William walked up to them and said, 'There you are. I've been looking for you everywhere. Oh, sorry, Beth. I didn't see you. We wanted to get a photograph of everyone. I'm not disturbing anything, am I?'

'No, that's fine,' said Josh. He stood up. 'I'll be back in a moment.'

'I need to go; they asked me to cover a late shift,' said Beth.

'Oh, right,' said Josh flatly. 'See you tomorrow?'

'OK,' said Beth. She walked off, glancing back at Josh. He was standing, staring at her. He waved, and they both had a sad smile.

'Come on, we need to get that photo done,' said William. He was hopping around from foot to foot.

Josh looked at his dad and shook his head, then said, 'Right, let's get it done.' He headed off and took some group photos.

As the party was also a farewell to Hilda as she moved on from the tearoom, more surprises came. Karl had organised the Somershire Singers to come and serenade them all evening. He also brought in some of the of the dancers from the local college who had taken part in the musical. This time there was no stopping Hilda from joining in. She danced and pranced around. Several people watching marvelled at her energy.

The biggest surprise was the impromptu concert by Lionheart, Jura, and Purple Knight. They played together so well that there was talk of them having a comeback tour. Even though only two of them had ever played together in the past. They only performed two songs. One of them, 'All Across the USA,' Jura's best known and loved number, Hilda had to join in. It reminded her of the trip she had shared across America with Pearl.

At the end of the evening, Hilda arranged a line-up of people on either side of the doorway as a farewell to Pearl. Some of them had party poppers. They had warned Pearl. They didn't want her collapsing again. Others in the line-up had bubbles to blow. Hilda, William, Louise, and Josh stood near the door. Josh stood at the end of the row as Pearl walked down, ready with his camera. He took many photos of Pearl kissing people, hugging, and being showered in bubbles. There were shots of her flinching as party poppers went off. The best shot was Pearl halfway down the line, smiling faces on both sides, streamers, and bubbles overhead, Pearl smiling and ducking.

On reaching the door Pearl got the biggest hugs and kisses from Louise and Hilda. There was a present for her. She opened it later. It was a framed photo montage of all the best photos of her times with Hilda. As Pearl opened the taxi door outside the tearoom, she glanced back. Smiles and waves greeted her. Her own tears were echoed in the eyes of Hilda.

Chapter Nineteen

November 1998

Villa Junto Al Mar, South America

Mildred Russell knew nothing of the sad goodbyes in England. Even if she had, it would just cause her to sneer. She was sunbathing on a beach in South America. Her own private beach outside her luxury villa, Villa Junto Al Mar. According to the locals, that meant 'house by the beach.' Very appropriate, given its location. She luxuriated in the warmth and sunshine, oblivious to everyone. Giving no thought to her husband and any consequences he might face from her actions. Only her own fate concerned her. She was certain that she had escaped from Penelope Kendal. Living under an assumed name, with the proceeds of her crime, the theft of council funds. She felt very safe indeed.

As far as she knew, the council had no way of knowing she stole their money. But the council had discovered the fraud and set in motion actions to recover it. Her trail was more visible than she realised. She had been responsible for the building of the new council offices just outside Plympton-on-Sea. Which had given her authority over the contracts and accounts. Of course, the council weren't irresponsible. They had checks and balances in place. She needed two other signatories and the authorisation of the chief executive to allow any transactions. But she was becoming very good at forgery. The chief executives, signature was one at which she excelled. As for the other two signatures, she just chose two of her staff who asked few questions.

The money transfer had been the trickiest. That's where her two old school friends came in useful. They were unwitting parties to the fraud. Tim was on the legal side and her bank manager for helped with the actual transfers. She transferred all the money from the council accounts to personal overseas accounts in South America. Much as Tim and the bank manager had shared in the illegal activity, they did not share in the reward. They could never believe she would do anything illegal. To them she would always be, 'little Milly,' the girl they were infatuated with from school days. The bank manager would find that to be a poor defence in court.

Little Milly was lying back on a sun lounger outside her luxurious home. She smiled and closed her eyes, enjoying her illicit gains. The sun shone down, proving what it says in the Bible, 'The sun shines on the righteous and the unrighteous.'

Police Station, Meedham, UK

Over in the UK, they finally released Lord Lenard Russell from the Meedham police station. He'd been arrested and questioned for 48 hours. His solicitor had worked hard to clear Len of all involvement in Mildred's crimes. The investigating officer could only find the one document as proof Len was involved. But they discovered that the witness was false and accepted Len's story that he didn't know the full breadth of his wife's crimes. They saw Len as weak and foolish.

When they discovered Len was Penelope Kendall's son, it caused great excitement. They thought he must be complicit in his mother's crimes. But further investigation showed that he'd been left, as a baby, to be brought up by others. She had merely bought him a new life under a false name. The first he knew of his mother's involvement had been a few days earlier. Mildred had told him on the day she left. He still didn't believe his own mother could be an international criminal. He was shocked to hear that she was serving time in a California State Prison. They didn't know what to make of him.

Then a lady turned up at the front desk wanting to speak with the chief investigating officer. After she left the Chief Inspector called his team together and shared all the information that Hilda Shilton had given him. They spent the next few hours checking it out. Everything was accurate and added greatly to their investigation. Leonard Russel was released with an apology and a great deal of pity from the arresting officers. Their efforts changed into catching Councillor Mildred and Penelope Kendall.

The full extent of Mildred's involvement with Penelope Kendall and The Conglomerate took longer to unpick, Hilda had only worked out part of the picture. But on visiting Len and Mildred's home, the police found that Mildred kept meticulous records of her dealings with The Conglomerate. Records that would enable international law agencies to shut down Penelope Kendall's network. Records that her trusted patsy Tim had looked after her. He shared them with the police in return for leniency.

Although Mildred had escaped to a country with no extradition treaty with the UK. What she didn't know was that the foreign office was just completing talks with that country's government to change that. Negotiations were at the point of a final treaty change.

Villa Junto Al Mar, South America

At the time her husband Len was being let out of a police station in the UK. Mildred was enjoying another day on the beach outside her villa. It had become her daily routine. Breakfast of orange juice, cereal, and coffee. Then a walk along the beach until the sun was fully up. Followed by a couple of hours basking on her beach until it was too hot. Lunch and a siesta, after which she would pop into the local town for a bit of shopping at the market stalls. In the evening, she often ate out at one of the local hostelries. A few of the local men had taken notice of her. There were one or two that she noticed in return. Then a bit more sunbathing in the afternoon.

As she lay on the beach that afternoon, a dark shadow crossed her face. Clouds passed across the sun occasionally, even in such a wonderful place. But this shadow stayed; she opened her eyes. A man and a woman were standing there. They were not dressed for the beach.

'Mrs Mildred Russell?' asked the man.

'No,' lied Mildred.

He held out a copy of her passport photo and repeated, 'Mrs Mildred Russell, I'm from the UK police. My colleague here is a local law enforcement officer. I have a few questions for you.'

'There's no extradition treaty with the UK,' said Mildred, sitting up.

'That was the case until two days ago,' said the local officer. A smile played on the edge of her lips.

After some questioning at a local police station and various applications for extradition, they put Mildred on a plane back to the UK. Some months later, at her trial, they her found guilty. Mildred's jail sentence, though not long, was very unwelcome. It lacked the charm of her beachfront villa. After a few months and some complex investigation, the council regained most of their stolen assets. The house Mildred had bought, sold for more than its purchase price. Making up for some of the money she had spent on luxuries.

***

When they eventually released Mildred from prison, she had an additional shock. A solicitor's letter. Len filed for divorce. He had found someone else to marry. Mildred found that all her old friends now shunned her. They said that she was not the woman they had thought. She headed north to find a new life, hopefully an honest one.

Meedham and Plympton Canal Basin, Meedham, UK

A few days after the goodbye party at The Hidden Garden Tearooms, Josh met up with Beth. They met at their favourite place. The local canal basin. Not a popular place with many other people, perhaps not a surprise. So, they were alone. They had their cameras around their necks as usual and walked hand in hand. The morning was frosty. But wrapped up in their love and warm coats, they didn't feel it.

They both stopped to look at a pretty, icy puddle. The sun glinted on the frozen surface and mud in such a glorious way. After taking a few photos and admiring the beautiful sight. Josh turned to an even more gorgeous vision. Beth radiated warmth, love, passion, and enchantment. Josh breathed deeply. Beth's chest rose and fell almost in unison with his. Josh gripped Beth's hands tightly and said, 'I love you so much. I want to spend the rest of my life with you. You're the one who makes me complete.'

Beth's eyes glistened. She gazed into Josh's eyes and asked, 'Is that a marriage proposal or a movie line?'

Josh smiled and said, 'a movie line, of course. But seriously, will you marry me?' He dropped to one knee into an icy puddle. 'I don't know why they always do this. But it seems the norm.' He didn't notice the cold water that he knelt in. He looked around anxiously. 'I don't have a ring. I'm not a planner.'

Beth pulled him to his feet and kissed him. Then said, 'Yes, I will. We can sort a ring out later.'

Early December 1998

William and Louise's House, Meedham, UK

Hilda agreed to the idea of only temporarily moving in with William and Louise. They settled she would be with them for Christmas and into the New Year. While she waited for her new bungalow in the retirement village of Seaview, at

Faringsea. She had so enjoyed living in the seaside town of Plympton and was glad to be just moving up the coast.

Hilda therefore spent Christmas 1998 with her son and daughter-in-law. William said that she had brought far more with her than needed for a brief stay. But Louise told him to be thankful it would all leave with her. They put most of her furniture in storage until her permanent home was ready. It didn't end up being a boring Christmas.

***

After Hilda had unpacked, she found a letter that she picked up from the doormat as she left the tearoom. An early Christmas letter from a school friend. She opened it and read:

"Deans Manor, Little Hampton, Dandsbury,
4th Dec 1998
My dearest Hilda,
I hope this letter finds you in reasonable health.

Our children are doing well. You may have heard that Sadie got married to a lovely lad called Luke. He's a top film producer from Hollywood who happened to be visiting. Making something called a 'Blockbuster' I think. They plan on living in Beverly Hills most of the time and having a modest home in the Cotswolds to stay in when they visit us. We visited a few properties with them. But it's hard to find a six-bed property in the Cotswolds these days with a couple of acres of paddock and stables adjacent. After all, Sadie needs somewhere for her horses.

Do you remember our grandson Freddie, the one who used to chase you around with a water pistol? Ironically, he is now studying hydro dynamics at Oxford. He's seeing a beautiful *young lady at the moment. She does a bit of modelling. More as a hobby than anything. You probably won't have seen her as I don't think you read Vogue.*

Our granddaughter Viola has just got a place at Covent Garden. We have high expectations of her. But then, so does the director of the Royal Ballet.

Still, as with everyone, we have problems. When we moved to our new house, we had to wait six months for the builders to fit the pool. Then three more months for the jacuzzi. I won't even begin to tell you the problems I had with the marble kitchen worktops. Anyone would think Italian marble was hard to obtain. The new guest room with its en-suite has been an ongoing nightmare. I only asked for a walk-in shower and the builders have made a complete meal of it. As for the new shagpile carpets, well, you probably know the issues around those.

You mentioned in your letter visiting us in the new year. That may not be possible. We are away in the Bahamas for Christmas and New Year. Then we are on a cruise in February and March. Easter the family descends en masse. May is Chelsea Flower Show, June is Ascot of course, end of June beginning of July is Wimbledon. August, and September, we have the family visit or visit them. By October, we are usually desperate for a break and need a rest at our little Villa in the South of France. November is Thanksgiving and December is Christmas and the family visit. So next year is out, I am afraid.

I hope your darling little family is well.

Love Sir Nigel and Lady Barlestone.

PS you will have noticed Nigel got his knighthood, at last. That is a tale for my next letter."

Hilda walked through to the lounge holding the letter. She sat on the sofa, seething. William walked in. He took one look at her red face and began to leave, but she saw him and said, 'Some people!'

'Which people in particular?' asked William. He sat on a chair next to Hilda.

'My old school friend Virginia Wriggleton or as she now is, Lady Barlestone!' said Hilda.

'Bit of a step up,' said William. He sat back in the chair.

'She used to be so nice at school. Pearl and I both liked her,' said Hilda. She got up and walked around.

'Things change. It was a few years ago now,' said William. He watched his mother pace.

Hilda stopped and handed William the letter. 'Look at this letter, boast, boast, boast.'

After a short time, he handed it back, laughing and said, 'People always exaggerate in round robins.'

'Round what's dear?' Hilda held her head to one side and pursed her lips.

'Round robins. They are Christmas letters telling everyone how well everyone is doing,' said William, as he got up.

'Hold on, what do you mean, exaggerate?' said Hilda. She looked at William with a frown.

William had reached the door. He turned to look at his mother and said, 'That's right. People always exaggerate in round robins.'

Hilda went quiet, not a state William was used to seeing her in unless she was asleep. William headed to the kitchen and Hilda followed him. Louise was preparing breakfast.

'Morning, ready for breakfast,' said Louise. She was laying out toast and cereal. Then she poured boiling water into a teapot.

'Morning,' said Hilda, sitting down.

'You're looking very thoughtful this morning,' said Louise. She put the teapot on the table.

'I have just been thinking,' said Hilda, as she buttered some toast.

'Is it to do with the round robin?' said William. Louise raised an eyebrow. Hilda just tapped the side of her nose. It was an unusually peaceful breakfast that morning.

Week before Christmas

A few weeks later, William received a letter that puzzled him. Over breakfast he chatted about it with Louise and Hilda, saying, 'I had a letter today; it must be a con. Apparently, I am now Laird Montgorn of Fife and you, Louise, are Lady Montgorn.'

'Excellent, perfect, can I see it please?' said Hilda. She held out her hand. William handed the letter to her.

'Mother, what have you done?' said William suspiciously.

'Just bought a square foot of a Scottish estate. It gives you ancient rights to a long-dead title dear,' said Hilda. She read the letter, nodding, and smiling.

Josh arrived, and as usual, didn't knock, but walked straight in. He was red-faced and flustered, having rushed around from his flat. Walking straight up to Hilda, he said, 'is this a practical joke, Gran?' He passed her a certificate.

Hilda took the certificate and read it: 'This is to confirm that Joshua Howard Shilton is now an ordained Bishop in the Church of Catherine's aunt.'

'Perfect, magnificent,' said Hilda. She kicked her legs in delight.

Just then, the doorbell rang. William answered it. There were two packages, one for William and one for Louise. He brought them through and handed Louise hers.

'I didn't order anything,' said Louise. 'Maybe it's an early Christmas present.'

'Nor me,' said William.

They all went through to the lounge. William and Louise sat on the sofa next to each other and opened their packages. William sat staring at a new door sign that read, 'Montgorn Castle.' In Louise's parcel was a document that declared she had adopted a lion cub at the local zoo. They both looked up towards Hilda, but she had gone.

They got up to search for her and found Hilda back in the kitchen, sitting at the table. She was writing a letter. She glanced up at them and said, 'Ah, there you are.'

'What's going on?' said William.

'Just sit down, and all will be clear,' said Hilda. All four of them sat around the kitchen table and Hilda read out her letter:

"Written at Castle Montgorn.

My dearest Lady Barlestone,

I am sorry for the delay in replying; it has been such a busy few weeks. I visited Buckingham Palace a few weeks ago and, of course, couldn't keep a certain person waiting."

William interrupted, saying, 'Wait a minute, I remember you visiting Buckingham Palace with Pearl, not to see the Queen.'

'Yes, and I didn't want to keep Pearl waiting when I popped into the toilet, so I was quick. I don't mention the Queen, just a certain person.'

William looked unconvinced as he shook his head.

'If I can please continue, said Hilda:

"You'll notice we have moved; this was because of my son William inheriting some land with a title. Lord and Lady Montgorn have decided that the best use of their estate is to keep lions. To that end, my daughter-in-law, Lady Montgorn, has already obtained her first lion.'"

William, Louise, and Josh were all smiling at the realisation of Hilda's planning.

"'My grandson Josh, whom you probably remember running around your feet, is now a Bishop. He is to be married in the new millennium at St Paul's.'"

'Gran, I'm getting married at the local church...' started Josh, then a light came on in his eyes. 'Of course, it's called St Pauls.' Hilda smiled, then carried on:

"I'm afraid that it will only be dignitaries and close family invited. Although we hope to make room for our close friends, The President and First Lady of the USA."

Everyone laughed at the mixture of truth and fiction in that.

"It won't be a problem not visiting you next year as spring and summer we are busy remodelling Castle Montgorn. Then, of course, as you say, we are back to November and December, which is a busy time. I do hope your little family are alright."

"All the best, dear, Lady Hilda Shilton"

'Mother, you are very sneaky, but having read your friends over the top letter, I like your response. Well done. That will make your ostentatious friend sit up and take notice.' William stood up, turned to Louise, and held out his arm saying, 'Well Lady Montgorn, may I take you through to the parlour in Castle Montgorn?'

'Absolutely my Lord,' said Louise. She stood and took his arm.

Josh stood, bowed to Hilda, saying, 'M'lady Shilton, are you ready to join his Lordship?'

'Yes, my Lord Bishop, I think I am,' said Hilda. She stood and took his arm.

The distinguished family proceeded into their lounge, sat down, and switched on the television. Coincidentally, a programme on the Royal Family was just starting. As the pseudo-stately family settled down to watch the programme, little did they know just how long Hilda would stay with them. Had they known, would William have beamed as brightly as he said, 'Another sherry, anyone?'

One thing is certain. It would be a fun and interesting time. When Hilda is around, that is guaranteed.

***

Hilda will be back in book 3 – '*Millennium Mystery.*'

Also By Mike Nevin

If you enjoyed this book, would you please leave an honest review on Amazon.

Other Books by Mike Nevin

Book 2 *Teacakes and Murder*
Book 3 Millennium Mystery
Coming Soon: Book 4 Double Dealing

Find my Books Here: